TRIAL by
FURY

KG MacGregor

Bella
BOOKS

2016

Bella Books, Inc.
P.O. Box 10543
Tallahassee, FL 32302

Printed in the United States of America on acid-free paper.

First Bella Books Edition 2016

Editor: Katherine V. Forrest
Cover Designer: Judith Fellows

ISBN: 978-1-59493-492-6

Other Bella Books By KG MacGregor

Anyone But You
Etched in Shadows
The House on Sandstone
Just This Once
Life After Love
Malicious Pursuit
Mulligan
Out of Love
Photographs of Claudia
Playing with Fuego
Rhapsody
Sea Legs
Secrets So Deep
Sumter Point
T-Minus Two
The Touch of a Woman
Undercover Tales
West of Nowhere
Worth Every Step

Shaken Series
Without Warning
Aftershock
Small Packages
Mother Load

Acknowledgments

In every publisher's toolkit is something called the "All Persons Fictional Disclaimer," a standard paragraph reminding readers they're embarking on a work of fiction, that any resemblance to persons, living or dead, is purely coincidental. That applies here.

And yet...sometimes the events seem all too common for any of us to claim they were conjured solely from the writer's mind. A 2015 study by the Association of American Universities found that almost a quarter of women on campus had been victims of sexual assault or sexual misconduct; eleven percent reported penetration by force, threat or incapacitation. By conservative estimates, that's over one hundred thousand women, one hundred thousand stories. Far too many to conclude the events in this book resemble only one.

Like most of you, my understanding of the legal process comes from television. Since nearly all of that is wrong, I turned to fellow Bella author and real-life attorney Erica Abbott for guidance. She tried valiantly to keep me from embarrassing myself, but no one's perfect. Any errors you find are mine alone.

Thanks as always to my Book Machine: editor Katherine V. Forrest; my cleaner-uppers, Karen Appleby and Jenny; and all the crew at Bella Books.

CHAPTER ONE

"Make room for the lady with the money!" Theodora Constantine squeezed down the hallway with their payment.

The conference room at Constantine and Associates held a table that seated thirty-two. It wasn't unusual for every chair to be filled during a strategy meeting, since Theo took only the most important, most visible civil litigation cases. Prominent clients, pressing social issues, nearly all related to women's rights. In fact, the firm was predominantly women, and racially diverse, as were most businesses in Atlanta.

Today, the table was overflowing with congratulatory flowers and buckets of champagne on ice. Every major case culminated in this room, either with a celebration like this one or a soul-searching assessment that took on the pall of a wake.

Theo waved the courier's envelope high above her head as she entered. "Whose turn is it to do the honors?"

All eyes fell upon paralegal Jalinda Smiley, a plus-sized African-American in her thirties, whose name bore no resemblance to her usual gloomy face. Of the forty-six people who worked in their high-rise office in downtown Atlanta, Jalinda was by far the quietest, the most mysterious. Superb at her job, she rarely interacted socially with her co-workers.

"You can skip me. Go to the next person." Typical Jalinda, shunning the spotlight.

Theo had expected that and was ready with the next name. "Kendra Kershaw then. Step right up and tell us what we've won."

Kendra, tall and angular, shimmied through the group to snatch the envelope. A striking, dark-skinned woman twenty years out of Emory Law School, she was a partner at the firm. Her caseload typically focused on issues of special benefit to women of color. She was taking the lead on their next big case, a class action suit charging BoRegards, a regional family restaurant chain, with wage theft.

She ripped open the envelope and read aloud, "Seven million, six hundred thousand dollars and zero cents."

A cheer erupted around the room. That was their settlement with TNS Cable News on behalf of Teresa Gonzalez, a female reporter who'd been fired after breaking off an extra-marital relationship with the network's lead anchor. Theo had argued the firing was the result of sex discrimination. The case had dragged on for over two years, with Theo demanding reinstatement, lost wages and punitive damages large enough to head off such behavior in the future. When it became clear from the evidence that TNS likely would lose in court, they'd negotiated a settlement. Constantine and Associates would collect a third of the total along with a subsequent check covering expenses. A handsome payday for a small firm like theirs, one that would bring a surge of positive publicity.

Corks popped one after another and clear plastic cups were filled to the brim. They'd share thirty minutes of revelry, after which most of the crew would get back to work on the wage theft case.

As Kendra waved the check around, Sandy Thornton snatched it out of the air. She'd been Theo's accountant for ten years, and her miserly attitude was the reason the firm was on solid financial footing.

Theo raised her glass in a gesture to a young woman across the room, Sabrina Dawson, who'd served as her second chair on the case. An attractive brunette with an athletic body, she'd cut her teeth on last year's sexual harassment suit against a defense contractor. Originally from Savannah, she had a charming demeanor that allowed her to connect with a jury of Southerners. After six years at the firm, she was bringing in her own clients and on track for promotion to partner.

And unfortunately, off-limits for anything else. Though Sabrina identified as bisexual, Theo didn't need a sexual harassment suit of her own.

Philip Vogel, the other partner, and one of only five men in the entire office, clinked his cup against hers. "Another home run, Theo. You had them on the ropes from day one." An avid triathlete, he could hardly express himself without sports metaphors.

"Come on, it was one of the most blatant cases I've ever seen. Jalinda could have won it." In fact, she'd encouraged her favorite paralegal to go on to law school, but Jalinda was content to remain in the shadows. "That was a brilliant move, by the way, linking the anchor's salary to punitive damages. It gave the jury a solid rationale."

An expert in valuation, Philip worked on every litigation case to justify the amount of actual damages and punitive awards. He had a gift for knowing what a judge or jury would find reasonable.

No matter how important their casework, Theo was determined to keep the practice small and manageable, focusing not on billable hours but on the importance of their mission. "It's a firm, not a farm," she always said. A family atmosphere made for loyal employees who would stick around and grow. Together, they'd be judged by their body of work and the social strides they made, not their ambition.

On days like this, she considered herself the luckiest attorney in Georgia. Thanks to the dedicated work of her handpicked staff, she was, at thirty-nine, already a millionaire several times over, a luxury that allowed her to choose only those cases with the potential to shake up the status quo for women. Her high-profile work had made her a national celebrity and frequent guest on cable news. That notoriety, coupled with her made-for-TV looks, had once earned her a mention as one of *People* magazine's 100 Most Beautiful People.

But she wasn't without controversy. Her reproductive and lesbian rights cases always guaranteed rowdy pickets at the courthouse, as did her status as an out and proud lesbian. She took pleasure from knowing her victories and accolades made her critics' heads explode.

As she sipped her champagne, Theo scanned the room for her longtime friend and advisor, Gloria Hendershot. Gloria, now in her mid-sixties and working as a part-time consultant, rarely missed a settlement celebration. A renowned women's studies scholar from Atlanta's Harwood University, she provided the research and historical context they needed to make their clients' stories resonate. For plaintiff Teresa Gonzalez, she'd shown with statistics the difficulties women encountered in securing similar employment in the television news industry after having been let go.

"Have you seen Gloria this afternoon?" Theo asked.

Philip shook his head. "She said something about an alumni luncheon with the board of trustees. She was bummed when she heard the check was coming in this afternoon."

"Coming through, coming through." Theo's administrative assistant Penny Lowrey held her arms out to part the crowd as she snaked her way across the room. "Theo, there's this…a *person* in reception who says…they need to see you, and only you. But they won't say what it's about. And they won't give their name."

A person who was a *they*. Theo was intrigued, but she rarely spoke with walk-ins because she'd been burned twice by celebrity stalkers hoping for an autograph or photo. "Did you suggest they call back and get on my calendar?"

"There's something different about him…or her, maybe. He's kind of feminine…but trying not to be." She leaned in close enough to whisper, "I think it might be a man transitioning from a woman."

* * *

Celia Perone straightened her necktie and tucked a loose strand of hair back under her fedora. The disguise came courtesy of the theater department's wardrobe, and was undeniably a ludicrous charade. She couldn't risk being recognized, not at this critical point in her career.

"You can wait here. Ms. Constantine will be with you shortly."

She gazed around Theodora Constantine's plush office with interest. It had all the personal touches of someone in the lofty role of champion of women's rights. A framed cover of *Ms.* magazine celebrating one of her victories…smiling photos with Ruth Bader Ginsburg, Meryl Streep and Gloria Steinem. Those were in prominent positions behind her desk, clearly placed so potential clients would know how important she was.

As if the woman needed any more publicity. She was a fixture on cable news talking about her cases and providing expert commentary on issues relevant to women or the LGBT community.

The large mahogany desk held a laptop computer and phone, along with a small framed photo propped in the far corner. Against her better judgment, Celia stepped around the desk for a better look. It was Constantine with three young men. While the woman's blond hair, cut to her collar in soft layers, set her apart, it was obvious the four were siblings from their strong jaws and deep-set, crystal-blue eyes.

Celia wondered if the men in the family had made their mark in the world the way their sister had. It took a special kind of upbringing to produce a woman capable of arguing before the Supreme Court at the age of thirty—albeit four years older than Sarah Weddington, who, at twenty-six, had argued the landmark abortion case *Roe v. Wade*. Constantine's case was *Crossman v. The Town of Jeffersburg, Georgia*, which set a precedent regarding maternity leave. Jeffersburg had held open its city manager's position until assistant manager Kimberly Crossman went on leave, after which they hired a man under her supervision, one who lacked her experience and qualifications.

What impressed Celia most wasn't that Crossman was handed the promotion and back pay. Rather, the sweeping ruling had put cities across the country on notice that the practice would not be tolerated. That's why Celia had come to Constantine and Associates—she needed someone to make waves, someone who could take on a case with a sledgehammer that would strike fear into every university in America.

Voices in the hallway startled her and she scurried from behind the desk to take a seat in one of the wingback chairs upholstered in deep green.

Constantine entered and closed the door. She was larger than life in person, her hair lighter, her eyes brighter. Already taller than most women, she wore heels that made her even more imposing. A navy blue dress, its high round collar draped by a string of pearls, hugged her slender body like a diver's wet suit.

"Hello, I'm Theo Constantine. How may I help you?"

Celia took the offered hand, noticing the woman's eyes as they drifted downward, likely in response to the incongruous softness of her skin against the absurdity of a man's dress. "I know what you're thinking."

"Perhaps not," she replied, a small smile turning up from the corner of her mouth.

"I look ridiculous, but I promise you there's a good reason for this getup. I can't let anyone know I'm here."

The attorney guided her back to the chair, and instead of moving behind her desk, turned the adjacent chair to face her. When she sat, she crossed a leg comfortably and placed her hands in her lap as if ready to chat with an old friend. "In this day and age, it's hardly unusual to see a woman dressed as a man...or vice versa. I already assumed you had a good reason."

Even with her experience onstage in costume—playing everything from a medieval witch in *MacBeth* to a drag king in *Victor Victoria*—Celia couldn't help feeling ridiculous in front of such an accomplished woman as Constantine. Especially since her disguise had crumbled the moment she opened her mouth.

"I was worried about security cameras. They're all over your building. You never know who has access." She listened to herself and sighed. "Shit, now I sound paranoid. Maybe I am."

"What brings you here?"

"Okay, I'm an idiot." Celia removed her hat and shook free her shoulder-length dark hair. Then she loosened her collar and tugged off the necktie in hopes of also shedding her lunacy. "I'm Dr. Celia Perone. I teach performance studies at Harwood University. The disguise is because I'm up for a promotion this year. Full professor. I can't afford to jeopardize that, but I have to tell somebody what's going on there. It needs to be stopped."

"Something related to your employment?"

"No, it doesn't have anything to do with me."

It was unlikely Constantine had heard of Hayley Burkhart, a lovely, talented performance studies student with a smile so grand it could be seen from the balcony. Her suicide had come the same night the Harwood Hornets had won the national championship in basketball. Atlanta's media, focused on the celebration, had relegated Hayley's story to less than an afterthought.

* * *

Though she'd known all along Celia Perone was a woman, Theo was stunned by the transformation when she removed her meager disguise. There was something familiar about her face… the sparkling green eyes and dainty, round lips. However, the name didn't ring a bell. She certainly would have remembered a woman so attractive.

"One of my students killed herself last week. They found her in the bathroom of her sorority house the night Harwood won the basketball championship. She'd slit her wrists and bled to death. Hayley Burkhart was her name. I don't suppose you read anything about that?"

Theo had been in Tampa taking depositions from BoRegards executives for the wage theft case. She'd watched the game in the hotel bar with Kendra and several of the paralegals, some of whom were loyal alums. "No, I'm so sorry to hear that. I was in

Florida last week. It's difficult to keep up with local news when I'm on the road."

"Not that you'd have noticed. Or that anyone else would," Celia added bitterly. "Harwood obviously cares more about sports than the lives of its female students. Hayley came to me for help after she was raped."

The mention of rape caused Theo's light demeanor to shift. "Tell me what you know about the details."

Celia visibly relaxed as she fell into her story, as though relieved to get it off her chest. "It happened a couple of months ago at Henderson Hall on campus. That's the jock dorm. There was this big party after the Vanderbilt game, and Hayley went with one of her friends. Michael Fitzpatrick's his name...he's one of my students too."

A story so profound surely had many layers. While Theo wasn't concerned at the moment with specific details, she noted the degree to which Celia remembered them.

"The last thing she remembered from the party was running into a couple of her sorority sisters. She woke up the next morning in one of the common areas on the third floor. Her panties were gone, and she could feel that she'd been violated." Her expression hardened to a snarl. "When she turned on her phone, the bastards had taken a picture of her half naked, sprawled out on the couch. She showed it to me."

Cases like this one sparked a deep rage in Theo. Nonetheless, they were criminal matters for the prosecutor's office. There was little—if anything—her firm could do. "Did she go to the police?"

"Yeah, but as soon as she told them where it happened, they backed off...said they couldn't do anything without proof." She drew a thumb drive from the pocket of her blazer. "So about a week later, her friend Michael got hold of a video from a secret list only the basketball team could see. It shows exactly what happened. It was three players. You can see them plain as day—Matt Frazier, D'Anthony Caldwell and Tanner Watson."

Theo recognized all three names as stars on the Hornets' national championship team. She took the drive and walked around her desk to insert it into the USB port on her laptop. "Is it possible this video is ambiguous? Or that it's been edited in any way...perhaps to remove a segment where Ms. Burkhart suggested consent?"

"Just look at it!" Celia said sharply. Then with obvious contrition, she added, "No way she consented to this."

The video, a mere twenty-three seconds long, was sickening, one of the starkest pieces of criminal evidence Theo had ever seen. A young woman lay prone on a couch—her eyes closed, mouth open and one arm hanging limply to the floor. There was no question she was completely out of it, incapable of consent.

A young man grunted and laughed as he hunched over her. From his distinctive shaggy red hair, this indeed was Matt Frazier, Harwood's All-American point guard. The others— Caldwell and Watson—jostled in front of the camera arguing playfully over who was next.

"Hayley took this to the campus police as proof. You know what they said? That they talked to the players and all of them said she was into it, that *she* came on to *them*. That's a bunch of bullshit. I knew her and it's not who she was."

As far as Theo was concerned, the video was damning proof of sexual assault. Someone in authority at the university needed to step in and force the campus police into action.

"Dr. Perone, you need to take this to the administration at Harwood. All the way to—"

"I did that. I thought they'd listen because they all know me from the faculty senate. We see each other at cocktail parties, for Christ's sake." She shook her head with disgust. "They wouldn't touch it. As far as they're concerned, the police looked into it and the case is closed. That's why I came to you. You have to do something."

Though she roiled at the desperation in Celia's voice, Theo's legal mind shot through several alleys of dead ends. With the young woman now deceased, it was difficult to imagine a legal cause of action.

"Look, Ms. Constantine. Hayley killed herself because of what they did—the guys who raped her, the cops who looked the other way...and then the assholes in the administration who wanted to make sure they got their basketball trophy." Her voice shook with fury as her face reddened. "They threw her out like garbage. Until somebody makes them pay, no woman is safe at Harwood."

"I get it," Theo said, nodding pensively as she recognized the potential impact of this particular case. Coddling athletes who committed sexual assault was a national problem, its ramifications serious enough to warrant at least an assessment from her firm.

Wrongful death was difficult, if not impossible, to prove after suicide. From a financial standpoint though, they could inflict some damage. Frazier and Caldwell were projected as first-round picks in the upcoming NBA draft, and on the cusp of becoming multimillionaires. They'd probably settle quickly to avoid a high-publicity civil trial.

"It's possible we could file a case against the individuals in this video...maybe get a settlement for Ms. Burkhart's family. The administration though...that's a much tougher case."

"Even if they intimidated people into keeping quiet?"

"Intimidated how?"

"Hayley said somebody called her...warned her she could be expelled for making false allegations. And when I went to see Earl Gupton—he's the chancellor—he'd called in Harwood's attorney and the chairman of the board of trustees. I got freaked out so I recorded the whole thing on my cell phone, which was probably illegal." She nodded toward Theo's computer. "It's on there too, that second file."

Considering she'd come to the office in disguise, it wasn't surprising she'd also made a surreptitious recording. "Actually, you're in the clear. Georgia's a one-party permission state. As long as you're a participant in the discussion, you're entitled to record it. You don't need anyone else's permission."

"So you should listen to it. I'm telling you, it felt like an ambush. Once I realized they weren't going to do anything about it, I mentioned maybe talking to Jack Trendall, the basketball coach. But they told me the attorney for the players was threatening a defamation suit, that I could be sued for telling anybody what Hayley said happened to her. They said I'd be personally responsible, that the university wouldn't support me because they'd determined there was no wrongdoing."

Theo was familiar with the tactic—a SLAPP suit, short for strategic lawsuit against public participation. Aggressive parties used them to compel someone's silence under threat of a defamation suit.

"I can assure you their threats don't legally bind you from talking about the allegations unless you know for certain they're false," she said, leaving her desk to return to the chair next to Celia's. "Unfortunately, rape often comes down to 'he said, she said.' That's a problem here because you have a group of men willing to back up each other's claims that the sex was consensual against a woman who's no longer here to speak for herself."

"But it wasn't consensual!" Celia's knuckles turned white as she gripped the arm of her chair. "And now a girl's dead!"

Theo recognized the righteous indignation. She saw it in the mirror every time she found herself up against a force that wouldn't move. And it always made her more determined to push harder.

The problems with this case were practical—she had a weak cause of action and virtually no leverage within the jurisdiction. The insular nature of a university campus created barriers at every turn. Any campus police department could deliberately reject criminal complaints, thereby holding its crime rates artificially low so parents would believe their kids were safe. Harwood's motive in this case was even more suspect—they may have deprived Hayley Burkhart of due process in order to ensure their players would be allowed to compete for a basketball trophy. Now they were protecting not only their reputation but their financial windfall from the championship.

"I get why you're so angry at the system, Dr. Perone. It seems obvious a young woman you cared about was treated horribly. But I have to ask you…if everything were proven to have occurred exactly as you've described it, what would you like to see happen next?"

"I want the rapists in jail. I want the chancellor fired. And the chief of police too." She pounded out her demands in the palm of her hand. "The chairman of the board of trustees too. They're animals, every last one. And I want a promise from Harwood University that this will never happen again, that every girl who reports a sexual assault gets a fair hearing with the presumption that she's telling the truth."

In other words, she wanted to lay waste to the system and everyone responsible for it—a scorched earth approach. That happened to be Theo's favorite strategy too, especially when she allowed herself to get emotionally involved in a case.

After a measured silence, she leaned forward and pressed her fingertips together. "I need to be honest with you here. Unless the university changes its position on investigating, I'm afraid it's doubtful anyone will go to jail. It's a question of jurisdiction." With shared frustration, she presented their legal dilemma, which she drew from having represented a group of women two years ago who were arrested during a protest of Harwood's decision to invite a misogynistic radio personality to speak on campus.

Celia threw up her hands. "But Harwood's in the city limits of Atlanta. If the campus police won't do anything, can't the Atlanta Police Department step in?"

"Technically yes, but they probably won't. It's a professional courtesy. Harwood operates under a memorandum of understanding with the city and the county—any crime on campus falls under the university's domain. If they don't press charges, the criminal case usually dies there because nobody wants to come in and step on their toes."

"Their own little fiefdom," Celia groused.

"I'm afraid so. While we can't force the police to take action, you could always try your luck with the district attorney's office." Though Theo seriously doubted the DA would risk alienating Harwood's fan base during an election year. "I should warn you however...I believe she too will be reluctant to claim jurisdiction at Harwood unless she's invited in by law enforcement or the board of trustees."

The desolation on Celia's face was crushing.

"As far as the administration goes," Theo continued, "I'm not sure anyone can legally force a private university to fire its chancellor and board chair. Only the trustees have that power. It just isn't something we can sue them for."

"So that's it? These players lie through their teeth and get away with rape? Those bastards are responsible for her death. All of them." Celia abruptly collected her belongings as if to storm out.

"No, that doesn't have to be the end of it," Theo said, catching her arm and urging her back to her chair. For a case as egregious as this one, she was willing to dig deeper to explore what avenues of retribution might exist. "The video is compelling. It's difficult to believe anyone could see it and not conclude Hayley was assaulted. But right now we have more questions than answers. I need to have my staff look into it to see what we can do."

"Does that mean you're going to take the case?"

There was no case. But Theo couldn't bear to turn away someone as passionate as Celia Perone. A kindred spirit in the fight for justice and equality.

"Our practice is about women's civil rights, Dr. Perone. We have experts who can turn this case inside out, people who can get to the bottom of what happened and find a way forward. We can't make this right for Hayley Burkhart, but if we decide there's a victory to be won for other women like her, we'll take your case."

CHAPTER TWO

Hank Maloney had literally hundreds of contacts in law enforcement, from the FBI in Quantico all the way to parking enforcement in Dekalb County. A former detective with the Atlanta Police Department, his ruddy complexion and gray crewcut gave him a veteran's grizzled look younger cops respected. At sixty-two, he'd been with Constantine and Associates for seven years as their chief investigator. He had a knack for getting insiders to talk off the record, when they were most likely to inadvertently hand over information not available to the general public.

"I got nothing," he grumbled as he tugged the wingback chair closer to Theo's desk. One flimsy document was his total booty from a day on campus. "Just a copy of the suicide report. Nothing exceptional about it. The girl bled out in a shower stall sometime after midnight while everybody else was out partying in the street. Real neat-like so all the blood went down the drain. They didn't find her until three a.m."

"And nothing on record about the rape? Are you sure you got the date right? February third, the night Vanderbilt played Harwood here in Atlanta."

"I checked it. I went backward and forward a whole month in case it got entered under the wrong date. Nada."

As he leaned back in the chair, his bulging belly parted his sport coat, revealing what appeared to be a large coffee stain on his yellow shirt. That hardly bothered Theo as much as his gray stubble—not a fashion statement, but the product of several days without shaving. She preferred a more professional look around the office because the prominence of her cases and clients meant the press could show up at the drop of a hat. He resisted though, arguing that police officers were notoriously put off by slick suits. They had to trust him before they'd open up.

"But there's definitely something fucked up about it," he said.

She'd totally given up on policing his workplace language.

"I got this guy on the inside. A black kid, Bobby Hill, a rookie on their force. I worked with his pop at the APD back when Bobby was just a twinkle in his pants."

And on cleaning up his euphemisms.

"Anyhow, I got Bobby to let me look over some of the other reports for that day. They get filed by number, and two-ninety-two was missing. If I had to guess, I'd say somebody pulled it."

It wasn't exactly a smoking gun, but the coincidences were adding up. "Did you notice the time?"

He checked his notes. "They wrote up a burglary in one of the dorms at eight sixteen a.m. and a scuffle over a reserved parking space at ten fifty. And here's another screwy part—they couldn't put their hands on the call logs for that day. I know from the reports that got filed which officers were on duty, but there's no record of what they were doing between the burglary and the scuffle."

Someone, it seemed, had gone to a lot of trouble to wipe out the paper trail.

He looked at her wearily. "So what's the next step, chief?"

"Dr. Perone told me Hayley went to student health services as soon as she left the dorm. Apparently they did a rape kit, so we need to find out if they still have it. Since the cops didn't bother to investigate, it ought to still be there."

There were strict rules about the chain of custody for rape kits. If the police collected it for evidence to prosecute, they were required to cover the cost and there would be a receipt indicating who picked it up.

Theo scribbled a note and pushed it across the desk. "Take this to Sandy and see if you can pry some petty cash out of her, a thousand dollars. I don't want that kit destroyed because nobody paid the bill. And make sure they retain it in proper storage."

When he left, she added the suicide report to the file that contained Celia's thumb drive and her written statement on everything she could remember about her meetings with Hayley. Now convinced the school had covered up a crime to protect its players, Theo wanted badly to take this case.

Celia had stuck her neck out to right a wrong. Theo responded to that kind of courage, especially women helping other women.

She scrolled through the directory on her computer and opened the audio file Celia had made of her meeting with administration. Sonya Walsh, Harwood's general counsel, was the one who'd spelled out the risks of a defamation suit, but Chancellor Gupton had added his own threat.

"Harwood faculty have a contractual obligation to protect the image of the university. Should these allegations result in a defamation suit, it would disparage Harwood's reputation. The board of trustees might consider that grounds for dismissal."

Celia hadn't mentioned they'd also threatened her job.

She slapped the intercom button on her phone. "Penny, where's Gloria? I haven't seen her in three days."

"I heard her arguing with Philip about five minutes ago. I'll track her down and send her in."

Arguing with Philip was one of Gloria's favorite pastimes, and the subject hardly mattered. Their office debates—

everything from economic philosophy to the perfect vintage of California red wine—were notorious. His Harvard training as a litigator withered when she buried him in factoids and obscure statistics off the top of her head. She'd have made an excellent attorney because she always played to win.

Two minutes later Gloria swept flamboyantly through the door. Fresh off a color appointment with her stylist, her ginger hair lit up the room like a blazing birthday cake. "I swear, it's like I can't step out of your sight without you having a panic attack. What is it this time?"

"Last time I checked, you still work for me, Gloria. I'm entitled to your infinite wisdom whenever I push this little button," Theo shot back smartly, pointing to her phone. "I need your take on something. What's the thinking on campus rape these days?"

"You mean, is it one in four or one in forty?" Dressed in flowing linen slacks, Gloria flopped into the upholstered chair and swung her legs over the arm, the pose of an insolent child rather than a sixty-four-year-old woman. "The studies vary, but suffice it to say it's an unacceptable percentage of women, whether we're talking inappropriate contact or violent rape. The problem is a lot of those incidents take place in off-campus housing, so the stats are murky. Are you specifically asking about what happens on campus?"

"I'm looking for the number of sexual assaults that fall under the jurisdiction of a typical university's police force."

She nonchalantly studied her nails as she answered. "That varies too. I don't know about typical universities, but Emory reported twenty-six sexual assaults last year. Harwood had four."

It constantly amazed her how Gloria was able to keep so much information at the ready. Besides her knowledge, she'd have a unique perspective on this potential case as a loyal alum of Harwood who'd taught in their women's studies department for over thirty years.

"That's a helluva difference. What do you think is behind it?"

"Hmm…both Southern Ivy, enrollment about the same." The so-called Southern Ivy schools also included the likes of Duke, Vanderbilt and Tulane, all prestigious and private. "Harwood may have better security, but my guess is it's tied to their policies prohibiting alcohol parties on campus. And strict enforcement. That's the largest category, you know. Sexual assault while incapacitated. Some of those date-rape drugs are easier to buy than a bag of M&Ms. Apparently they're pretty easy to hide in a party drink. But if you don't have alcohol parties, you don't have party drinks."

Except Hayley's rape had taken place at an alcohol-fueled party on campus, and Celia was adamant she'd been drugged.

"Some schools use their honor court, which is made up of fellow students. Harwood does that, I think, as long as it's not a violent incident. Students can be suspended or even expelled, depending on the circumstances."

"Hunh…I wonder if they consider it violent if the victim's unconscious and can't fight back." It was a rhetorical question, as it was clear Harwood didn't even consider what happened to Hayley an assault. "Is it possible some schools don't take reports as seriously? Maybe their numbers are deflated by their refusal to prosecute."

"Well of course," Gloria answered with a huff, as if even an idiot knew that. "It's an out-and-out conflict of interest to ask colleges to report their own rape statistics. If parents knew what the real numbers were, they'd never let their daughters go to school there."

Theo took no pleasure from sharing Celia's story, plus the details Hank had discovered about what appeared to be a deliberate coverup. By the time she'd gotten through the narrative, Gloria was mournfully silent, no doubt stewing about the actions of the institution where she'd spent more than half her life.

"I have a video of the assault…it's pretty graphic. There's no way anyone could look at this and call it consensual." She swung the laptop around and clicked it to play.

When the clip ended, Gloria sprang from her chair and started to pace, as if ready to spring into action. "That's one of the most horrendous things I've ever seen. What kind of person films a rape like it's a souvenir?"

"Someone who ought to be in jail."

"We need to take this straight to Earl Gupton. He's a friend of mine, you know. One of the kindest, most honest men I've ever met. I'll make an appointment for us. If anyone can get to the bottom of this, it's Earl."

"Forget Gupton. I've also got him on tape blowing it off. Worse than that, he and Norman Tuttle—and Sonya Walsh too—practically threatened Dr. Perone's job if the allegations got repeated. If I had to guess, I'd say they wanted this buried because those guys were basketball players. The rape happened right before the NCAA tournament."

Gloria scrunched her nose with obvious distaste at the mention of the board chair. "I never liked Tuttle. He spits when he talks." She took a long moment to absorb the news, a mar on the university she so loved. "I have a feeling this is going to get very ugly, Theo."

"I know, but we can't just let it go. Not with all this evidence. They did this to her—the players, the cops, the administration. They might as well have held the knife that slashed her wrists."

"Causing a suicide? Won't that be tough to prove?"

"I'm afraid so. I looked for some wiggle room in the *Appling* decision. Harwood had to know Hayley would suffer emotionally if she didn't get justice. We could argue that makes it foreseeable."

"Fine, but since when is wrongful death in our wheelhouse?"

Theo played the rape clip one more time. "Maybe it's time we put it in our wheelhouse. Somebody has to answer for this woman."

* * *

"*He started it.*"
"*Did not.*"
"*Did too.*"

Celia's home office shared a common wall with the Fowlers' eight-year-old twins, whose words came through as clearly as if they were in the next room. She couldn't wait until the family saved enough money for a down payment on a larger home.

How they managed to live in a two-bedroom townhouse with two rambunctious boys and a newborn was beyond her.

Sitting at her desk, she turned on the TV to drown out the yelling. Not that cable news was much of an improvement, with their hyping of sensational stories that had absolutely zero relevance to the lives of real people.

"…bringing to a close the nineteenth GOP-led congressional investigation into the 2012 attack on the Diplomatic Mission in Benghazi. We'll be back after this brief message with a report on some inflammatory charges against Illinois Senator Jim Collingwood, who filed for divorce on Monday from his wife of twenty-one years, after reporters here at TNS broke the story of his longtime affair with a Costa Rican beauty queen. Stay tuned."

"Who cares about Jim Collingwood's divorce? It's none of our business," she shouted at the TV, giving the Fowler boys a dose of their own medicine.

She needed at least another hour to finish changes to the syllabus for Introduction to Theater, or as she called it, Sixty-Five Freshmen in Need of a Humanities Credit. With any luck, her promotion would come through and the fall course would be given to one of the assistant professors so she could teach something more interesting. A craft class on TV directing, or maybe a seminar—anything that let her work with upperclassmen. Twelve years of teaching mostly fundamentals to freshmen and sophomores had gotten old. To say nothing of the fact that she drew mostly theater courses, when the department head knew her interest and expertise were in film and television.

"We're back with news on the Jim Collingwood divorce. Following an anonymous report the senator was attempting to conceal his financial assets, his wife, Loretta Gordon Collingwood, hired famed women's rights attorney Theodora Constantine to represent her in divorce filings. Constantine held a press conference this afternoon in our nation's capital."

Celia leaped from her desk and crossed the room to stand in front of her TV while repeatedly clicking the volume button on her remote.

Flanked by Mrs. Collingwood and her children—three daughters and three sons—Theo stood at an outdoor podium before a throng of reporters. The stiff collar of her suit, black with white piping, made her look like a military officer.

Her eyes blazing with undisguised contempt, she began, "It has been confirmed that, during the weeks prior to filing for divorce from the mother of his six children, Senator Jim Collingwood moved stocks valued at eighteen-point-six million dollars to a holding company headquartered in the Cayman Islands, and transferred his interest in a forty-million-dollar real estate group to Miss Roberta Castro, a citizen of Costa Rica with whom he's alleged to have had an illicit affair that has now spanned four years."

It was a made-for-TV spectacle, clearly designed to humiliate the senator and extract quick concessions in their divorce settlement. Theo was famous for stunts like these, and that's why women called her when they wanted to sue rich, powerful men.

She'd spoken unabashedly about the practice in the interview with *Ms.* magazine, the one that was framed and displayed in her office. Outcomes were often decided in the court of public opinion, she said, where the winner was the one who controlled the narrative. Calling out bad behavior disrupted the systems powerful people used to silence their victims.

"Not only has Senator Collingwood attempted to hide assets that are undeniably joint property and therefore subject to equal distribution, it is apparent he also failed to report these transfers to the Internal Revenue Service—in violation of financial disclosure rules governing members of Congress. My client is seeking a contempt of court ruling placing Senator Collingwood in custody until these assets are returned to the US."

Jim Collingwood was toast. Not only would he lose at least half of his fortune in a divorce settlement, he was likely to be censured by his peers in the Senate and turned out by Illinois voters in the next election.

Theo Constantine played hardball. Her take-no-prisoners style usually won enormous settlements in high-profile cases, nearly all of which featured men behaving badly. The Silicon Valley CEO who fired his administrative assistant after she cut her hair. The paternity suit against the televangelist. The drunken TV star who groped a flight attendant.

That's why Celia had gone to Theo in the first place. But with rich and famous clients like those, it made little sense Theo would take on a case for a nobody like her. Or for a nobody like Hayley.

No wonder she hadn't called back.

* * *

"Flight attendants, prepare for landing."

Theo pretended to focus on her notes as she draped a hand over the seat divider to squeeze Jalinda's fingers. The paralegal had worked hard to overcome her fear of flying, but takeoffs and landings made her especially uneasy.

The trip home from Washington's National Airport had taken less than two hours, getting them into Atlanta just before nine p.m. Too late to make any more calls.

"I have a feeling Collingwood's attorneys will present us with an offer within the next twenty-four hours," she said, attempting to divert attention from their bouncing descent into a thick cloud cover. "It would be nice to get the preliminaries wrapped up by midweek. Then I can send Sabrina back to DC to handle the paperwork."

"I'll check her schedule in the morning to make sure she's available."

"Thanks. I appreciate you coming with me on such short notice today."

Jalinda closed her eyes tightly as they hit another bump. "I actually prefer these spur-of-the-moment trips. There's no time to dread the flight."

Theo chuckled and glanced out the window. "We're breaking through the clouds. I can see the lights downtown. We should be on the ground in another couple of minutes."

"Speaking of tomorrow, you wanted me to remind you to check with Hank on the status of the rape kit, the one for the Harwood student who killed herself."

The case had been on Theo's mind all day. A young woman who had taken her own life over a rape that had gone unpunished was a haunting reminder that no matter how much she accomplished on behalf of her clients, there was still so very far to go.

"What do you think of that case, Jalinda? Did you ever get a chance to look at the evidence?"

She nodded. "It was disgusting. And if the university refused to investigate to preserve their basketball championship hopes, it's an egregious denial of due process. But I read your notes… it'll be hard to make a cause of action against the perpetrators without a victim to testify. You'd have to argue wrongful death."

That was their problem in a nutshell—existing case law simply wasn't on their side. The Georgia courts had never held a defendant culpable for someone's suicide. Still, it was an intriguing case, not only for its legal challenges, but because it cried out for justice.

"Several facts are in our favor though." Theo released Jalinda's hand so she could count on her fingers. "Number one, the precipitating behavior—the rape—was clearly illegal. That makes this case different from *Parsons*, the online bullying case. Number two, the rape, the university's denial of due process and the threats toward a faculty member amount to intentional, not merely negligent, tort. And three, according to Gloria, thirty-three percent of rape victims have suicidal thoughts, and thirteen percent attempt suicide. Any research university with a gender studies department has these statistics at hand so they have no excuse for not knowing the risks. After viewing the incontrovertible video evidence, they were morally obligated to assess the potential for damage to the complainant, who sought counseling services at the student health center following the rape. That makes the outcome foreseeable."

Who was she trying to convince—Jalinda or herself? Hayley's family might recover damages from the players in a civil suit, but Celia wanted the university held responsible too.

A judgment against a prominent school such as Harwood would send a message that all universities had an obligation to protect female students from sexual assault, to prosecute violators with force, and to implement programs and practices that deterred the behavior. Those were the sweeping cases Theo relished, where she could make a difference against systemic bias.

There was more to this case than she wanted to admit, more than the righteousness of winning justice for Hayley Burkhart. Something about Celia Perone compelled her forward, even against her better judgment. It always came back to the same thing—she was a woman fighting for other women, and Theo wanted to be on her side.

CHAPTER THREE

Gloria's lecturing tone carried the authority of her thirty years at the head of a classroom. "It doesn't matter if she personally calls herself a feminist or not. Her work is postmodern feminist in the sense that it casts women as individuals apart from their contrast to men."

"But her themes are universal. You could flip the genders of her characters, tweak their details and still end up with the same final score." Philip was over his head discussing Toni Morrison and gender theory with Gloria, but Theo gave him credit for his willingness to try.

"Which is exactly what makes it postmodernist."

Theo cleared her throat. "Boys and girls, please. Take a chair. Let's get some resolution on this Harwood case."

Jalinda was seated to Theo's left, her files of evidence and legal reviews organized with color-coded tabs. Sandy sat to her right with a tablet computer ready to calculate costs. Hank occupied the head of the massive conference table, Theo's usual chair.

Kendra and Sabrina had also been invited to sit in. They'd be tied up for months with the wage theft case, but Theo wanted their legal opinion before she threw herself into this complaint.

"I've given this case a lot of thought. It's a long shot...very possibly a loser. But we're going to take it anyway."

"Cause of action?" Philip asked.

"Wrongful death." She studied their faces for a reaction. "We're going to argue the rapists and the university conspired to deprive Hayley Burkhart of her civil rights, that the trauma of the rape and subsequent lack of police action caused mental distress, and the mental distress led her to take her life."

Kendra nodded slowly, which Theo took as a positive sign until she said, "You're right, it's a loser."

"There's no case law in Georgia to support it," Sabrina added.

"I'm aware of that." She rested her elbows on the table and proceeded to stare her colleagues down. "But sometimes a situation comes along that makes you question whether or not the existing case law is all-inclusive. I believe it's possible to carve out an exceptional set of circumstances for which parties can be held culpable for suicide."

She explained the nuances of her case as she'd articulated them to Jalinda on the plane. With each argument, their skepticism appeared to fade, though not much.

Sandy raised a finger to inject her point. "As your accountant, I'm going on record to say money-losing cases are not good for our bottom line."

"I don't expect a significant drain on our resources. My team is limited to Jalinda and Hank, with input from Philip and Gloria."

"If we're playing moneyball here," Philip said, "I'd like to know what sort of damages you're seeking. Was Ms. Burkhart on her way to a multimillion-dollar career that her survivors are now deprived of?"

"That's for you to figure out, but compensatory damages may not be relevant. We're arguing her complaint was ignored in order to protect Harwood's prospects for a basketball championship. Therefore, we demand disgorgement of profits."

His mouth formed a perfect O.

"In an average year, it's estimated the NCAA champion—especially one from a major conference like the South Ten—enjoys a windfall of at least thirty million dollars from TV rights, ticket sales, merchandising and fundraising. Profits obtained by illegal or unethical acts are considered unjust enrichment, and we want them surrendered."

Sandy began nodding vigorously. "For that kind of return, we can do this."

For Theo, it wasn't about the money. She wanted justice—and change.

* * *

The hardwood floors of Sammy's Pint held years of Irish ale and celebration. The pub's late hours and proximity to the community theater made it a favorite watering hole for cast and crew following performances. While Celia didn't care for the creamy taste of Irish brew, she was a sucker for their turkey reuben sandwich.

She'd come by MARTA, metro Atlanta's rail system, straight from her lecture, looking every bit the professor in a skirt and blazer. With irony, she remembered wearing this same outfit the day she'd met with Gupton and the others.

The pub was far enough from campus that she wasn't worried about running into anyone she knew from the university. She still felt silly for having gone to the attorney's office in costume. In retrospect, it was a wonder Theo Constantine hadn't dismissed her as a paranoid kook.

But was it paranoia if her fears were real? Sure, there were whistleblower protections even for private institutions, but it wouldn't be difficult for the university to manufacture other reasons to disrupt her promotion—or even fire her—if they knew she was going behind their back to deliver trouble to their doorstep. While seeing those players punished for what they did to Hayley mattered a great deal, so did keeping her job.

A balding businessman who looked to be in his late forties slid from his barstool and sauntered to her table. "A smile sure would light up that pretty face of yours."

Even under the best of circumstances, Celia bristled at men who presumed her face was theirs to comment on. But as a trained actor, she'd perfected a cold-hearted glare that usually stopped them in their tracks.

He threw up his hands and backed away. "Sorry...guess it's your time of the month."

Too bad Theo Constantine wasn't here to respond to his sexist remark. Something told Celia that would be a treat to see.

From their brief encounter at the law office, Theo was every bit as impressive as her celebrity profile suggested. It wasn't only her imposing look. She'd taken command of the conversation from the get-go as if already plotting her legal strategy. It would be thrilling to see her in action in a courtroom...as it had been thrilling to be in the same room with her. Theo Constantine came across as engaging on television, but in person she was captivating. Authoritative, passionate. Though embarrassed to admit it, Celia had found herself starstruck.

Her tall bar table in the back corner afforded a clear view of the pub's front door. She nursed her chardonnay, needing to make it last in order to justify taking up a table in case Theo was late. She couldn't order another, or she'd be half-drunk before their meeting ever started.

It was hardly worth choosing a clandestine meeting place, as Theo came through the door wearing an expensive-looking slate-gray business suit and carrying a leather portfolio. Anyone with eyes could guess she was a potent attorney. Or definitely a potent something.

"I halfway expected you to send someone else, Ms. Constantine," she said as Theo slid onto the opposite stool. "I'm sure your time is valuable."

"Please call me Theo. And as I recall, you were pretty insistent about speaking only to me."

They were immediately interrupted by a waitress who took her drink order.

"Whatever she's having is fine," Theo said, gesturing toward the glass of white wine. When the waitress left, she folded her hands on the table and looked Celia squarely in the eye. "I'll cut to the chase, Dr. Perone. I've reviewed the material you gave me and done some digging of my own. The circumstances of this case bother me a lot. But as I explained in my office, we aren't in a position to bring criminal charges against the four young men involved."

"Four? There were only three in the video."

"Someone held the camera. In the eyes of the law, if a crime was committed, he too was a participant."

"*If* a crime was committed? You can't be serious."

"Unfortunately, it isn't officially a crime unless they're charged. The best way to facilitate that at this point would probably be to convince the DA to get involved, or ask the Department of Justice to look into whether or not these men violated Hayley's civil rights. As I explained in my office, it's my experience that neither of those agencies wants to trample on the judgment of local law enforcement except in the most egregious circumstances. To be honest, this very well could meet that threshold, but only if it gains traction and produces enough outrage."

"You've seen the video. It doesn't get any more outrageous than that."

They stopped talking long enough for the waitress to deliver the drink. When Theo declined to order food, Celia reluctantly did the same. It wasn't actually food she wanted, but a chance to discuss the case thoroughly. Now she had to hope Theo wouldn't zip through her talking points and leave her hanging as she rushed out the door to her next appointment.

"A massive public outcry might make the DOJ more likely to act. For that to happen though, Hayley's story would need to go viral. Get the news media talking about it, get people signing petitions that put pressure on the authorities. That could work since the men involved are popular public figures. The problem is we can't stir up the outrage without releasing the video. The question then becomes how cruel that might be to the people who cared about Hayley. The least anyone can do for her now that she's dead is treat her with the dignity these young men and the university denied her in life."

An honorable sentiment, but meaningless if it meant the players would go unpunished. "Couldn't her face be blurred? That's what they did in the Steubenville rape case."

"We'd have to do that anyway," Theo replied. "It's against the law in Georgia to identify rape victims. The original is still out there though. If the story goes viral, there's a very good chance it'll end up posted online somewhere. So before we take a step like that, I want to feel certain it's in the best interest of justice. We don't want to exploit someone who's already been victimized enough."

Celia knew at that moment she'd made the right decision to take the case to Theo's firm. They weren't experts in women's rights because of law books and legal maneuvering—they led this crusade because they believed in the morality of what they were doing.

"Does that mean you're going to take this case?"

Theo tightened her lips in what looked like a pained expression. "Yes, but I have to warn you we're on shaky ground, at least from a legal perspective."

"How can that be when you have a video of them doing it?"

"Because we're not charging them with rape. Only the police or district attorney can do that. We're suing them in civil court for causing Hayley's death. All of them—the players, the cops, the university administration—everyone who played a role in the rape, or in the decision not to prosecute."

Everyone who played a role. Celia couldn't wait to hear Theo call them out by name in front of a dozen microphones on the steps of Harwood's administration building.

"I'll be honest, Celia…this case won't be easy. But right now it's been swept under the rug. This gives us a chance to bring it into the light. That's the key—convincing the public they've done something wrong."

"You mean convincing a jury."

Theo paused to take a sip of her wine. "We may not have to. You told me what you wanted from this—for the players and the school to be punished. And for Harwood to put policies in place to make sure this never happens again. Remember saying that?"

She did, and at that moment, realized how much of her wanted vengeance for Hayley.

"There are several ways that can happen. Ninety-five percent of civil actions never make it to trial. Most of them end with a financial settlement. Sure, we'll ask for money, because that's the only language everybody speaks. But there are other ways to get what we want."

"For instance?"

"Ah, this is where it gets fun." Theo leaned back and flashed a cunning smile. "First we make enough noise to get the public outraged. They'll turn up the heat. If Harwood's police force doesn't respond, that could put pressure on the district attorney's office to step in with their own criminal investigation. Right behind them will be the Department of Justice asking if Hayley's civil rights were violated. And don't forget the Department of Education. They're investigating sexual assault as a Title IX violation at more than a hundred universities right now. I can't make guarantees, but my gut tells me we can make everyone who had a hand in this pay dearly."

* * *

It was a boastful claim, but Theo was convinced an aggressive strategy would generate federal interest in the case. The White House had raised the issue of campus rape to prominence with its grant to develop prevention programs at universities across the nation. What better way to show they were serious than to prosecute rapists and pressure schools to get in line?

She was sick and tired of reading about cases like Hayley's. Young women incapacitated by alcohol or date rape drugs, their bodies assaulted and debased. Some were further humiliated on social media by strangers and even their so-called friends, but the ultimate violation—the cruelest twist of all—came when their cries for justice went unanswered.

"I've talked this over with several of my associates, and we all agree wrongful death is the best approach. We name as defendants everyone involved in the chain of events, and we seek damages as well as redress."

"That would be so freaking awesome!" Celia's voice rose with excitement, but then her eyes narrowed to a sneer. "As long as redress means hoisting them all up by their…whatever."

Theo stifled a chuckle. She didn't dare say she found Celia's principled rage delightful, a word she'd never used before to describe a client or witness. Googling their bios was standard, but she'd gone so far as to read up on Celia's scholarly work, and peruse photos from academic conferences and community theater performances.

But this was supposed to be about business.

"Redress means the court would force the university to implement a system that guarantees this won't happen to any more students who report a sexual assault. There needs to be an ironclad system that allows claims to proceed and victims to appeal to independent agencies. Harwood University is too invested in its reputation—and in this case, its athletics—to police itself. For starters, the campus police officers who failed to investigate this should be fired, along with everyone in the police department who was part of the decision to sweep it under the rug. And there's no question your chancellor should be forced to step down, as well as the chairman of the board of trustees."

"So you're actually going after the administration in court? I figured the scandal alone would force them to resign, and we'd at least get decent people to take over at the top. The main thing is catching the bastards who did this and putting them in jail."

"All of them did this, Celia. The players, the cops and the brass who glossed over it so it wouldn't disrupt their national championship. They were more interested in preserving their image so they could fundraise and sell school merchandise."

Blurting out her first name was a professional slip, but Celia didn't seem to notice. Her eyes were now wide with panic. "Will you have to involve me in this? I mean, you have the video and all. I didn't really have anything to do with it."

"But you *are* a key witness. You're the only one who can testify about taking this issue to the chancellor, about being threatened if you went public. That's a critical piece of our narrative, the only real piece that implicates the administration in the coverup."

Celia tipped her head forward and massaged the back of her neck as if chasing away a nervous headache.

"Look, I get why you don't want to be in the middle of this, why you'd be worried about people seeing you come to my office. It takes courage to bring cases like this against powerful people and institutions. I respect that. That's how Hayley felt when she pressed her complaint with the police. These were popular basketball players, heroes on campus. It was gutsy."

That was a sucker punch and she knew it, to borrow one of Philip's sports metaphors. A little guilt went a long way in getting women to stand up for themselves.

She went on, "The university deprived Hayley of due process. It happens all over the country because our institutions are set up to enable this kind of behavior, to write it off as boys being boys and girls being sluts. It's not enough to punish one group of ballplayers when this kind of thing impacts women on college campuses all across the country. We have to shut the whole system down at Harwood. That puts every school in America on notice that they're next if they allow this sort of thing to happen on their watch. And Haley gets more than justice—she gets a legacy."

"Right, right. I get it." She buried her head in her hands and groaned.

Theo had seen this reaction before. Clients who suddenly realize they're getting exactly what they asked for, and then get cold feet.

"I'm going to lose my job over this."

"On the contrary." Theo grasped her forearm and gave it a

reassuring squeeze. "If you testify as to what you were told in your meeting with the administration—and we play the tape that backs you up—you'll have the safest job at Harwood. They wouldn't dare cross you again because they know they'd have to deal with me in the courtroom." Another bit of braggadocio, but it sometimes helped give clients and witnesses the confidence they needed to come forward. "In case you haven't noticed, I've made a career out of suing people who bully women."

"I can't believe I've gotten myself into this." Celia shook her head and looked away. Then abruptly, she said, "But you're right. This is about Hayley and all the other women this could happen to. So what do I need to do now?"

Theo was relieved. It would have been possible to proceed without Celia's cooperation, but much easier if she was fully on board with their strategy. The more she'd discussed this case with Gloria and the rest of her team, the more they were convinced it represented an opportunity to lay a critical cornerstone for the rights of women on campus.

"Nothing for now. We need to contact Hayley's next of kin. My investigator looked up who that is." She checked the notes inside her portfolio. "Belinda Burkhart, her mother. Technically, she's the only one who has legal standing to sue for wrongful death."

Celia's face fell. "Uh-oh...that could be a problem."

CHAPTER FOUR

It was obvious from her wrinkled forehead that Theo's earlier optimism was gone. "Are you seriously telling me Hayley herself was the product of a rape?"

"Apparently. I just found out this morning."

"Who told you this?"

"Hayley's friend Michael, the guy I told you about who went to the party with her. He's gay. And also one of my students. Theater kids…they're close-knit. They tell each other stuff they don't tell anybody else. He said Hayley hadn't even seen her mother since she was about seven."

Theo scribbled the notes on her legal pad with the backward slant typical of left-handers. Her irritation seemed to grow worse.

"Is it that bad?" Celia asked.

"I don't know yet. I'm just annoyed my investigator didn't tell me this."

Something in her voice made Celia glad she wasn't that investigator.

"Okay, the address we have for her mother is in Macon," Theo said. "Do you have any idea who she lives with?"

"I'm guessing it's a group home for developmental disabilities. But that's not where the rape happened. Hayley was born in Brunswick, so her mom must have been in a facility there at the time. Michael said she was raped either by another resident or a staff member. They never found out which. The family filed a lawsuit against the state and got a settlement. Hayley's grandmother didn't believe in abortion, so when Hayley was born, she took custody and raised her. But then the grandmother died five or six years ago and Hayley had to go to a foster home till she finished high school."

Celia had thought it an incredible story, one that explained a lot about Hayley's lack of emotional support as she struggled with the trauma of her attack. Sadly, she also knew that brand of isolation all too well.

"There has to be a conservator, somebody who makes decisions on the mother's behalf. An aunt or uncle, a cousin? Or maybe it's just a social worker."

"Not a clue."

"We'll need to interview Michael. He probably has a lot of firsthand information about the night it happened."

Celia shook her head. "I'm not sure he'll do it. Don't get me wrong—he's totally on board with telling us whatever he can about Hayley. He just doesn't want to get called to testify. I'm pretty sure he's protecting a boyfriend, somebody on the basketball team. That's how he got hold of the tape."

"That's absurd—and it's not going to fly, Celia." A surprisingly curt reply, followed by what seemed like a deliberate softening. "It's just that we can't make our case without the video, and we can't present it without telling the court how we acquired it. I take it his boyfriend's in the closet."

"That would be my guess."

"Clearly the video bothered both of them enough to come forward, and they had to know the authorities would eventually see it. Now they need to understand what's at stake here. I can play hardball if I have to—leak it to the press and name names—

but I'd rather have them on our side willingly. Will you try to set up a private meeting for me? I'll need both Michael *and* his boyfriend. Somewhere out of the way where they'll feel safe to talk. I can meet them."

"I'll see what I can do." She had access to a backstage dressing room at the community theater house. "This could ruin their lives, you know. Not Michael—he's out. His boyfriend though…we can't possibly know what he's up against at home. Or how the rest of the team's going to react."

"That's why we do everything in private. We weigh one against the other." She held up her cell phone. "Privacy matters now, Celia. No communicating with me by text or email. Pick up the phone if you need to talk. Not just to me—anyone else involved in the case. That goes for Michael too. And don't ever leave anything but a callback message. It doesn't matter how many times we talk to each other, but they can't know the substance of what we say."

Theo went on to explain their legal circumstances—the fact that Celia was a witness, not a client, meant they weren't entitled to privileged communications. That was true also of her written messages with Michael. Everything was subject to discovery if the defense claimed she was conspiring with Michael to make false allegations.

"Believe me, Celia, they'll do everything they can to discredit you, or to intimidate you into withdrawing from the case—especially when they realize you made this audiotape."

Celia slumped in her chair, her mind racing with the potential ramifications. But with Theo ready to do battle on a dead girl's behalf, it seemed trivial to worry about her own fallout. "I guess that's part of their game. It's not enough that they trashed Hayley. They have to drag all her friends through the mud too. No wonder people don't come forward when shit like this happens."

"You came forward, Celia. If Hayley gets any justice at all, it'll be because of you."

* * *

Frustration and helplessness were common among the women she represented, Theo reflected—even those like Celia who weren't actually victims. A deflated sense of self-worth was so ingrained that many of them felt defeated before their claims were ever argued. Sometimes it was all she could do to convince them not to settle for crumbs.

She rested her chin on her hands, readying herself for the speech she gave everyone before formally launching their case. It was important to prepare victims and witnesses for what was coming. "I won't kid you, Celia. No case is ever a slam-dunk, even when all the evidence is in our favor. The administration is going to fight us every step of the way, and so will the players. They'll say terrible things about Hayley. They'll twist your words so hard, your own mother will think you're lying."

Celia sat solemnly, her expression like that of a teenage girl who was being scolded.

"We have to stay focused, no matter how difficult it gets. Once we go forward, we're all in—no letting up. This isn't just for Hayley. It's for the right of women on campuses everywhere to control their bodies. For their right to feel safe and to know our laws and institutions will protect them." She jabbed her finger into the table to emphasize her words. "The universities, the police, the courts. We're sending a message that says there will be hell to pay if you turn away and let this happen."

"I'm in already, Theo. You don't have to convince me."

She hadn't realized until that moment she'd been gritting her teeth, lecturing Celia as she would a jury. "Sorry, I get carried away sometimes. What I'm trying to say is I've been down this road before and they don't scare me. I promise you we'll be ready for them."

"I have no doubt." Celia smiled for the first time since they'd met, tipping her head to the side in way that made her look girlish.

Theo sensed it again, that feeling she'd had in her office that she knew Celia from somewhere else. "This is totally off the subject but I can't stop thinking you look familiar. Is there any chance we've met before? Were you ever on one of my juries? Or at a civic club or something where I spoke? I give talks every now and then to women's groups."

"Definitely not. I would have remembered meeting you." The words carried a suggestive tone, and Celia's eyes widened. "Because you're famous, I mean."

"Hmm…I forget that. But I'm pretty good with faces. If we've never met, then you have a twin somewhere."

Celia hissed in a deep breath and held it for a second. "Okay…it's possible you've seen me before, but it would have been a long time ago. A very long time…and I've changed a lot." She winced, apparently contemplating whether or not to spill a secret.

"That's it. Now you *have* to tell me." She hadn't intended to meet with Celia for more than a few minutes, but found herself in no hurry to go.

"You know I teach performance studies, right? Acting, directing, stage management, TV craft." Celia stared sheepishly at her hands as they twirled her wineglass. "I grew up in LA. When I was a kid, I had my own TV show on KidStop."

The mention of the children's network triggered an avalanche of memories, namely Theo fighting with her brothers over the remote control. "Oh…my…God! You're *Little CeCe*. I watched you every day after school. I can't believe this. I wanted to be just like you."

"No, you wanted to be like *her*. She was a Hollywood illusion. Sorry to crack the fantasy, but the real Celia was a screwed-up kid who went to work every day in the showbiz cesspool. And like most kids whose mothers whored them out to Hollywood, I went home to a cesspool too."

That didn't sound good—and Theo wanted every last detail. "I always wondered what happened to you. And why the hell did they cancel your show? It was the biggest thing on TV for girls my age and all of a sudden it just vanished."

Celia brazenly cupped her breasts and lifted them. "Because Little CeCe started getting these boobs when she was only eleven."

Theo felt somewhat guilty that she'd already noticed Celia's breasts, which strained against her top. They were quite large for such a slender woman.

"There were a couple of sickos on the production team who found that development a little too interesting, if you catch my drift. But the network brass didn't want an after-school show about puberty. Thank God for small favors."

"Seriously? You had your own TV show and you're complaining about it? That's every kid's dream."

"Trust me, it isn't what it's cracked up to be. Imagine being eight or ten years old and working all day on a set where everybody forgets that you just want to play with your friends or watch some TV of your own. And your mom feeds you carrots and celery for lunch so you won't get fat and lose your gig. I was the golden goose, the one who paid the mortgage. That's a lot of pressure for a kid."

Miraculously, the animated expressions and powerful voice were still the same after thirty years. At least they seemed that way to Theo, who was ticking off her favorite episodes in her head.

"I feel like a fangirl meeting my idol. You're not going to believe this, but watching your show is what made me realize the world treated women differently. Before that, I thought it was just because my brothers were jerks. Remember that episode about the baseball team? The boys kept jumping in front of the girls to make all the plays. And one of them snatched the ball out of your hands before you could throw it. You got all the girls together and told them just to stand around, not to even swing when you were batting. The boys ended up having to beg for your help, and then you made the game-saving catch."

Celia laughed and nodded along. "I remember, but again… that wasn't me. It was Little CeCe. The real Celia Monroe never played baseball a day in her life."

"That's right. Your name used to be Monroe. You changed it."

"I changed it back to my birth name," she explained. "Kyle Monroe was my stepfather. And my manager. Turned out he embezzled most of my earnings and left my mom and me flat broke. We could have used a Theo Constantine back then."

"Where is he now? I'll kick his ass."

"Probably out in the Nevada desert somewhere under a pile of rocks. We only found out about the embezzling because some goons came looking for him after he racked up a bunch of gambling debts in Vegas. The asshole didn't even show up for my mom's funeral." She glanced away pensively and shook her head. "Between them, they were a real Hollywood power couple—she was alcohol, he was cocaine."

Theo's initial perception of Celia Perone was effectively shattered. She was no helpless damsel in need of a knight to fight her battle, but a gutsy survivor who'd probably been forced to scrape for everything she ever got. No wonder she was outraged by what happened to Hayley Burkhart. Both of them had overcome so much to get where they were.

"This is going to take a little getting used to," Theo said. "It's not every day I get such a blast from the past. Seriously, what happened after your show? Did you work on anything else?"

"Not that anyone would remember…at least I hope not. Ever hear of *Bloody Night in Hell*? One of those teen slasher flicks. Unfortunately, I did the sequel too."

"I missed those." Theo couldn't resist scribbling the title on her notepad. "But I'm going to download them this weekend."

"Oh, please don't do that—for your own sake. They were worse than awful. You'll never get those four hours back."

"The more you protest, the more determined I am to see them." Admittedly, she'd never been a fan of the horror genre. Too much violence against women, many of whom were scantily dressed—if they were dressed at all. "You aren't running around naked, are you?"

"God, no! I was only fourteen. But one of the older girls— Suzy Flynn—she had to do the bathtub scene where the killer looked in the window, and she ran out with a towel the size of a washcloth. I remember her saying the director made her shoot that scene about twenty times. Such a creep."

"Misogynistic pervert." Theo couldn't allow herself to dwell on that, or she'd get fired up and want to file suit against the film industry too. There was enough on her plate already. "That's a truly fascinating story. So how did you get from Little CeCe to Dr. Perone?"

"After my mom got rid of Kyle, we finally had royalties coming in from international, and it was enough to get me through college after she died. It was crazy to stay in the business, but I guess I had Stockholm Syndrome. I went to UCLA and ended up going for my PhD in performance studies. That's what I knew. I was addicted to it."

"You don't have to explain that part to me. Everyone should follow their bliss. I was the same way about law school. What I don't get is, if you had the showbiz bug, why'd you leave California for a place like Atlanta?"

Celia drank the last of her wine. "I'll need another drink to tell you that story."

"Sounds like a plan. Is the food here any good?"

* * *

"...and in the last year of my PhD, I got involved with Gina Worley. You might recognize that name. She was the assistant coach for the women's basketball team at UCLA, but then Harwood hired her away. Her first head coaching job. She got me an interview here that year. In fact, I got hired as part of her deal...one of those spousal placements, since we were living as domestic partners. It was a plum job for somebody right out of a doctoral program. I wasn't all that crazy about living in Georgia, but Harwood's the kind of place you can get used to in a hurry. Everything's first class."

Theo shook her head in an exaggerated double-take. "Excuse me, I'm still trying to wrap my head around the fact that Little CeCe was a lesbian. No wonder I liked that show so much."

Celia laughed with delight. From the moment she'd revealed her childhood identity, their conversation had shifted from business to personal. "How do you think she got all those girls to go along with her?"

"Wait! What if I wasn't even gay before that? What if you made me this way?"

"I've been known to have that effect on women," Celia said almost flirtatiously, doing her best not to crack a smile.

If anyone could make a straight woman jump the fence, it would be Theo Constantine. Perfect white teeth that lit up her whole face when she smiled. Hypnotic blue eyes. Thick blond hair with dark streaks underneath…perfect for gripping during sex.

The second glass of wine had gone to her head, Celia realized with panic, and her meal hadn't yet smoothed its effects. It was a miracle she hadn't blurted out her thoughts.

"So what happened with you and the coach? Did you get benched?"

"Other way around. She got canned a couple of years ago. Took the Harwood women to three Sweet Sixteens and a Final Four. Then she hit a wall and had six losing seasons in a row. Now she's coaching at some little state college in Ohio. No thanks, not moving to Ohio." The way she said it made it sound worse than it was. Neither she nor Gina had been particularly sorry when their relationship ended. "We were already more miss than hit by that time. In fact, she tried to blame me for her last three losing seasons. Said I didn't support her enough, that she was distracted by her home life. Could have been true, I guess. Once she started losing, she wasn't a whole lot of fun to be around. I started working with the community theater so I wouldn't have to come home at the end of the day. Sorry if that makes me a bad person."

"Those things happen. Sometimes people grow apart."

Celia had gone online and read dozens of profiles of Theo—and yet none of them had gone into great detail about her private life. Beyond her confirmation she was a lesbian, she'd given nothing away. Was there a partner lurking in the shadows? Children? She'd told *The Advocate* she thought it best to keep those close to her in the shadows, given the controversy that followed her.

"That's enough about me. I looked you up on Wikipedia. I want to know how you got rid of your Jersey accent without picking up a Georgia drawl. That's one of the toughest things to teach theater students."

"South Jersey's more of a Philly accent, not so noticeable. What I had, they neutralized my first year at Barnard. They're big on diction."

"Barnard...and then Columbia Law. That's right, I read all about you," she confessed. "What I don't get is why you'd pick a place like Atlanta after so many years in New York. You're hiding your talents down here."

Theo grinned and pushed her empty plate aside. She looked completely relaxed now, having removed her suit jacket and tucked her scarf into the pocket. The sleeves of her white silk blouse were rolled to her elbows, revealing an expensive gold watch and delicate chain bracelet. Not a ring in sight. "Hiding my talents, huh?"

That was more of her wine talking, Celia realized, trying to be complimentary without coming right out and gushing over what a rock star Theo was in the legal world. "New York's the biggest stage on the planet. You just don't strike me as someone who'd be at home down here in the Deep South."

"Fair enough. Turns out I ended up here the same way you did—I followed a woman. We met at Barnard, and when I was finishing up at Columbia, she got a job teaching philosophy at Spelman. Shonnie Thurman's her name." She said it with unmistakable affection. "We moved down here together and I hung out my shingle. I like Atlanta. The pace is a little slower than in Manhattan, but it's got its own sophistication. Besides, there's Harwood, Emory, John Marshall, Georgia State...it's a good pipeline for young, smart attorneys."

"Spelman." Celia had worked on a community theater presentation of *Showboat* with several members of their drama department, all of whom were African-American. "So you've been together for..."

"Oh, we're not together now. What you said about New York, about it being a bigger stage...you're right. But it's more than that. It's a whole different culture there. Cosmopolitan. Shonnie and I fit together well in the city, but not so much here in Atlanta. She found a better kinship at Spelman…closer to her cultural roots."

"I guess that makes sense." Though it made no sense at all someone would throw over Theo. "So you got your heart broken."

Theo shrugged. "It worked out for the best. She has a wife now. I went to their wedding last year. We're still friends…not as close as I thought we'd be though. We're different people now."

So where did that leave Theo? Most likely on the receiving end of women throwing themselves at her. She was rich, successful and gorgeous. And fortunately for Celia, the effects of her wine had faded, enabling her to think that without saying it aloud.

Instead she managed something more benign. "And now you're married to your job, I bet. Just like me."

"Feels that way sometimes. Good thing I love what I do. Do you?"

"Most of the time. I'd like to be teaching TV classes instead of theater…and seniors instead of freshmen. But it's fun seeing students get excited about the performance arts. Kids like Hayley and Michael. Hayley had real talent…maybe even too much of it for her own good." A shudder ran through her as she recalled their last conversation. "She told her sorority sisters what happened to her. Apparently some of them thought she was just being dramatic, that it wasn't as bad as she made it out to be. Ironic, huh? You're so good at something that it kills you."

Theo's smile faded, and Celia realized hers had too. Here she'd sat chatting up a woman who piqued her sexual interest when the whole reason they'd met in the first place was a girl who'd killed herself after being raped.

* * *

After a full glass of wine, Theo had been careful to watch the clock—an hour since her last sip. It wouldn't do for someone of her notoriety to get pulled over for DUI. The press would eat it up.

"Where are you parked?" she asked as they stepped onto the sidewalk. In the last few days, the humidity had crept upward, reminding everyone in the city that summer was on its way.

"At the MARTA station in Dunwoody. You couldn't pay me to drive in this city."

That meant they were heading in opposite directions, unless... "I can give you a ride to your car if you like. I'm in the garage around the corner."

"Thanks, but it's probably easier on both of us if I take the Red Line. Pretty hard to beat a sixteen-minute ride."

"Very true." To say nothing of the fact that it probably wasn't a good idea to feed her attraction to someone who was practically her client. She hadn't been drawn to a woman so quickly since the first time she met Shonnie. Something compelled her to say so. "I don't mean to be crass about this...considering we met because of Hayley's assault, that is. I've enjoyed talking to you, hearing your story. It blows me away that I watched you on TV when I was a kid. Maybe one of these days...if our circumstances are different, I wouldn't mind seeing more of you."

Celia stopped abruptly. Eyebrows up, mouth agape. She was Little CeCe all over again.

"Geez, that sounded pretty arrogant, didn't it?" Though she hadn't expected Celia to be shocked.

"And we can't see each other now because...?"

So it wasn't shock after all, though it left Theo with what felt like a sterile explanation. "Because of your involvement in this case. It would be way too easy for me to forget how important you are as a witness. If we file this suit, I need to focus on my legal obligations to Hayley." As difficult as that might be. It was critical she keep her objectivity about Celia's credibility and potential effectiveness, and not let herself be swayed by personal feelings that had nothing to do with the case.

"*If* we file this suit? I thought you'd decided."

"I meant when."

That was the sum of Celia's response—a deflection to the case. Nothing to suggest she was interested in seeing more of Theo outside of their work, or even flattered by the idea.

"I assume you'll hold one of your famous press conferences."

"Damn right. You'd be surprised how many people decide to settle the minute they see me on the news."

"Doesn't surprise me at all. I saw the one you did last week for Loretta Collingwood."

"That was fun." And effective—they'd been called back to DC the next day to meet with the senator's attorneys and expected a very generous divorce settlement. "We'll definitely launch Hayley's case with a bang. The more noise we make, the more likely someone will step in and prosecute."

Given the difficulty of proving wrongful death by suicide, it was quite possible their only victories might come from public outrage. She had to hope it would be enough to upset the status quo at Harwood.

"So when will you file?" With every question or comment, Celia was making clear her intent to keep their relationship professional.

"Not for a while, I'm afraid. We have a lot of work to do first. Securing the best plaintiff, making sure we've identified all the defendants, lining up witnesses and evidence. But I promise to keep you posted on the benchmarks."

"Thank you...for everything." Celia's girlish smile appeared again. "You can't possibly know how much I appreciate you taking this case. You're just...just a hero in so many ways."

A hero. Not exactly an invitation for something personal, but at least it was a compliment. "Have a safe ride home. Let me know about Michael and his basketball player friend. But remember what I said—no emails, no texts."

"Got it." She made a phone gesture with her thumb and pinky as she turned and walked away.

Theo found herself dazed. When had she started wanting to kiss her witnesses goodnight?

CHAPTER FIVE

In the passenger seat of Hank's ancient Chevy Suburban, Theo scanned the first draft of their complaint, which at this point contained a brief outline of events, the state jurisdiction, and an exhaustive list of named defendants, from the young men involved in the rape all the way to Harwood's board of trustees. Hank also had identified the two officers who took the original complaint at the student health center and the head of campus police.

She turned to Jalinda, who had raked all the garbage in the backseat to one side so she'd have a clean place to sit. "Did you bring an extra copy of this? We'll probably need to leave one they can put in Belinda's file."

"Right here." Jalinda patted her rolling briefcase, which was stuffed with all the documentation they'd gathered so far.

Theo had planned to spend the day reading the latest round of wage theft briefs from Kendra and her team. Instead, they were riding to Macon to meet with Belinda Burkhart's custodian, whoever that turned out to be. Until they secured cooperation from Haley's family, they had no plaintiff—and therefore no case.

As a boutique firm with limited resources, Constantine and Associates rarely waged more than two or three major cases at the same time, though she frequently jumped into the fray when a high-profile client called. It kept her services top of mind and made the phones ring—to say nothing of the fact that famous clients usually found themselves involved in seven- or eight-figure disputes that paid hefty fees.

A semi-truck roared by on the left, causing their vehicle to waver.

"Jesus, Hank! You drive slower than my grandmother. Does this bucket of bolts even have an accelerator?"

He cast an indignant look from the driver's seat. "Don't complain. It's paid for."

For what she'd paid him last year in bonuses alone, he could have bought a brand new one for cash. At his core, he was still a crusty gumshoe.

"What did you learn about Belinda Burkhart?" she asked.

"Social services wouldn't tell me squat, but they gave me a number for her uncle. That's the grandmother's brother, a guy by the name of Donald Lipscomb. I talked to him on the phone last night. Sixty-six, divorced. He used to be a developer of some sort...strip malls, I think. Nothing major. And not all that successful either. Two personal bankruptcies and a lien on his house. He paid all his debts off about four years ago with some cash his sister left him and retired. Lives in Atlanta out by the airport."

"Sounds like he could be our kind of guy." For some, money was a stronger motivator than justice. "What did he know about Belinda?"

"He said it was some kind of prenatal accident where she didn't get enough oxygen. They put her in an institution when she was twelve because she got too difficult to control at home."

"Anything on her rape?"

"He didn't know much." He checked his sideview mirror and signaled to change lanes. Inch by inch, they overtook a dilapidated pickup truck driven by a bent woman who could barely see over the hood. "There was a lawsuit against the state, but nothing in the records about the perpetrator. They settled for eight hundred grand."

"Sounds like the state was protecting itself. Either she was raped by an employee, or it happened while she was unsupervised. Maybe she wandered off and they found her after it happened."

"I don't get it," Hank said. "Are there guys really that hard up for somebody to have sex with? Who gets off on doing it with a woman who doesn't even know what's going on?"

"If that's a serious question, I happen to have a list of names right here." Theo slapped the complaint against her knee.

"Nah, that's different. This campus business…it's way worse if you ask me. It takes a real creep to go gangers on a girl who's passed out and then take pictures of her. If I ever caught my son doing something like that, I'd make him sorry he was ever born."

"You won't though, because Mark's not like that."

Despite his generally boorish manner, Hank redeemed himself regularly as a fierce protector of women. Raised by a single mom who'd worked two jobs and practically dared him to misbehave, he carried a chip on his shoulder when it came to women who'd been taken advantage of, no matter the circumstances. His career as a police detective had given him the tools to right the wrongs, while Theo gave him the opportunity.

"Here, one of you read me this," he said, thrusting a crumpled page of directions in her hands.

Jalinda poked her head forward over the console and said, "You know, the new cars have tiny people living in the dashboard who tell you how to get wherever you want to go."

"You're starting to sound just like her," he snarled, jacking his thumb toward Theo, who called out the turn-by-turn instructions. The scribbled note led them to the end of a cul-de-sac and a neat split-level brick house with tan siding. A white van was parked in the driveway in front of what appeared to be a converted garage.

"This is it," Hank said. "According to state records, it's licensed for four ambulatory adult clients. I looked it up—that means no wheelchairs. Doug and Debbie Robeson are the foster parents."

Theo could honestly say she knew little about adult foster care. Had she been hired to represent someone like Belinda Burkhart in her rape case, she'd have demanded enough to cover the costs of private care for the rest of her life.

The door was answered by a heavyset woman who identified herself as Debbie. She wore what looked to be nurse's scrubs—blue drawstring pants and a floral V-neck shirt. "Are y'all the ones who called about Belinda?"

"Yes, thank you for seeing us," Theo answered. "We'd like to speak with her if we can…ask her a few questions."

"Sorry, she don't talk. What do y'all need to know?"

For all practical purposes, that was the sum of it. If Belinda was nonverbal, she likely was incapable of standing for herself as a plaintiff in her biological daughter's wrongful death case. Still, it was necessary for Theo to conduct her due diligence.

"If we could just sit with her for a few minutes…and it would be helpful if we could record our conversation. Is that all right?"

"I guess." Debbie gestured toward the sofa in the well-kept living room. "Y'all have a seat. I'll go get her."

"I get the feeling we're going to need the uncle's address too," Theo whispered to Hank.

He patted the chest pocket of his sport coat.

When Debbie returned, she was holding the hand of a woman in her late thirties—about the same age as Theo. With her oval face and prominent brown eyes, she bore a distinct family resemblance to her late daughter, who'd been a pretty young woman.

"Can you wave to these nice people, Belinda?"

The woman's hand went up and down in a mechanical motion, though she never made eye contact.

"She's calmed down a lot since they took her off Keppra. That stuff was making her act out…screaming all the time. She'd hit herself and throw stuff. And push everybody. I'm telling you, it got scary for a while there."

Though it was likely Belinda couldn't understand the meaning of Debbie's words, Theo was nonetheless uncomfortable speaking about her as if she weren't present. "How are you now, Belinda? Do you feel better?"

"She still gets seizures 'bout once a month. He wants to start her on Dilantin again. Last time she took it, it made her sleep all the time. But it's better than seizures 'cause she can fall and hurt herself."

Jalinda, ever efficient and capable, took notes with one hand and held out her digital recorder with the other.

Hank leaned forward so he was in Belinda's line of sight. "Belinda, do you know who Hayley is?"

"Oh my goodness, that's her daughter, the one who killed herself. The social worker told us all about that. They said they were gonna put her school money in Belinda's account."

So much for seeing if Belinda might react to hearing her daughter's name. There was no apparent recognition at all, even after Debbie interjected and explained who she was.

"Mrs. Robeson, is Belinda getting all the services she needs? Doctors, therapy?"

She squinted and tipped her head thoughtfully. "I guess. The only real problem she has are the seizures. She eats good, sleeps good."

"And what about material things?" Theo made note of Belinda's clothing, a Georgia Bulldogs T-shirt tucked into elastic-waist jeans, and bright-white sneakers with velcro straps.

Debbie shrugged. "She pretty much has all-new everything. We buy her clothes and bathroom stuff out of her account two or three times a year. I cain't think what else she'd need."

Their case for legal standing was on shaky ground. Belinda Burkhart wasn't competent to make a wrongful death claim on her own. Even if her uncle was convinced to sue on her behalf, the argument for financial compensation would be weak. Belinda didn't even know her daughter and could hardly claim pain and suffering from her loss.

Theo's head was already spinning the options for a backup plan. It was inconceivable these monsters would get away with what they'd done—she'd practically promised Celia she wouldn't let that happen.

* * *

"O, devil, devil! If that the Earth could teem with woman's tears, each drop she falls would prove a crocodile. Out of my sight!"

Duncan Tripp, a sophomore who'd barely passed Celia's Intro to Theater class as a freshman, delivered the lines with all the emotion of an ax handle. It was a mystery why he'd signed up for Fundamentals of Stage Acting.

"Whose voice is that, Duncan?" she asked, walking across the stage to face the students in the front row of the tiny theater. "Yours?"

"It's supposed to be Othello's."

An Othello who sounded like Duncan. "And what is he feeling?"

"He's upset."

"What could he possibly be upset about? He has power as a general, and he's married to a beautiful woman who loves him."

The silence went on long enough for her to know he'd memorized the lines without comprehending the story. He was bailed out by Hayley's friend Michael. "He believes he's been betrayed by Desdemona."

"Correct." She spun back toward Duncan and noticed several of her students had begun stowing their scripts and notes, as the hour had ended. "We'll give this another try on Monday. A little practice in front of the mirror, everyone. And read the script—several times if you have to. Acting is about occupying these characters."

Though she'd managed not to completely humiliate Duncan for his abysmal performance, she still felt guilty for calling him out in such a negative manner. It wasn't her usual teaching style.

"Duncan." She strolled deliberately toward him with her arms folded across her chest. "You're the only one in class who got all the lines right. Good job. We'll work on that delivery next week."

"Dr. Perone?" Michael had lagged behind waiting for the others to leave.

A gifted stage actor, he had delicate features she could only describe as pretty. His future as a leading man would be enhanced if he added muscle to his slender frame and grew some facial hair.

He produced a thumb drive. "I got what you asked for—all the IMs from Hayley since the rape—but I deleted the name of the guy who gave me the video. That needs to stay confidential." He must have noticed her confusion because he clarified, "Instant messages, Facebook. A couple of gmails too, but what's weird is that all the stuff we sent through our student accounts is gone. It was mostly notes for class, nothing personal. Looks like Harwood deleted her account. That makes sense, I guess, but I thought it was weird they even wiped the ones I sent to her."

"It's not weird to me, Michael. I think the university's trying to get rid of all the evidence against the players. That video you gave me...I had a copy saved on the computer in my office and now it's gone. Wiped off Harwood's server. Good thing I still had it on the stick."

"Joke's on them then. Like I said, practically every time we talked about private stuff, it was IMs on Facebook. They're all here, including the chat we had the day after it happened. She told me everything she remembered, and then all about what they did at the health center."

After hearing the video had been erased from the folder on her computer, Theo had asked her to help collect preliminary information that might be relevant to their case. She'd get access to everything else through discovery, she said, but only if she could convince a judge they had a legitimate cause of action. She'd be glad to get her hands on these messages.

"Michael, this attorney I told you about...she really needs to talk to you and your friend in person."

He shook his head adamantly. "No way. I'll give you everything I have, but I can't be involved any more than that."

"You're already involved." She guided him toward the wings of the stage where their voices wouldn't carry. "You're the one Hayley talked to most. There's a process called discovery. It basically means the players who did this are legally entitled to know how we got our hands on the evidence—especially the video. Not only that, they can ask a judge for permission to look at all of your emails and messages with Hayley…and anyone else who might be related to the case."

"That's not fair!" He literally withdrew, taking a step back as though separating himself from both her and the case. "Hayley's been my best friend…like, forever. What we talked about is private. Secrets other people have no right to know."

Alarmed by the panic in his voice, she closed the distance between them and gave his shoulder a reassuring squeeze. "Michael, it's going to come out anyway if we go forward with the case. That secret list the team had, it'll be subpoenaed. They'll be able to determine who posted the video and who shared it with you. But all the attorney cares about at this point is what happened to Hayley. Anything else you talked about… nobody has any reason to make that public." Even as the words left her lips, she knew she couldn't make that guarantee. The university administration had already shown its capacity for dirty tricks.

"But they'll—God, they can't do that. Somebody's going to get hurt."

"Look, Michael. I get it. You're protecting someone on the basketball team, right?"

He looked as though he might cry. "You have no idea what the rest of those guys are like. They'll make his life miserable. I promised him I wouldn't tell."

"Michael, they raped your friend and she killed herself."

"He had nothing to do with it. Don't you see? He tried to do the right thing. But if they find out, they'll beat the crap out of him, Dr. Perone. And then Coach T's going to kick him off the team."

"For doing something brave? He's a hero for standing up to those guys. So are you." She couldn't bring herself to shame him for wanting to hide, not after first going to Theo in disguise so it wouldn't cost her a promotion. "Michael, I didn't want to be involved either. There's a very good chance I could lose my job over this, but we both know that's not what matters here. We have a responsibility to Hayley. We can't stop caring about her now, not until we make those people pay for what they did to her."

His face contorted with anguish, but she could tell she was getting through.

"I'll talk to the attorney and tell her how important your privacy is. I'm sure she'll do everything in her legal power to protect you." That much she could promise. "I know it's tough right now, but someday you'll look back on this and be so proud you did the right thing. Your friend will feel the same way. It's who you are."

* * *

Theo was pleased Celia had followed her directions to leave a callback message that gave nothing away. Pressing a finger to her ear to shut out the road noise, she shouted, "You do good work, Doc. If they sack you at Harwood, I can probably find a place for you in the firm."

"Doing what exactly? You guys need a drama coach?"

"Uh, not really…but how's your driving?" She glanced over at Hank, who was creeping down the interstate again. "Never mind. You were right about Belinda Burkhart. She can't help us at all. We're heading back to Atlanta to talk to the grandmother's brother."

She proposed meeting Celia for a drink to pick up Michael's thumb drive.

"I dropped it off at your office this morning. I didn't know you were out."

Theo was both pleased and disappointed. Pleased to know Celia had gone out of her way to deliver the data, and disappointed they had no pressing reason to see each other again, at least not right away. When she ended the call, she heard a distinct chuckle from Hank.

"What?"

"Didn't say nothin'."

She glanced back at Jalinda, who was wearing earbuds so she could transcribe the recording she'd made with Belinda. She'd missed the conversation.

As Theo played the words back in her head, her face began to burn. Admittedly, she'd broken from her usual professional protocol with the cheery and personable chitchat, enough that Hank had noticed and interpreted it as flirting.

Which it was, despite her declaration to Celia that it was a line she couldn't cross. After their conversation at Sammy's Pint, she'd gone home and studied the Georgia Bar Association's guidelines, which she already knew by heart. Dating a witness wasn't strictly prohibited as long as it didn't compromise her representation of her client. So why did it feel sleazy?

"You know what, Hank? Just shut up and drive."

They followed the directions on her smartphone, and by late afternoon arrived at a small brick house in Forest Park, a suburban community of small square homes enclosed within chain-link fences. A rusted SUV that looked like it could have been their Suburban's older brother sat in the driveway.

A plane roared overhead, leading her to conclude they were directly underneath the flight path for Hartsfield-Jackson International Airport. Probably one of the cheapest neighborhoods in the Greater Atlanta area.

"Let me do this," Hank said. His knock on the weathered wooden door brought a throaty bark from inside.

An old dog, if Theo had to guess, and a big one. She clutched her portfolio to her chest as if it were a shield.

Jalinda held up her phone. "I assume you want me to record this one too."

A yell from inside quieted the eruption and a man answered the door. He was thin and drawn, dressed in gray work pants with a plaid shirt. "You Hank Maloney?" he asked.

"Sure am. Donald Lipscomb?" Hank stuck out his fat hand for a shake and slipped into his detective persona. "Thanks for meeting with us. As I told you on the phone, we're working on a case that involves your niece. Your great-niece, I mean. I was hoping we could ask some questions."

He introduced Theo as an attorney who was looking into possible legal action, and Jalinda as her assistant.

"What kind of legal action? They told me she killed herself."

Theo girded herself against a possible dog attack and followed him inside, where the stench of cigarette smoke nearly choked her. She passed on the offer of an upholstered chair in favor of a wooden stool he likely used as a side table for his ashtray and beer. The instant she sat down, a gray-bearded black lab began sniffing her feet.

Watching the dog warily in case it lifted its leg, she asked, "Were you aware your great-niece had reported being raped a month before her suicide?"

He answered with a look of disgust. "I hadn't heard that. Do they know who did it?"

She was careful with the details, doling them out slowly so he'd grasp the horror of Hayley's death. "Are you a Harwood sports fan, Mr. Lipscomb? Did you happen to see them win their national basketball championship last month?"

"Watched it right here in this chair," he said. "Kentucky never knew what hit 'em."

"So you recognize these names—Matt Frazier, D'Anthony Caldwell and Tanner Watson." She waited for his nod. "They're the ones who raped her. We're absolutely certain. We acquired a video they made while they were doing it. All three of them were laughing and talking about Hayley like she was a slut. They wanted to show it to their friends and brag about it."

"She was unconscious, Don," Hank chimed in, leaning forward as if to emphasize they were talking man to man. "They slipped her a Mickey that made her pass out, and then they took turns with her. One of them even used her phone to take a picture of her without her clothes when they were done. When she came to, she went to call for help and that picture was staring back at her. Can you imagine what kind of low-life does something like that to a girl?"

Lipscomb's fists curled and released as his agitation grew, and his knee began to bounce. "What's going to happen to them?"

"That could be up to you," Theo said calmly. "They should be held responsible, don't you agree?"

"Damn right."

She went on to explain the process Hayley followed, from the student health center to the police, and then to a trusted professor. "The police and the administration refused to help her. We think it was because they were ballplayers. Harwood didn't want them arrested because they couldn't win with their best players in jail. People don't want to cheer for them, don't want to buy those championship T-shirts. So they just ignored that evidence—I'm talking video proof they raped her while she was passed out—and took the players' word for it that she wanted to have sex with all of them."

"But she couldn't have given consent because she wasn't even conscious," Hank reminded.

"No one believed her, Mr. Lipscomb. After she told a couple of her sorority sisters, one of them said she was just being a drama queen. They told her if she didn't shut up, she was going to cost them the championship. They didn't care about her being raped. They just wanted to win that trophy. So they turned on her even though *she* was the victim. On the night the Hornets won—you were probably sitting right here in this chair when it happened—she went into the bathroom at her sorority house and slashed her wrists. She died all alone thinking nobody cared what happened to her."

The man's eyes filled with tears that he hurriedly wiped away. "What are you going to do about it?"

Theo opened her portfolio to the cause of action document, its space for the name of the plaintiff blank. "You were her great-uncle, the only real family she had. As the next of kin, you're the only one entitled to speak on Hayley's behalf. It's up to you to make them pay."

CHAPTER SIX

Harwood Street, marking the northern edge of the antebellum campus, was the epicenter of the university's social and commercial activity. Bars, restaurants and T-shirt shops, one after another, all catering to students on a budget. The Bistro was a cut above, and thus a popular lunch place for faculty and administrators.

Celia had run into a friend unexpectedly in the campus bookstore and they agreed to get lunch.

She recognized the waitress as a former student from her Intro to Theater class and smiled at her. "I'll have the chicken caesar, dressing on the side, please."

"Make it two," said Kay Crylak, the women's softball coach. "But you can drown mine in dressing if you want."

Though only in her mid-thirties, Kay's face already showed signs of her years in the sun—leathered skin with deep red spots on her face and arms. She wore her dark hair short enough to tame what would otherwise have been a mass of curls.

Celia had met her through Gina when she arrived at Harwood eight years ago from a successful stint as coach of a junior college in Florida. After three semi-serious relationships, Kay was once again single and had made clear her romantic interest in Celia. Unrequited interest, as it were, since Celia felt nothing but friendship. To Kay's credit, she'd handled the rejection with her easygoing manner.

"I was surprised to see you," Celia said. "I figured you'd be on the road recruiting all summer."

"I'm heading up for a couple of tournaments in the Smokies in August, but mostly we're set for next year. Twelve scholarships and eight walk-ons." Kay looked around and lowered her voice. "Provided two of my scholarships pass remedial algebra in summer school. It's hard enough to coach 'em in softball without having to get 'em through math and English. And then I have to figure out how I'm going to keep 'em eligible for four years."

"I hear ya." The diction training from her early TV career went out the window after only a few minutes of being exposed to Kay's Southern drawl.

"A lot of homework on the bus, I reckon."

From living with Gina for ten years, Celia knew all about the NCAA's rules for academic progress. More than once, she'd been pressured by someone in the athletic department to grant exceptions that allowed players to make up work so they wouldn't fail her class and lose their eligibility for sports. "You wouldn't believe how many calls I get from coaches wanting special considerations for players."

Kay chuckled and rolled her eyes. "Why wouldn't I believe it? I've made my share of calls like that. Then I have to go build a fire under my girls' britches so they don't cut class and make me look like an idiot."

"I don't mind them missing class as long as they're serious about making up the work. I know they have travel schedules and can't be there all the time. But some of them think they ought to get a pass just because they play for the school. I'm not going to hand out grades for nothing—especially if they act like they're entitled."

Frazier, Caldwell and Watson must have felt especially entitled when police officers took their word for it that Hayley had consented to gang sex even after seeing video of their brutal assault.

The details of Hayley's rape haunted Celia every day. To wake to the horror of knowing something awful had happened—she knew that feeling all too well—only to have it confirmed in the worst way. Then to have her trust shattered by those who didn't seem to care she'd been violated.

"...to be proactive in class," Kay went on, bringing Celia back to the present. "They're supposed to go meet with all their professors at the beginning of the semester and figure out the conflicts. I tell 'em to read ahead and take exams early whenever they can. And every time we hit the road, travel time is study time. No iPods, no video games. Just homework."

"Gina was the same way." In fact, Harwood's female athletes had always been far more conscientious about stopping by her office to talk about how to offset their participation in sports. "You know, I'm trying to think of the last time one of the football players came in for a meeting like that. Or anybody from the basketball team. Maybe twice in twelve years."

"Don't you know, girl? The rules are different if you have dangly bits, especially if you play one of the big money sports. Hell, those coaches don't even teach their own classes. They have grad assistants do it for 'em. It's no wonder the players screw around. Sports is all they care about. They're just following the example their coaches set."

Women's basketball wasn't exactly big money, but it was considered a major sport—certainly more visible than women's soccer or softball. Gina had felt a lot of pressure to succeed on the court, sloughing off her teaching load on her assistant coaches as well. The AD—athletic director—actually encouraged it. "Gina wasn't exactly a shining example as far as teaching her classes, but she never let her girls get away with anything. Not on the court, and not in the classroom either."

"I'm the the same way."

Gina also kept her team's business in the locker room. Squabbles between players and coaches, academic struggles and love triangles—all of it took place out of the public eye. "You ever have a player get in trouble, Kay? I remember a couple of Gina's underage girls got caught with a bottle of tequila in their dorm room. Then another one got into a fight with somebody at a bonfire. She always dealt with that kind of stuff herself… benched them for two or three games."

"The worst thing I ever had to deal with was when my starting left fielder accidentally *borrowed* somebody's bike off a rack at the library. That was just last year. We talked the cops out of pressing charges, but I still suspended her ass for two games. Talk about tough love—that killed us because she was hitting four-fifty."

Celia was intrigued by the mention of the police. "How did you manage to get the cops to drop it?"

"There's this guy we're supposed to call. The AD handed out a bunch of his business cards at a meeting a couple of years ago." Kay opened her wallet to find it. "Here it is…Austin Thompson. I think he went to law school here a few years ago, but apparently he works now at Hubbard-McCaffrey. I guess that's one of the law firms downtown. All I know is he's in with all the big shots in the AD's office. And the boosters too. Pals around with the players…you know the kind—a jock sniffer. He shows up like a genie out of a magic lamp whenever one of 'em gets in trouble with the cops. Bar fights, DUIs, shoplifting. I bet the football team has him on speed dial."

So that's how it worked—an attorney on call who ran interference for all the athletes. Apparently the basketball team had him on speed dial too. "Who pays him? The athletic department?"

Kay paused her story while the waitress delivered their lunch.

"Beats me. I just know I called him like they said and he turned a bike theft into a lost and found."

If Celia had to bet, he also had a hand in turning a gang rape of an unconscious woman into consensual sex.

* * *

Theo twisted in her chair at the massive conference table where she and Jalinda had splayed more than a dozen law books open to cases relevant to wrongful death. The State of Georgia made it all but impossible to hold another party responsible for suicide, no matter how ugly the circumstances.

"For the sake of argument, let's assume we get past the issue of standing," Theo said. A formidable assumption, since the defense would argue Donald Lipscomb was not Hayley Burkhart's closest surviving relative, and therefore not eligible to sue anyone for her loss. "What's our best way around *Appling*? Hayley didn't lose the ability to behave rationally during the thirty-day period following the rape. No rage, no frenzy, no loss of control. The defense will argue there's no proximal cause of death. Case dismissed."

Jalinda reviewed her notes, which were tagged as usual with multicolored tabs linking them to the evidence they'd collected so far. "So we'll need to document her state of mind. Interviews with friends, sorority sisters. Establish a change in personality or demeanor during the window."

"Good, good." She'd gotten some of that in her interview with Michael, which Celia had arranged. As they'd suspected, his boyfriend, Gavin Sandifor, played for the Hornets and was part of the players' secret group where the video had been shared. "And since she reported the crime to the student health center and campus police, followed up when she received the video, and ultimately took it to one of her professors when the police refused to charge her assailants, we can also show that *she* believed the university was equally responsible for her state of mind."

It was a stretch but Theo couldn't cut new law out of whole cloth—she had to shape the facts of the narrative around existing cases. The key was convincing first a judge then a jury that Hayley's feelings of being violated—along with frustration at the university's lack of action on her behalf—had created a sense of hopelessness. When her rapists were glorified after their championship win, she suffered a sudden mental breakdown that led to her impulsive act.

Jalinda's nose wrinkled with uncertainty. "What if they say she was already unstable? That the circumstances of her birth and the loss of her grandmother made her unable to cope. Or she suffered remorse after engaging in sex with multiple partners. Or maybe she was just acting out a dramatic scene because of her interest in performance studies."

Already unable to cope. Without realizing it, Jalinda had just given her a brilliant idea.

"Damn, Jalinda. I'm going to use that to argue her suicide was foreseeable. I wish you'd think more seriously about my advice to go to law school. You're a natural."

"It's not natural. I get it mostly from you and Kendra. I listen when you practice your arguments. Some of it rubs off."

Penny appeared in the doorway and rapped her knuckles gently on the door. "Theo, I have KDP News on the line. They're doing a segment tonight on a study just released that shows male nurses are paid more than female nurses. They want you for a live interview around seven. I checked…you have a royal blue top and white necklace hanging on the back of the door in the studio."

Good thing, since she was wearing a forest-green dress, which would render her transparent against the computer-generated backgrounds some news stations used for remote interviews. "Tell them yes, but not to leave me hanging like they did last time. I'm out of here if we haven't started by seven thirty. And see if you can get me a copy of that study. No, get me Gloria for about an hour this afternoon. Have her review it so she can tell me what I need to know."

Hank squeezed past Penny into the room, surprisingly clean-shaven and wearing a crisp white shirt with a dark sport coat.

"What's up with you?" Theo asked. "You have a date or something?"

Scoffing at her remark, he slid a piece of paper across the table. "I just talked to the nurse at the student health center, the one that comes in for all the rape cases. Her official title is Sexual Assault Nurse Examiner. She said the campus cops picked up the rape kit the same day Hayley Burkhart came in. In fact, they called twice asking if it was ready."

Why would they be so anxious to pick up the rape kit if they had no intention of charging the men responsible?

Theo examined the form, a copy of the receipt the courts required to establish the chain of custody. The scrawl on the signature line was illegible. "Any idea whose chicken scratch this is?"

He drew a small notepad from his chest pocket. "I know he's about five-nine with dark hair and a mustache with flecks of gray. That puts him at forty-five or so, and he had a couple of bars on his collar. Probably makes him a sergeant."

"But he was too shy to leave his name. What do you make of that?"

"Raynelle...that's the nurse's name, Raynelle Willis. I knew her back when I was at APD and she worked over at Emory. She said the cops treated this case like it was a big emergency, like they were really going to nail those guys. She couldn't believe it when I told her they never even filed charges."

So he knew Harwood's rape specialist from his days on the police force. And apparently he'd wanted to make a good impression on her, since he'd cleaned himself up.

"And by the way, Raynelle couldn't tell me much because of the privacy laws, but she let it slip that Hayley Burkhart showed signs of sexual trauma consistent with multiple assailants."

Theo did her best to fight off a visible shudder.

"So the police now have the rape kit?" Jalinda asked as she started a new page of notes.

"Funny you should ask." He leafed through his notepad. "After I talked to Raynelle, I called Bobby Hill at the police station, my rookie contact. He took a look around the evidence room, including their cold storage. I'll give you three guesses what's not there. These guys've got some brass ones, all right."

The conspiracy grew more brazen at every turn. Everyone involved in the case was acting with impunity, certain there would be no accounting. Even Celia, who'd witnessed the duplicity firsthand, would be shocked to know the coverup ran so deep.

* * *

Celia arranged her dinner on a tray with a small salad and glass of chardonnay. Her evening ritual—a "gourmet" meal in a disposable dish from the microwave, eaten in front of the evening news.

The teaser had promised a story about the salary discrepancies between male and female nurses, which was in the news because of a recent national study. Ever since she'd read about Theo and the work of her law firm, anything remotely related to equal rights for women got her attention. But she hadn't expected Theo's face to suddenly fill half her screen alongside that of the baritone news anchor.

"...if you could explain why these researchers concluded this is the result of *systemic* bias. What exactly does that mean?"

Theo's response was delayed by a couple of seconds while his question transmitted over the airwaves. "Right, systemic bias involves human *systems*, such as those in place at work, at school or within a consumer transaction. One of the ways it manifests in the workplace is when employees are judged not by their skills, knowledge and performance, but by their characteristics—in this case, by their gender. The importance of this study is that it proves men in the nursing profession are paid more than women across the board for the exact same jobs, even when their skill sets and experience are identical."

The blue blouse picked up the color of her eyes, which looked especially bright in the studio lights. Small white earrings that matched her necklace peeked out beneath her blond hair. She truly was an attractive woman, worthy of her vaunted inclusion on *People* magazine's list.

The news anchor challenged her in a voice that suggested he took her implications personally. "There's a counterargument however, one that says their jobs aren't identical, that men are called on to perform more physical tasks, such as lifting patients or controlling those who become unruly."

With a hint of a condescending smile, Theo waited patiently for him to finish. "Female nurses are called on also for such duties, but they aren't paid extra when they do them. In fact, they perform the same jobs as male nurses day in and day out. Some may even be physically stronger than men, but the point is we don't measure their strength and use those results to set their salaries. Let's assume we did, however. No matter where they scored on the strength measure, they'd still be required to lift patients and perform other physical duties. For those who scored lower, the work would be more difficult. What sense would it make to pay them less?"

The anchor tried to jump back into the conversation but Theo hardly took a breath.

"In our society, women more than men are socialized to nurture others and dispense compassion, qualities that are universally recognized as essential in the nursing profession. Yet they aren't paid more for possessing those qualities. It goes without saying there are plenty of nurturing, compassionate men, just as there are women who are physically strong. But studies have documented that men aren't called on as often as women for emotional support. Why is it we value physical strength over compassion when we assess someone's worth?"

"Zing!" Celia shouted.

"Furthermore," Theo went on, "women are far more likely to experience social assaults in the workplace or abusive treatment from patients, doctors and administrators. Yet female nurses who have to put up with those things are paid less—more than five thousand dollars a year on average. That amounts to as much as two hundred thousand over a career, twice that when you consider the lost opportunity to grow wealth. That's blatant sex discrimination, all because the *systems* in which nurses work overvalue the perceived skills of men while undervaluing those of women. Such discrimination is against the law."

With cold, hard facts, Theo had practically laid out a legal case for the taking. The news anchor could only manage a contemptuous scowl as he grudgingly thanked her and introduced the commercial break.

Celia hit the rewind button and watched the interview again, paying special attention to Theo's emphatic expressions and confident voice. She was almost robotic—fact, fact, fact, fact, conclusion. An unbending pragmatist, she'd shut down the anchorman's argument with the same bluntness as she'd dismissed any notion of dating Celia. While it wasn't exactly endearing, there was a certain appeal to her candor and precision when it was directed toward someone else.

Admittedly, she'd become frustrated with Theo's professional demeanor. Their only contact since talking on the phone the day she dropped off Michael's thumb drive had come through her administrative assistant, Penny Lowrey—confirmation they were proceeding with the case and thanks for setting up the meeting with Michael and his boyfriend. Not a word about what she'd learned from their interview. Considering how deeply Celia was invested in the case, she surely deserved to be kept in the loop.

But it wasn't only case updates she wanted. Now that Theo had briefly opened the door, she wanted to throw the rules out the window. If not now, then she wanted a promise for later when the case was over. Women like Theo didn't come along every day. Or every decade.

CHAPTER SEVEN

"Right here's fine," Theo told the Uber driver as she passed him an extra five bucks.

Parking on Harwood's campus was nearly impossible for visitors, even now that spring semester was officially over. At least the ride from her office in the backseat had given her time to review Jalinda's notes on the woman she was set to meet. Sarah Holcomb, Hayley's sorority sister and roommate, the girl who'd found her in the shower. She was a junior from Chattanooga majoring in computer science.

According to Michael, Sarah had been supportive of Hayley after the rape, unlike some of her sisters.

Jalinda was waiting at the designated meeting point, sitting on a low wall that lined the sidewalk in front of Jackson Library. "She's waiting for us in a study room on the third floor."

For someone who seldom interacted socially with co-workers, Jalinda had an uncanny ability to relate to total strangers. Her no-nonsense approach made them feel as if they were compelled to answer, when in fact, their testimony wasn't required unless they'd been served a subpoena.

"Is she cooperative?"

"Traumatized is more like it. I got the feeling she found it therapeutic to talk about it."

To blend in better on campus, Theo had dressed down for the day in ankle pants and a light blazer with the sleeves pushed up. No doubt the university would take umbrage at her trespassing so she could gather information to sue them.

Sarah sat behind a small table facing the door. "Just a second," she said in greeting as she finished messaging on her phone.

Jalinda set up the recorder and readied herself with a blank legal pad while Theo studied their subject. She looked like hundreds of coeds on Harwood's campus—trim and athletic with straight dark hair pulled tight in a ponytail. A starter on the volleyball team, according to Jalinda's notes.

"All done." She set her phone aside. "I guess you want to talk about Hayley. Do I need a lawyer or anything? I'm just a witness, right?"

"That's correct. We're just trying to get some background information about Hayley's state of mind last spring. We're talking with lots of people who knew her." Theo introduced herself as an attorney representing the family. "Jalinda tells me you and Hayley were roommates."

"Just this past year. Not best friends or anything, but we got along okay. I was the one who found her in the shower."

They listened patiently as she described her personal aftermath of Hayley's suicide. To this day, Sarah felt guilty for being wrapped up in a "stupid" basketball game while Hayley suffered. And still wishing she could have done something to help her.

Through a series of probing questions, Theo got some of what she needed—confirmation that Hayley's overall demeanor had changed dramatically in late February.

"She started doing everything with Michael Fitzgerald, a guy she knew from the drama department. He wasn't her boyfriend or anything like that. Everybody knew he was gay. But he was a nice guy...I met him a few times. He was practically the only one she'd talk to. She came back to the room a couple of times and it was obvious she'd been crying. Or she'd be really quiet like she was worrying about something. It was like that for three or four days before she finally told us what happened."

According to Gloria's research, it wasn't unusual for women to keep their sexual assaults secret. The stigma attached to being a rape victim was more than some could bear.

"You seem certain of the date. Why does it stand out for you?"

"It was right before spring break. She was supposed to come with us to Daytona but she backed out at the last minute. And wouldn't say why at first. But then she did."

"How did the other women react when she told them about the rape?"

Sarah's face fell. "Not everybody believed her. It happened at a party—most of us were there, and everybody was pretty wasted. People always celebrate after big games. Things get kind of wild, you know? You lose control…you forget stuff. Nobody saw anything like what she said happened."

"What exactly did she say?"

"That she went with Michael, but he ran into somebody he knew. Probably a guy. The last thing she remembered was talking to Morgan Hunter and me right after she got there. Morgan's in our sorority too. She lives two doors down on our hall."

"Do you remember that conversation? With Hayley and Morgan, I mean."

"Yeah, we were standing by the big TV."

The more details, the better. "Was Hayley drinking anything?"

"We all were. There was a big table near the door where they were passing out drinks when you came in."

Theo turned to Jalinda. "Go back to the people we've talked to already and see if anyone has photos from the party. It would be good to know who was handing out those drinks."

"I can answer that," Sarah said, suddenly sitting up straight. "It was Ruben Vargas. They always make him do stuff like that, serve drinks and clean up, on account of he's a freshman."

Vargas was a reserve shooting guard, not otherwise implicated in the assault.

"I still want photos, Jalinda. Anything you can get." To Sarah, she said, "About Hayley's story...did you believe her when she said she was assaulted?"

"Not at first. Sawyer Niles—she's our president—she thought Hayley was being a drama queen, like she was playing a role. And a couple of them, like Morgan, kept telling her not to say anything because the guys could get kicked off the team."

So far, it was completely consistent with what Hayley had revealed in her messages with Michael.

"The thing is, we were all there and nobody saw anything. But I *do* remember she stayed out all night. It wasn't like her to do that. And then later she said somebody made a video of it—the rape, I mean—but she never showed it to any of us. I honestly didn't know what to think, but it was obvious to me *Hayley* believed she was assaulted," she mumbled, her voice hardened with regret. "I could have been a better friend about it."

As Sarah paused to compose her cracking voice, Jalinda produced a bottle of water from her shoulder bag.

The young woman went on to describe the party atmosphere in detail. Lots of booze and loud music, everyone in a joyous mood because they'd just beaten Vanderbilt. She couldn't recall seeing Hayley when the party began to break up.

Leaving aside the fact that being wasted meant a woman was incapable of giving consent, there was still a question of how much alcohol Hayley had consumed. According to Michael, she wasn't into it.

"Did Hayley drink a lot?"

"Not that I knew of. I never saw her drunk or anything. Or even buzzed. She wasn't much of a partier. She only went to things like that because it was a sorority event for all of us to go together—she was a good sister that way—but she usually left parties early, especially the wild ones."

Theo pressed on. "Did Hayley have any boyfriends? Did she ever talk about her sexual experiences?"

Sarah shook her head. "The only guy she ever mentioned having a crush on was Michael. That was her freshman year before she found out he was into dudes. But let's face it—even if she'd wanted to have sex with somebody, it wouldn't have been with three guys at the same time. That's what she said, that they took turns. I can tell you, she wasn't like that at all."

It wasn't enough to get Sarah's opinion. Theo needed examples of things Hayley had said or done that supported that characterization. With prodding, Sarah recounted conversations about dating and sex, the sort of girl talk roommates shared when they were drifting off to sleep.

"Tell me what you remember about Hayley's behavior in the weeks after the incident. Was she depressed? Angry? Frustrated?"

"All of those. Some days she was hysterical. Like the day they called her from the dean's office. I was sitting right there with her in the room. They told her how serious it was to make false allegations...something like that. She could be expelled."

That also tracked with the other evidence from her notes to Michael. Sarah's independent corroboration was an important addition, but not a smoking gun. A threat delivered by phone could have come from anyone—an administrator, a coach or even another student who wanted to protect the basketball program.

"One of her professors told her to go see a therapist so she did. Three or four times maybe. I don't think it helped all that much though. Her prof was going to report what happened to the chancellor. But nothing ever came of it—they didn't do anything at all."

As a last effort to confirm the version of events Celia and Michael had cobbled together, she asked for the names of everyone in their sorority who might have talked with Hayley about what happened. In particular, she needed to substantiate the claim that Hayley's state of mind deteriorated as a direct result of the school's inaction. That was critical in order to hold the university responsible for her death.

"...and Jordan Cooke. Now there's somebody you *really* ought to talk to. She's a Chi Omega but we're all friends. She was super pissed about it on account of it happened to her too, like a month ago. Not a whole bunch of guys like Hayley, but he did practically the same thing—put something in her drink while they were watching the tournament at Theta Pi house."

"A month ago, you say." The timeline was striking, but not as much as the fact that Jordan Cooke also had been drugged. "Did she report it?"

"Why bother? She saw how they handled Hayley. Those guys know all they have to do is say it was consensual. That's it. No more questions."

Theo looked at Jalinda, who nodded as she furiously made notes. They definitely wanted to talk to Jordan Cooke.

* * *

Celia cleared a corner of her desk for the cardboard box. "I appreciate this, Duncan. I packed that way too heavy to carry all the way from the faculty parking lot."

Duncan had been eager to help in any way he could, though his brown-nosing was for naught. She'd already submitted her final grades for the semester.

"Anything else I can do?" he asked.

"Relax already. You got a B-minus."

He pumped his fist and said a silent prayer skyward.

"But I'll be honest with you. A lot of that was for effort and for turning in your work on time. Acting requires a fair bit of natural aptitude, and I don't really think it's your grace. If you're set on a career in the performing arts, you might want to look on the business side."

"Don't worry. I promise not to sign up for any more of your classes. I'm a broadcast journalism major. I thought it would help if I had some performance experience, but Shakespeare doesn't exactly jibe with SportsCenter."

"And vice versa," she added with a chuckle.

As she arranged the research materials on her desk, she took another opportunity to look at the embossed letter that had arrived that morning in campus mail. Her promotion to full professor had been approved by Harwood's board of trustees, effective immediately. Finally, she could breathe a sigh of relief.

"You want me to unpack this for you?" Duncan asked, indicating the box.

"Sure, just stack it all on that middle shelf for now. Thank you."

The migration from home to office was routine, and one of the few days she drove her car to campus. During spring and fall semesters, she kept regular office hours but did most of her scholarly work at home where she wouldn't be interrupted. Summers were different. With the Fowler twins next door out of school for the summer, her office in Forbes Hall was quieter. Since there was nothing on her teaching schedule, she could come and go as she pleased and work undisturbed on campus. The third edition of her widely-used text, *The Television Actor's Handbook*, was due back to the publisher by the end of August. She'd submitted the book as the centerpiece of her promotion packet.

The irony was, despite her expertise and text, most of Harwood's TV performance classes were taught by someone else—a longtime adjunct—while she was relegated to theater courses. She hoped her new promotion would change that, along with ending her responsibility for the spring theater production.

"Did you see the *Daily Hornet*?" Duncan asked, his reference being the student newspaper. "They say Sacramento's going to take Matt Frazier with the number one pick. Then D'Anthony Caldwell could go second to Detroit. One and two from Harwood—how awesome is that!"

The mere mention of their names shattered her upbeat mood and made her want to spew obscenities. The endless accolades from the media—how Frazier and Caldwell's hard work had paid off, how they were good kids, good role models—sickened her. No one in the sports media, not even the outsiders who wrote provocative blogs, had written a word about their monstrous behavior, despite the number of people who knew about it. Somehow every whiff of allegation about the rape had been squelched.

"Duncan, did you happen to catch any rumors about those guys being involved in an incident last winter at one of the dorms? Something about a woman at a party?"

"Yeah, it turned out to be bogus. Some girl said she was raped, but all the people who were there said it didn't happen like that, that she made it all up to get the players in trouble. The cops didn't press charges, so there must not have been anything to it."

"I heard there was a video."

He shrugged, clearly oblivious.

It was infuriating how quickly the controversy had vanished, how the players' denial had completely shaped the narrative. People shut out the stories they didn't want to be true. Willful ignorance. Celia felt she was as much to blame for that as anyone, having given in to threats from the chancellor and board chair not to go public right away with the allegations.

How many others had been intimidated into silence?

* * *

Theo held the phone to her ear as she walked. "I'm on campus. Would it be all right if I stopped by your office?"

After a measured silence, Celia replied, "Oh, what the hell. Sure."

Even after Celia had agreed to proceed as a witness, her anxiousness was unmistakable. It said a lot about her commitment to the case that she was willing to meet in public.

The visit to campus had paid off so far. Sarah Holcomb proved an excellent witness, accurately chronicling Hayley's fall from a happy, friendly sorority sister to one who refused to socialize. One who cried frequently and suffered nightmares. And who grew especially despondent once she felt she'd exhausted all avenues of retribution.

That was the thrust of their case—the rape had thrown her into a depression that could have been mitigated had the university stood beside her and punished the men responsible. Instead, they'd further victimized her with overt threats of expulsion if she continued to tell her story. Their treatment of her amounted to depraved indifference.

Strolling across the azalea-lined campus, she took in its elegant beauty. It was a costume, not unlike the one Celia had worn to her office to disguise her identity. Underneath its veneer of Southern charm, Harwood was a bastion of misogyny.

Dropping in on Celia unannounced wasn't a professional necessity, but the temptation had proven too strong to resist. Ever since Hank had remarked on her flirtations, she'd kept her distance, waiting to see if her interest in Celia was only a passing fancy, something that would naturally fade if she didn't indulge it. Instead, she found Celia invading her thoughts each time she uncovered a new piece of information or identified a new witness. Justice for Hayley was her goal, but winning for Celia had become her motivation.

Unfortunately their case was still tenuous with a razor-thin margin for error. If they failed to prove the rape and subsequent coverup had caused Hayley to take her own life, Celia and the others would have sacrificed themselves for nothing.

She paused in the foyer of Forbes Hall long enough to view the building's directory. Faculty offices were on the third floor.

The antebellum building was as well kept as the university grounds. Marble stairs, glossy tile floors, mahogany wainscoting polished to a reflective shine. The aura of tradition and privilege was undeniable. No wonder Celia valued her position.

A young man, obviously a student, emerged from a room near the end of the hall, never looking up from his texting as he passed.

Theo continued to the open office to find Celia arranging things on a shelf, her back to the door. Clearing her throat, she leaned against the doorjamb. As Celia turned, her eyes lit up and she briefly smiled. "Playing hooky from your office, counselor?"

"Sort of," she said with a chuckle. "I came by for an interview with one of Hayley's sorority sisters. Thought I'd stop by. Are you sure you're okay with me being here?"

"Of course." Despite her statement, she scooted behind Theo to close the door. For obvious reasons, she didn't want to be overheard talking about a lawsuit against her employer.

The room's centerpiece was an L-shaped desk covered with folders that surrounded a computer monitor and keyboard. Bookshelves lined the opposite wall. The only decorative piece in the room was a framed poster for *The Pirates of Penzance*.

"I take it you're a Gilbert and Sullivan fan," Theo said, her eyes drifting downward to note that Hayley and Michael had starred in the production. She'd hardly recognized them in costume.

"We staged that a year ago last spring. I wouldn't call it my favorite, but it's hard to find quality musicals that fit our theater budget. We picked that one because all the Gilbert and Sullivan work is out of copyright." She arranged the armchairs in front of her desk so they faced each other. "I thought I'd hear from you sooner. I know you're busy, but…"

Theo had no choice but to come clean. "To tell you the truth, it took me a few days to get over myself and start focusing on the case instead of my sudden infatuation with Little CeCe. I'm really sorry about that. It was unprofessional…and not something I usually do. Or ever do."

"Don't worry about it." Celia's thin-lipped smile was hard to read, but she definitely wasn't annoyed. "I enjoyed talking with you at the pub."

"Good…so did I. But I want you to know my head's back on straight and Hayley's my priority now."

Celia gestured toward one of the chairs. Then she took the opposite seat, crossing a leg to show half of her thigh beneath a black denim skirt as she leaned across the desk to grab a piece of paper. "I was planning to call you later anyway. I got this letter today. It's a done deal."

Theo smiled to read of the promotion. "Congratulations. This puts that issue to bed. I bet you're relieved."

"You have no idea." She pushed the letter aside and instantly shifted to a businesslike tone of her own. "So how did it go with Michael and Gavin?"

"I got what I needed for now," Theo said, making a conscious effort not to let her eyes drift downward toward Celia's exposed leg. "I've also talked with several of Hayley's friends. I think we'll be ready to file soon. Just a few loose ends." She updated Celia on the case so far. "I stopped by because, well…we're putting together a strong case, but I want to make sure you're clear that it's not a sure thing—not by a long shot. We're going to make a helluva lot of noise when this goes public. First is a press conference in front of the entrance to Harwood University, timed so it hits the evening news cycle. Then if all goes as planned, I'll spend a couple of days in our teleconferencing studio doing all the news shows. This will be a major story because the players are well known. You can expect to see it in all the papers, all the talk shows, practically everywhere."

"You don't have to sell me on it, Theo. I've seen you in action. Teresa Gonzalez. Loretta Collingwood."

"That's what I'm talking about. If we're lucky, the press conference alone will be enough to get someone to file criminal charges against the players involved—either the DA or the DOJ. The board of trustees will go into damage control. And I can all but guarantee you there'll be a Title IX investigation too. Those things have serious teeth. You end up with rape crisis centers and compliance officers scrutinizing every single reported case."

"Which is exactly what Harwood needs."

"Right." And that was the disconnect for Theo—the best outcome wasn't necessarily a judgment in a civil trial. "But the way it's all coming together, I honestly don't know if we'll have enough evidence to convince a judge to let us bring the wrongful death suit to trial. I just felt like I needed to be honest with you about that."

"I'm not worried about your honesty, Theo." Celia patted her hand, a familiar gesture Theo found charming. "Besides, it's what happens in the end that matters, isn't it? Like you said, this is going to stir things up. I just hope Gupton and Tuttle don't weasel their way out of this. If they covered it up, somebody ought to file charges against them too."

Theo savored Celia's touch, almost taking her hand. Yielding to that urge would only confirm her concerns about stopping by in the first place. Theirs was supposed to be a professional relationship.

She shifted and put her hands in her pockets. "I want those two to face the music as much as you do, and anyone else at

Harwood who had a hand in this. But it's a tough case to make if you're the prosecutor…legally speaking, that is. What they did was reprehensible, but it didn't break the law. And keep in mind, Harwood's going to do everything in its power to get the entire case thrown out. Even if we get to court, Hayley's uncle doesn't give us a whole lot of leverage. He won't garner much sympathy from a judge or jury because he didn't have a close relationship with her. They'll be reluctant to give him a large award for pain and suffering. The defendants know that, so they'll push us to settle for peanuts just to get this story off the front page."

"Such bastards." In a matter of moments, her gentle face had turned to an angry scowl.

"We've got one thing in our favor though. No matter what else happens, the facts as we know them will come out the moment we file. From a PR perspective, this will be a nightmare for Harwood. Think Sandusky at Penn State. Gupton could be pressured to step down. Tuttle could lose his seat on the board. Is that justice? No, but it's better than nothing."

Celia walked toward the window and folded her arms as she looked out. "They traded a woman's life for a goddamn basketball trophy."

A pithy line, which Theo committed to memory so she could work it into her comments at the press conference, minus the swearing. "We aren't conceding anything. I'm only trying to manage your expectations."

She answered without turning around. "I get it, Theo. It boils my blood how apathetic people are about this. Not just here—everywhere. Men do whatever they want, don't they? It's been like that since the beginning of time. People cover their ears so they can pretend it doesn't happen. That way they don't have to feel responsible, so they don't have to do anything about it."

After a thoughtful silence, Theo replied, "That's exactly why our firm exists, Celia. I promise you we'll take it right into their teeth."

"I know you will." She smiled weakly and returned to her seat. "I appreciate what you're doing. Not just for Hayley, for all of us. You make a difference, Theo."

Between the two of them, Celia was the real hero. It took a lot of courage to stand up to power, especially to those who controlled her livelihood. The fact that she'd done so to win justice for someone else made her someone Theo couldn't stop thinking about.

CHAPTER EIGHT

Theo had temporarily traded the sofa and chairs in her office for a small conference table. She needed a workspace, and all the common areas were now taken up with the wage theft case. As Kendra hit her stride, the interruptions grew less frequent, allowing Theo and her team of two to focus almost exclusively on Hayley Burkhart.

They were building quite a library of evidence for their case. Jalinda had catalogued the messages between Hayley and Michael, cross-referencing them with the known timeline and the relevant social media posts of everyone linked to the basketball team or Hayley's sorority. To that list, they added the recollections of the women who talked with Hayley after the assault.

Hank was working his sources to identify anyone in the DA's office who might be friendly to the idea of pursuing criminal charges. The last thing they wanted was an assistant DA who would give the illusion of a serious investigation, but then follow the campus police's lead and declare the sex was consensual.

Jalinda sat at the far end of the table arranging documents for their afternoon meeting while Theo scanned the *Atlanta Journal-Constitution* for updates on the Harwood players. Frazier and Caldwell were splashed across the front page in living color in a feature touting their promising NBA careers. The draft was two weeks away, after which both players were set to become multimillionaires. Rich, privileged rapists.

"Any more news on the whereabouts of the rape kit?" Theo asked hopefully.

"None that I know of, but Hank was supposed to check in with his friend again. Maybe it turned up."

If Hank didn't get his hands on it soon, the results could be moot in a court of law. It was bad enough the chain of custody was now suspect, since someone could have tampered with it while it was unaccounted for. Even if it suddenly appeared in the police's evidence locker, any proof that Hayley had been drugged would be gone if the biological samples suffered chemical breakdown because they hadn't been properly refrigerated.

The "maybes" were piling up too fast for Theo's comfort. Chief among them was the precarious relationship between Donald Lipscomb and his great-niece.

She flipped through several photographs Lipscomb had sent to prove their familial bond. The most recent was a Christmas gathering at his sister's house when Hayley was twelve. His only documented tie to the family, it seemed, was his conservatorship for Belinda, for which he was paid a modest administrative fee each year. Hayley's trust, the one her grandmother had set aside for college, had reverted to the state for her mother's care.

"Pain and suffering," she mumbled. That was their first avenue for recovery, so they'd have to prove Lipscomb was emotionally distraught over Hayley's death. She was, after all, his last living relative.

From a business standpoint, Constantine and Associates didn't stand to collect much unless they went to trial and won substantial damages or disgorgement. But could a jury be convinced to award that much money to someone like

Lipscomb? That was a question she tried not to think about. If the case had required more time and resources, it would have been difficult to proceed, no matter how much Theo wanted to win for both Hayley and Celia.

"Is there anyone else we need to interview?" she asked.

Wordlessly, Jalinda produced an interview log with names and addresses.

All were checked off except one—Jordan Cooke, the sorority girl who reportedly had experienced a similar assault. Now that spring semester had ended, she was traveling for the summer with her mother in Europe.

"Lunch is here if you're interested," Penny said. She rolled in a cart with a small tray of salads, sandwiches and sodas, a standing order from the café downstairs for anyone too busy to step out.

Hank followed on her heels and wasted no time helping himself to a corned beef on rye. Before sitting, he slid a thumb drive across the table.

"Check it out, Jalinda," Theo said. "Hell has frozen over. Hank Maloney just handed me something related to a computer."

He was notoriously anti-technology, favoring legwork and phones over computers. "It's not mine. Came from my son Mark. I asked him to help me out. He found something you need to see."

After taking a bite of a tuna wrap, she inserted the thumb drive into the USB port on her laptop. It opened to three numbered video files. "What have we got here?"

"Listen to the first one. It's our cameraman."

The clip in question contained a snippet of the rape video. *"Get out the way, man."* It was said to D'Anthony Caldwell, who'd lunged into the camera's line of sight to say he had next.

"Notice what he said. Not 'get out *of* the way,' just 'get out the way.' Now click on the second one. It's an interview after the Tulane game with Ruben Vargas, the reserve shooting guard. He's talking about D'Anthony Caldwell."

"He's a beast. We get him the ball down low and get out the way, man."

The third file was audio-only, looping the common line from both files over and over. The voice and inflection were indistinguishable.

"Looks like we found another name for our defendant list," Hank said smugly.

The voice file was convincing, especially with Sarah Holcomb's testimony that Vargas was the one handing out drinks at the after-game party. Still, they couldn't risk having their entire case thrown out over a mistaken identity. "Probably...but I don't particularly relish the thought of being sued for guessing wrong. Find him and talk to him. Let him hear this. Tell him we're having our experts track the digital fingerprints of the video to identify who recorded it. See if he'll admit to anything."

Hank mumbled as he scribbled on his notepad, "Track the digital footprints...whatever the hell that means."

"He'll figure it out." She turned to Jalinda. "Assuming we hold off on adding another defendant, could we be ready to file on Monday?"

Jalinda tipped her head from side to side as she studied her array of documents. "Yes."

That's why Jalinda was her favorite paralegal. She never hedged on a yes-no question, and once she gave her word, she made it happen.

Hank held up a hand while he hastily chewed and swallowed his sandwich. "What's your hurry, chief? I thought you were waiting for that Cooke girl to get back from Europe."

"She's not a witness to the events, and as far as we know, she didn't have direct contact with the victim." She tossed the newspaper so it slid across the table. "The NBA draft is two weeks from today. I want teams to think twice about picking these bastards. Let's get Hayley's story front and center while they're talking it over. We file Monday in time to make the six o'clock news, and we release the video to the networks so it goes viral. That'll give our allegations credibility."

The court wouldn't appreciate her poisoning the jury pool. But then, they never did.

The decision to file on Monday meant she should call Celia and give her a heads-up. Or better yet, see her. But first, there was something she needed to take care of.

She picked up her desk phone and dialed her assistant. "Penny, get me Bill Auger."

* * *

The brass walls of the Weller Regent Hotel's elevator cast a near-perfect reflection that allowed Celia to check her look. For her meeting with Theo on the fortieth-floor terrace, she'd raced home from her office to change into a sleeveless gray dress with a silver chain belt that cinched her waist. Other than the occasional reception for a visiting dignitary or scholar, she attended very few events that called for anything other than business wear. This particular dress was left over from a cocktail social hosted by the faculty senate for the outgoing chair.

Seeing Theo again called for flair, especially since they were meeting in a downtown cocktail bar at happy hour. Did that signal a change in attitude about dating? If Theo insisted on keeping their relationship purely professional, Celia intended to show her what she was missing. This case wouldn't last forever. When it ended, she wanted to be at the top of Theo's wish list.

Stepping onto the terrace, she immediately noticed several professionally dressed women—some of them representing the profession that hung around hotel bars at happy hour. Young and smiling, teetering on four-inch heels and showing lots of skin. Not a place she thought Theo would have chosen.

"I'm meeting someone. Theodora Constantine."

The sultry hostess, herself bound tightly in a black spandex minidress, lit up with recognition. "You must be Dr. Perone. Right this way."

Pleased to hear her name, she followed to a nearly deserted covered area of the terrace. With every step, she grew more certain of herself, throwing her shoulders back and lifting her chin. Determined to make Theo eat her heart out.

Theo sat at a cocktail table in the corner, where a bottle of champagne chilled in a bucket of ice. Tucking away her phone at the sound of their footsteps, she stood and took in Celia's appearance, giving away her approval with a smile. "Glad you could make it on short notice. I hope this is okay. I was afraid if we sat outside, we'd be fighting off drunken pharmaceutical salesmen." She wore a salmon-colored skirt and matching blouse that managed to look both elegant and businesslike.

"It's fine. Kind of reminds me of those movies where the gangsters have their own private table in the back of the ethnic restaurant."

"A lot of those end badly for the gangsters. Should I be worried?"

"Only if I wipe down my glass before I excuse myself to the ladies' room."

"Ah, fingerprints." Theo poured two glasses of bubbly and raised her glass in a toast. "To...gangsters in backrooms."

The lighthearted banter was reminiscent of their dinner at Sammy's Pint. Theo's mood was more upbeat, a pleasant departure from the rather pessimistic visit to her office, where she'd warned the case might not be winnable.

"I'm sorry about the other day, Celia. I only meant to catch you up on the case, not to bring you down with bad news. And I'm sorry I haven't stayed in touch. I think we've turned the corner on our preparation though, so I feel better about where we stand. And about everything else, if you want to know the truth."

Celia had no idea what "everything else" meant, but she liked this interesting new dimension that appeared when Theo allowed herself to relax. With one leg gently bobbing as it swung across her knee and her elbows resting languidly on the arms of a chair, she was the very picture of sex appeal.

Snapping her thoughts from that observation, Celia reminded herself this was supposed to be a business meeting.

Theo explained that they'd completed their preliminary interviews and were confident they could establish a cause for action. It was time now to file their case and blow the lid off the secrets at Harwood University.

The news stirred a surprising sense of apprehension. Celia had been ready to level charges the first day she'd gone to Theo's office, but since then had come to accept the slow wheels of justice. The thorough investigation, the meticulous planning. And warnings about all the things that could go wrong. Now everything was ready to explode. At least in the interim she'd gotten her promotion.

"I was just coming around to accepting the fact that our case was dragging out. I've been telling myself every day that patience is a virtue."

"And it is…or so I hear. I don't have any myself. You can chalk the timing up to my mean streak." Theo folded her arms across her chest. With a wily look, she said, "I decided we should get this out there a couple of weeks before the NBA draft—see if we can give those teams second thoughts about who they might be picking."

Celia sighed and shook her head. "Why? You think their fans won't support a rapist? Look at Harwood. They were more than willing to ignore what happened to Hayley so they could win a championship. What makes you think the NBA will be any different?"

"Because professional sports is big business. Teams look long and hard before they draft somebody with character issues. It's a risk, but nothing a good PR agent can't clean up. This case is different though. It would be downright reckless to spend your first-round draft pick on somebody who might be going to prison for twenty years."

She had a point—if it were true. "You honestly think that could happen?"

"There's always a chance. I've been looking at that video." She shook her head with disgust. "Once its makes the nightly news, a lot of alumni—especially women—are going to hit the roof. Don't be surprised if Harwood backpedals and decides to investigate. They'll have to do something to save face. And there will be talk of the DA stepping in. Even a whiff of criminal charges could torpedo Frazier and Caldwell's draft position."

Celia chuckled sardonically. "Wouldn't it be something if both of them dropped to the second round? Millions of dollars down the drain."

"And while that would be great news, it's just the tip of the iceberg. Remember, we're still going after them for wrongful death. Your boss included."

The reminder triggered a ripple of anxiety, the same one she'd fought before bringing the case to Theo in the first place. "Tell me again how I'm not going to lose my job over this."

* * *

If only she could laugh off Celia's concerns.

"That's actually why I wanted to meet this afternoon, to give you a heads up about next Monday so you'd have some time to prepare."

"You said they couldn't touch me."

"Mmm...they can't. At least that's my legal opinion. You're a whistleblower and you have tenure. With an academic contract like that, you're practically bulletproof, but that doesn't mean they won't hassle you. In fact, you might experience some blowback right away, so I wanted to put you in touch with a friend of mine." She produced a business card from her pocket, feeling immensely proud of herself for resolving this particular issue—for more reasons than one. "William Auger. Like me, he specializes in litigation."

Celia examined the card and handed it back. "I thought you were my attorney."

"I can't be your attorney, not if I'm representing Donald Lipscomb. You're a witness. That makes it a conflict of interest. But Bill's a good guy. He's expecting you tomorrow morning at eleven. He'll be your point person going forward."

"Just like that? I don't even get a say in the matter?"

She was taken aback by the sharpness of Celia's response. "Of course you do. I can make some other recommendations or you can find someone on your own. But whatever you do, you need to do it quickly. Your name won't be in our filing, but your testimony about the meeting you had with Gupton and Tuttle will. In fact, it's the linchpin of how we tie the university to the wrongful death. They'll know you're involved. You could very well find yourself locked out of your office as soon as they receive notice, which could be as early as Monday afternoon. Bill can help you if that happens."

"Shit."

"I'm sorry, Celia." She hadn't anticipated such a hostile reaction and blamed herself for taking so long to admit that Celia would benefit from having her own representation. That meant letting her go, something—for purely selfish reasons—she hadn't wanted to do.

Celia fell back in her chair and closed her eyes. "Jesus, this is really happening. I'm going to lose my job after all."

"No, you won't. You have to trust me. And Bill. Especially Bill. He's very good and he won't let that happen."

After an extended silence, Celia opened her eyes and shook her head as if clearing her thoughts. "In light of this wonderful, wonderful news of yours, can you possibly tell me why we're drinking champagne?"

Theo smiled triumphantly as she poured another glass. "Because…I was thinking…if you follow through with meeting Bill, it neutralizes any ethical considerations someone might raise about a conflict of interest."

Celia froze, a blank expression overtaking her face.

It suddenly occurred to Theo she'd never actually gotten a response to her overture about a more personal relationship. Since Celia hadn't objected to the possibility, she'd taken for granted she also felt an attraction. "Uh-oh…this is potentially embarrassing."

"What on earth are you talking about? What's embarrassing?"

"It's possible I've gotten ahead of myself again. I've been worrying all this time about how to handle a conflict of interest, and it might even be moot…because I never actually asked if you'd be interested in going out." Theo felt her confidence plummet under Celia's bewildered gaze.

"That's what this is about? You wanted me to have a new lawyer so we could date and there wouldn't be a conflict of interest?"

Embarrassing...humiliating. Meekly, she replied, "That was sort of my plan."

Celia abruptly snatched Auger's business card back from Theo's fingers and leaned back, raising the glass of champagne to her lips. "Why didn't you say so?"

CHAPTER NINE

Theo's navigation system delivered her to a small community of colonial townhouses, yellow brick with dark green shutters. She located Celia's and pulled into a short driveway in front of a one-car garage.

The neighborhood was pleasant enough but too suburban for her tastes. Tranquility and backyard barbecues weren't worth the commute. She didn't have an hour a day to waste sitting in Atlanta's crazy traffic. The only reason she'd driven out to Dunwoody tonight was because it struck her as rude to ask Celia out without offering to pick her up.

She adjusted the zipper of her aqua blue minidress to the hollow of her breasts and strolled casually to the front door while making a conscious decision not to be nervous. Up until now, she'd shared mostly her attorney persona with Celia—confident, capable, in charge. Tonight they were on equal footing, a pair of women on a first date.

The red door opened and Celia grinned back. "I give up. You found me." She was, in a word, a knockout. Her black spandex dress left one shoulder bare, and her shoulder-length dark hair followed the same line, parted on one side with long bangs angling across her brow. Two-inch platform heels brought her almost to eye level, since Theo, conscious of their height difference, had worn low-heeled dress sandals.

"Wow." The word tumbled out mindlessly as she eyed Celia up and down. "Sorry I'm late. Friday traffic is horrendous."

"Can't say I didn't warn you. I could have met you at the restaurant, you know."

"That just isn't a date in my book."

"I wouldn't have guessed you were old-fashioned." She stepped aside to invite Theo into the foyer. "You look wow too, by the way."

The small living room was done in vibrant hues—a pair of deep red love seats angled around a colorful rug, accented with pale yellow throw pillows that matched the opposite wall. The dining area, where an abundant array of fake wildflowers decorated a glass-topped table, was opposite a staircase to the second floor.

"This is lovely." And smaller than it appeared from the outside. Cozy would be the polite word.

"Thanks, but none of it's my doing. When Gina left for Ohio, we both sold everything and started over. This was the last of the sales models and I bought it furnished, all except for my office upstairs."

Theo's eyes came back to Celia, who waited by the door with a small beaded purse. She might not have been much of a decorator, but she certainly knew how to dress herself.

"How'd it go with Bill?" she asked once they'd settled in the car. It was actually none of her business, but she wanted peace of mind that she'd handed Celia off to the right person.

"Fine, I suppose. He seems like a pretty good guy. He advised me to clean out my personal effects from my office immediately just in case they change the locks after they find out I'm a snitch. So much for my weekend, huh?"

It was tempting to offer to help, but probably better if she kept her hand out of Celia's dealings with her attorney. Besides, she was intent on enjoying Celia's company tonight without the weight of the case hanging over them.

"I'm glad you like him. But now that we've got that out of the way, what do you say we make a deal not to talk shop tonight?"

Celia laughed. "Fine, as long as you promise me we aren't going to talk about Little CeCe instead."

"Not sure I can make that deal." Theo gave her a sidelong glance and noticed a prim smile. "What's wrong with talking about Little CeCe? You should be proud of her."

"For what I did when I was ten? That was a whole other world. It blows me away that you still remember it."

Theo decided against mentioning she'd watched a pair of episodes on YouTube the night before.

As they neared downtown on Interstate 85, vehicles slowed to a crawl across all five lanes.

"I don't know how people stand this. I'd go crazy if I had to drive in and out of the city every day."

"Why do you think I take MARTA?"

After less than a mile, traffic came to a standstill. Theo did her best to stay calm, all the while watching the clock. Their dinner reservation at the Ritz-Carlton's Atlanta Grill was for eight, and it was already ten till. No way would they get all the way across town on time. "Let me just make a quick call."

The hostess, though polite, was firm. "I'm so sorry, Ms. Constantine. We won't be able to hold your table tonight. We could reseat you at ten."

If she'd been alone in the car, she'd have offered the woman several hundred dollars just to keep their table open. But then Celia might think throwing money around like that was tacky.

"It doesn't matter," Celia said. "Someplace else is fine."

It mattered to Theo. She'd planned the perfect date—dinner at a five-star restaurant and then dancing at Compound, Atlanta's trendiest club. Friday was Ladies Night. The last time she'd gone—admittedly over a year ago—they'd arrived after ten thirty and had to wait forty minutes just to get in the door.

"Hold on. I'll make this work." She tried Park 75 at the Four Seasons—a wedding rehearsal banquet—and The Cafe at the Mandarin—nothing before nine fifteen.

"Seriously, Theo…I don't care where we eat. I came for the company."

A practical solution was staring her in the face—the Spring Street exit. Theo hesitantly cleared her throat and said, "My place is just a few blocks from here. If you'd be willing to skip the restaurant, I'm sure I could throw something together."

After a pause that reeked of trepidation, Celia answered, "Fine by me."

Or maybe that was Theo projecting her own misgivings. A first date wasn't supposed to be at one of their homes. It was too private, too personal. Too presumptive.

She had a rule about sex—not until the third date at least. That wasn't just an arbitrary number she'd pulled out of thin air. It took her that long to rule out any potential conflicts. In her profession, she couldn't afford to find herself in a compromising position. Virtually anyone who worked at another law firm was out. Ditto for drug users and those she deemed ethically challenged.

Naturally, that also included anyone associated with the people she was currently suing. But just because she'd already broken that dictate didn't mean the other rule was squishy too. Sleeping together on the first date was reckless, not only for the professional risks, but for the way it short-circuited getting to know someone. Sex was much better when she had time to develop feelings for a woman. Maybe Celia was right—she really was old-fashioned.

And here she was again making assumptions, this time taking for granted that Celia would even want to sleep with her. She'd only agreed to dinner.

* * *

Celia didn't know what to make of Theo's unusually anxious mood. Clearly she was annoyed about losing their dinner reservation, but that didn't explain the tension in her voice. Especially since it only started once they agreed to have dinner at her place instead of a restaurant.

One thing she knew—she was looking forward to seeing how Theo lived in the quiet of her own home, away from the staff that ran interference for her and the hostesses who gave her private space in their crowded bars. Did she have a softer side? A vulnerability? The jury was still out on that one.

"What's funny?" Theo asked as she navigated her way through the parking garage of a towering condominium building.

It was only then Celia realized she'd laughed aloud at her inadvertent jury metaphor. "Sorry, I was just imagining if we'd ended up at my place. We'd be calling out for Chinese. I don't cook. Not well enough for company, anyway."

They parked in a wide, well-lit space only steps from a sign directing them to the elevator.

"Anyone can cook. All it takes is a little imagination and practice." Theo swiped the small transponder attached to her key fob over a panel, opening a door that led to an elevator lobby. Inside, she punched in a four-digit code and pressed the button for the top floor.

"The penthouse? Seriously?"

"I know, it's a cliché. But it has an open terrace. Once I saw it, I couldn't be satisfied with anything else."

The appeal was obvious the moment they stepped inside. Her spacious living area had full-length glass walls that afforded a spectacular view of the city beyond the terrace. The floors were dark, glossy wood, and the low profile furnishings blended into taupe walls and rugs.

"Want the nickel tour?" Theo asked. "My cleaning lady was here today."

"This is amazing. If I lived in a place like this, I'd never leave."

"I say that too, and then I remember somebody has to work to pay for it." They crossed the living area to a hallway. "Guest room and office on this side."

The guest room was notably larger than Celia's master bedroom. And better appointed too, with a king-sized bed, chaise lounge and walk-in closet. The office had built-in bookcases dotted with photos and plaques. On a credenza behind the desk was a small statuette of a blind Lady Justice.

They crossed back through the living area, which included a dining table for eight.

"And this is the kitchen...obviously."

The top-of-the-line appliances suggested a cook who knew what she was doing. Black granite counters. Glass cabinets revealing white dinnerware and crystal, all lined up like soldiers.

"The master suite's on this side," Theo said with a hint of pride.

And no wonder—it was the stuff of decorating magazines. As in the living room, the wall that bordered the terrace was mostly glass. Near the double French doors was a sitting area with a love seat and an antique trunk that served as a coffee table.

"Let me rephrase that, Theo. If I lived here, I'd never leave this room."

"I spend a lot of time in here. I get home late sometimes and don't even bother to turn the lights on anywhere else. Everything I need is right here."

Celia noted the padded headboard of the king-sized bed. "I take it you read a lot in bed."

"You think?" Theo opened the door of the bedside table to reveal a stack of law journals. She led the way through a spacious bathroom—Jacuzzi tub, glass shower, toilet compartment, double sinks. At the far end was a pocket door that opened to another section. "My morning ritual."

It was a fitness room. On one side was a weight bench with a rack of dumbbells. On the other, a fit ball and yoga mat. In the center was a treadmill with an elaborate instrument panel, angled to face an enormous wall-mounted TV.

That explained why Theo looked so good, why her arms and legs were firm and her figure trim. "I'd have guessed a building this fancy had a fitness room."

Theo snorted. "I don't like to share. Besides, you haven't seen me when I've just rolled out of bed."

Not yet, anyway. That hadn't stopped her from trying to imagine it. There had been no one in her life since Gina, leaving her with pent-up sexual frustration she'd hardly noticed until Theo showed an interest in her.

"I promised you dinner. Let's go see what's in the kitchen."

Ten minutes later, Celia found herself stirring pasta into a pot of boiling water while Theo assembled the makings for what she called Greek spaghetti. Everything that went into the dish was high-end—Campari tomatoes, imported olives and feta, fresh parsley—all prepared using specialty cookware.

"You're pretty serious about your culinary habits," Celia observed.

"It's in my genes. My parents own a Greek restaurant in Cherry Hill, outside Philly. It's a busy place for lunch and dinner. We all worked in the kitchen growing up. My brothers and I, that is." She held up a dark bottle of olive oil, its entire label written in Greek. "This, by the way, is perfection in a bottle. My father imports it for the restaurant and keeps me supplied."

"How come you didn't end up in the restaurant business?"

Theo visibly shuddered. "No, thanks. This is as close as I want to get. My brother Gus is the only one who still cooks for a living."

"What about your other brothers? There were four of you, right?" It occurred to her Theo had never told her that, and she explained, "I peeked at the photo on your desk."

"That's right. George is the oldest. He's a trader on Wall Street…takes a train into the city every day so his daughters can grow up in Connecticut. Stefan plays saxophone in a jazz band. He's touring somewhere in Asia right now."

"And your parents…they're happy with the restaurant?"

"If you can call it that," she answered with a huff. "My father isn't exactly what anyone would call a happy man. Nothing's ever good enough, you know? And my mom just goes along with it. All of us were dying to leave home the day we turned eighteen. We love him to death but he made us all neurotic."

"I wouldn't call you neurotic. Fastidious maybe…but not neurotic."

After mixing the drained pasta in a skillet with olive oil and garlic, Theo tossed it with the other ingredients and served it up on dinner plates, which they carried outside to the terrace. While the pasta was cooking, she'd dressed the table with linens, flameless candles and flatware. A bottle of cabernet sat open and ready to pour.

"Theo, I hate traffic as much as the next person, but no restaurant in Atlanta could beat this table. It's divine."

"True, but we didn't get to order the New York strip, did we?"

The first taste of tomatoes and pasta exploded onto Celia's tastebuds. To her surprise, she noticed immediately the distinctive flavor of the imported Greek olive oil. "Oh, my gosh. This is wonderful."

Theo smiled, clearly pleased with the praise. "I guess all those hours slaving away in Papa's kitchen paid off."

"I'll say. Do you go back for cooking lessons?"

"Once a year, maybe. But just for a day or so. I try to meet up with George whenever I'm in New York, and we all try to see Stefan if he's playing nearby. By all, I mean Gus too. My folks don't really care much for jazz."

On the surface, it was a more conventional upbringing than the one Celia had, but there clearly was an undercurrent to Theo's glum description that suggested an emotional distance from her parents. "I bet they're proud of you. Who wouldn't be? Look at all you've done."

Theo shrugged. "It's fair to say they had something more traditional in mind. Definitely not a lesbian. More like a housewife with a bunch of blue-eyed progeny. They never planned for me to go to college. I did that on my own with loans and scholarships," she added cynically.

Not just to college, Celia noted. Barnard and Columbia.

The brothers had pushed back against expectations as well, Theo said. While the family had appeared privileged from the outside, they were as dysfunctional as anyone else. The result was all four siblings now leading their own lives, bound to one another through their shared upbringing, but with only a perfunctory closeness to their parents.

It wasn't at all surprising to learn Theo was a self-made woman. The interesting aspect was that she'd been driven in large part by her defiance of expectations. Little wonder she'd ended up in a career filled with battles against the status quo.

Celia raised her glass in a toast. "I'm glad you ended up here."

Theo smiled, her eyes twinkling from the glow of the candles. "And I'm glad you ended up *here*...as in right here, tonight. I don't usually have women over on the first date. Seems a bit presumptuous."

It was the third time she'd voiced concern about taking certain assumptions for granted. "For whom?"

"Ah, good question. Both of us, I guess." Theo stared back unflinchingly, the corner of her mouth turned up in a half-smile. "As you know, I have a knack for expecting you to say yes to whatever I suggest. I didn't actually plan tonight with an ulterior motive. In fact, I didn't plan it this way at all."

Celia studied her through narrowed eyes before folding her napkin and laying it neatly on the table. "I can't decide about you, Theo."

"How so?"

"You talk like you aren't sure what's going on here. Either you honestly don't have a clue—but it can't be that because you're too smart not to be perceptive—or you like to play it cool."

"Or there's a third possibility," Theo said, the softness in her voice giving away a hint of uncertainty. Her fingers walked across the table like a spider and grasped Celia's hand. "A good attorney never asks a question unless she's sure of the answer."

How could someone so daring in other arenas be anything but confident in her love life?

"Theo, I'm forty-one years old and I've been around the block a time or two. I agreed to come to your apartment. No hesitation, no apprehension." And no doubt about what she was getting herself into, or how she wanted their night to end. "I don't know how much clearer I can be."

"I know, I'm not as daft as I might look sometimes." Her look turned serious. "It's just that it's not often I find myself attracted to someone involved in one of my cases. You caught me off guard and it's taken me a while to figure out how to handle it— or if I should handle it at all, since there's the complication with you being a witness. Everything I know about you so far tells me you're worth the effort. If you feel the same way, I'll have to be more careful than ever. That's why I'm double-checking all the boxes."

It was a stunning admission for what had, until now, been a lighthearted first date. With a shift in tenor, Celia had no choice but to answer Theo's honesty with the same. "Then let me take some of the mystery out of this. I'm not feeling ambushed or manipulated. I'm here because you're the most interesting woman I've met in a very long time. Maybe ever... okay, definitely ever. Not only will I likely say yes to whatever you ask, I already have ideas of my own. So we can stop dancing in circles, walking on eggshells...whatever metaphor applies here."

Their eyes froze in a rapt gaze, all questions answered, all doubts erased.

"Speaking of dancing..." Theo glanced at her watch and tipped her head thoughtfully. "I'd planned on hitting Compound after dinner. But if it's all the same to you...I'd just as soon stay here and see what happens next."

With a gentle squeeze, Theo tugged her to the center of the table, where their lips met in a soft, motionless kiss that lasted no more than a few seconds.

"More of that," Celia whispered. "I want more of that to happen next."

CHAPTER TEN

Theo's designer couch, with its narrow seat and firm leather cushions, left something to be desired as a necking spot. After a minute or two of trying to get comfortably situated, she'd sent Celia to the love seat in the sitting area of her bedroom while she brought in their dishes and gave the kitchen a once-over.

"Stop stalling," she mumbled to herself, recognizing she was more nervous than usual. She'd entertained women like this before…women who ran their course through her life before she admitted there had to be more. Tonight was different—because Celia was shaping up to be the "more" she'd been waiting for.

After pouring two small snifters of Frangelico, she returned to the bedroom to find Celia sitting with her feet tucked beneath her, her shoes on the floor. If her dress rose one more inch, it might as well not be there at all.

"I was starting to wonder what happened to you," Celia said as she accepted the offered drink.

"Does it surprise you I like to keep things neat?"

After a noticeable pause, Celia asked, "Does that include me?"

"Not sure if I know what you mean. If it's your shoes on my floor...I can live with that." She gently pushed a strand of Celia's hair over her shoulder. "If it's your hair blocking my view of your lovely face, then no."

"You are a smooth one, Theo Constantine." Leaning forward, her lips parted to invite another kiss.

Theo took her time closing the distance. All the while, her eyes darted between Celia's hooded gaze and shimmering lips. Once they came together this time, there was no chance they would stop.

Training all of her focus onto their kiss, she separated the senses. The faint nutty aroma of the Frangelico, its sweet remnants still on Celia's lips. The warmth of her tongue and smoothness of her teeth. The barely audible clicks as they touched and parted.

When Celia pulled away long enough to set her glass on the side table, Theo did the same. Though it freed their hands for discovery, she wasn't finished savoring their kiss. With a strong hand, she guided Celia onto her lap, face to face. Celia's dress rose to her hips.

"You're a delight, Dr. Perone," she murmured.

Celia answered with a fierce kiss, her breasts crushing against Theo's.

Theo's hips began a slow, steady roll as her excitement grew. She cupped Celia's bottom, finding it bare but for the scratchy lace of her thong. How long could she last before she had to tear it off?

The decision wasn't hers. Celia leaned back and tugged the zipper of Theo's dress to her navel. With her hands snaking inside, she panted, "Enough of this. Take me to bed."

As they stood, Theo peeled the black spandex upward, bringing Celia's figure into view. With a shrug, she pushed her own dress off her shoulders and let it fall to the floor. Her bra and bikini panties followed.

Celia eyed her with obvious lust. "I could eat you up."

Moments later, they were stretched across the smooth cool sheet, where Theo worked the clasp of the black lace bra. As she pulled it away, Celia's ample round breasts fell to the side and her rose-colored nipples tightened.

Resisting the urge to ravage them, Theo returned to her mouth, deliberately forcing her senses to take in all the places where their bodies touched. Breasts together, her excited center straddling a smooth thigh. Celia's fingertips digging into her hips.

Their breathing grew ragged as she lowered her lips to a rigid nipple. From one to the other and back. Kneading the soft mounds and pushing them into her mouth as Celia flailed.

Crawling lower still, she slid her finger under the band of the thong and pushed it down, her head filling with the scent of arousal.

Celia helped, rolling the lacy cloth off her feet and opening her legs to reveal a smoothly waxed mound, its pink folds glistening.

Theo moaned at the sight. Instantly losing all sense of restraint, she dived forward to bury her face in the wet flesh. A hand on her shoulder stopped her short.

"Oh, no. You don't get to be first all by yourself," Celia gently scolded. She sat up and urged Theo's knee upward.

Following the not-so-subtle cues, she inched herself around until she could lower herself onto Celia's waiting mouth. Eager lips drew her in and began their impatient assault. Theo slithered as she sought the perfect spot, the ultimate friction. Then tearing her thoughts from the rippling sensations, she dropped her mouth onto Celia's center again, parting the slickness with one long swipe of her tongue.

Her concentration on the sweet wet nub was momentarily interrupted when she felt Celia enter her. She answered with two fingers, curling them so she could stroke the tightened walls.

Stiffening the tip of her tongue, she probed furiously until she realized Celia had stopped her motions. Hardened thighs, rising hips. Suddenly Celia let out a long low moan that vibrated against Theo's inner lips, and gripped her bottom with so much force, Theo was sure it would leave bruises.

She continued until Celia began to twitch each time her tongue touched a sensitive spot. Nuzzling into the apex of her legs, she bathed it with her warm breath, gradually allowing her focus to return to her own pleasure.

* * *

Celia held on tightly as Theo's orgasm started, even rolling with her as she tried to get away. Her persistence paid off with another, but then Theo lowered her hands to shield herself from the onslaught. Eyes closed, smiling, gasping for breath.

She was gorgeous. Soft skin covering firm muscles, the faint tan line of a bikini she might have worn weeks ago on a beach getaway.

"Come on, let's do that again," Celia said.

"It would have to be over my dead body, at least for the next hour or so."

A blast of cool air from the air conditioner vent above the bed caused Celia to shiver and pull up the sheet. Snuggling close to Theo, she reveled in the continued throbbing from her own climax. "Just promise me there are more where that one came from."

"Maybe a few…thousand." Theo rolled onto her side and arranged her pillow so they could see each other while they talked. "Would you believe it if I told you I hardly ever come the first time I make love with someone? It takes me a few times to get that far. I think it's because I sometimes have a hard time letting go."

"But you did…didn't you?"

"You were inside me. You know I did." Theo tickled her collarbone with her fingertips. "It's different with you. I want to know what it is about Celia Perone that makes me break all my rules."

Celia had her own reason for wanting this time to be different. She liked imagining she was the one Theo had been waiting for, the one she was meant to fall in love with. That they'd fall in love together. "Maybe it's just fate, counselor."

"Now there's an idea." Theo capped off her reply with a light kiss. "I knew there was something about you the first time you came to my office. Your Windsor knot…that fedora."

"Don't tease me." She still was embarrassed by her spectacle.

"Sorry. What if I told you I thought you were being brave? That I was impressed because you knew your job was at risk and you came anyway."

"Is that even a little bit true?"

Theo chuckled. "I notice women who stick their neck out. That's what it takes to shake things up. It was a selfless act."

Celia had been so starstruck that day, she hadn't even noticed being noticed. Sure, Theo had been attentive and kind, but she was all business. "Did you really feel something that day? Or was it the day you found out I was Little CeCe?"

"You remember when we met at the pub? You said you were surprised to see me, that you thought I'd send someone else." Theo began to nibble on her earlobe. "No way was I going to do that. I wanted to see you again."

"Hunh. That's funny. I never got that vibe from you until you said you wished we could date. That blew me away." But when Theo dismissed it, Celia had assumed it hadn't been important enough to pursue.

"Chalk it up to my poker face. Part of my training for the courtroom. I'm very good at controlling my emotions…just not with you, apparently. I shouldn't even have said anything, not before I worked out how we could do this without crossing any ethical lines. But I couldn't help myself."

Celia covered her hand and pressed it to her heart. "I like it better when you talk to me."

"I will from now on."

A wave of guilt coursed through her as she thought of how she'd felt that day in Theo's office. It was time to come clean with why Hayley's story had mattered so much. "Honesty isn't just telling the truth, Theo. It's also not hiding things that might be important."

"I know. I felt bad for not saying something sooner about what I was feeling…like that day I stopped by your office at the university. The bottom line was I wanted to see you again, plain and simple. But I was still trying to figure out a way to make it work."

"I've…I've been keeping something from you too. Something about Hayley," she blurted, feeling at once relieved to have opened the door. "Not about her, really. About me."

Theo didn't say anything, at least not with words. The gentle massage of her chest had stopped and a wrinkle appeared on her brow.

"It wasn't totally selfless what I did. I was trying to make up for not doing it when it happened to me."

She held fast to Theo's arm as she tried to sit up.

"You were raped?"

"Maybe. I'm not really sure what happened, but it wasn't nothing." For years, she'd kept her teenage trauma bottled up, not even telling Gina. "It was at a party in LA after we finished my last slasher film. I was only sixteen at the time. One minute I was sitting out by the pool with some of the guys from the crew. Next thing I know, it's morning and I'm waking up in a strange bed all by myself. No clothes, no memory of who I was with. And nobody around to ask."

"Were you hurt?"

She shook her head, recalling vividly the feelings of disorientation. "No, I didn't feel anything. It's not like I was a virgin…but it's hard to believe somebody would have knocked me out like that and put me to bed naked without doing something. I have absolutely no memory of what happened… but it couldn't have been as bad as what they did to Hayley."

"Celia, whoever did that to you was a lowlife…the worst kind of coward. Did you try to find out who it was?"

"I asked my friend Richard if he'd seen anything. He was one of the producers. It was his house. He said he had no idea. I know it wasn't him because he's gay, but that doesn't mean he didn't let it happen." Twenty years had mellowed her outrage but not her questions. "I told my mother. You know what she said? 'So some guy took advantage of you. Get used to it.' That was the Judy Monroe School of Parenting."

Theo snaked an arm underneath her and pulled her close. "I'm so sorry. I wish I could have been there for you."

"You and me both. Something tells me you'd have found out who it was and kicked his ass."

"Damn right." She planted a series of kisses on Celia's head. "It hurts me to know that happened to you, that you've been carrying it around by yourself for so long."

"I don't carry it all the time. It's just here right now because of Hayley. I usually try not to think about it too much because it only makes me imagine all the awful things that might have happened. At this stage of my life, I honestly don't want to know."

"I can understand that. I'd probably feel the same way."

Celia sighed. "I just wonder what I would have said to Hayley if she hadn't shown me the video proving those guys really did it. 'Tough break, kid. Shit happens.' I'd like to think I would have been more supportive than that."

"You would have. I see your anger, your indignation. It's like mine, just as intense."

Except Celia's had laid dormant until Hayley's horror brought it all back. Twenty-five years of skirting the fight while she folded herself into the establishment, becoming part of the hegemony. The reports she'd seen as part of the faculty senate had confirmed these attacks were happening, and the perpetrators were getting off with little more than a scolding from their peers on the honor court. Why hadn't she questioned that? Why had it taken Hayley's suicide to ignite her rage?

* * *

Though it wasn't yet seven, sunrise had overtaken the room.

Theo slid quietly from the bed, careful not to wake Celia, who was sprawled facedown without a pillow. Her arms and legs lay juxtaposed as though in the midst of a freestyle swimming stroke.

In her walk-in closet, she slipped on the Atlanta Braves nightshirt she would have worn had she slept alone. Her summer robe she saved for Celia, dropping it at the end of the bed as she tiptoed out to the kitchen.

Their night together had proven greater than any of the fantasies she'd conjured. Celia's somber revelation had interrupted their lovemaking, but by the time they talked it out, they were emotionally closer. When they kissed again, their passion was ready to burst.

Celia Perone *was* different. Whatever it was that had prompted Theo to toss out her rulebook was having the same effect on her heart. Until now, she hadn't believed in love at first sight, or love at first anything. Celia was making her think again.

"Is that coffee?" Celia had eschewed the robe, choosing instead one of Theo's crisply ironed white shirts. Its sleeves were rolled up and its tail just long enough to tease what she wore underneath. "I nicked some knickers from your drawer too, in case you're wondering. And I gave them a good sniff before I put them on."

Theo chuckled and held out her arms. "I tried to be quiet when I got up. You looked so peaceful. I could have watched you for hours."

"You must like looking at roadkill. The only reason I looked peaceful was because you wore me out."

"Believe me, I was tempted to wake you up so we could start over. You were so beautiful lying there."

Celia grunted. "Bed head and morning breath. Always a winning combination."

She seemed determined to deflect everything Theo said with self-deprecating humor. Either she wasn't serious about their night of lovemaking or she didn't think Theo was.

Theo placed a hand over Celia's mouth and said, "I thought you were gorgeous and I couldn't have been happier at waking up and finding you beside me. And now you're supposed to say, 'You're so sweet, Theo. I'm delighted to know you find me irresistible.'"

They both began to laugh, and when Celia finally tugged her hand away, she said, "I get the message. Delighted, enchanted… enthralled. I'm all those things."

"That's much more like it." She kissed her on the nose before presenting her with a mug of coffee. "Cream?"

"Black."

"Good, because I don't have cream."

"Man, you're spunky in the morning!"

Theo bit her tongue to keep from telling her to get used to it. Too presumptuous. "Let's sit outside. It won't get oppressively hot out there until about ten." She led the way and raised the umbrella over a chaise lounge. "Want to sit with me?"

Celia waited for her to get settled and took the space in front, leaning back against Theo's chest. "This is so nice, Theo. You might have a hard time getting rid of me."

"Who says I want to? And before you toss that off with another glib remark, you should know I'm serious when I say that. I liked waking up with you. We're going to have many, many mornings like this."

After a long silence, Celia began tickling the back of her hand. "How can you know that already?"

"I told you. It's different. You're different. I woke up this morning and felt it all over again." She swept Celia's hair back and laid a light kiss on her temple. "Last night was just the beginning as far as I'm concerned. This feels right. I can't explain it more than that…it's like trying to describe lightning. All I know is I'm not going to question it."

"Don't question it." Celia craned her neck upward so they could share a kiss. "Just run with it. That's what I'm going to do."

CHAPTER ELEVEN

Theo had hired a pair of limos to take her team to the press site. On the short ride with Jalinda, she finished a call with Penny. "I won't have time to go to Rhode Island this week. See if you can schedule a teleconference on Wednesday or Thursday. If she insists on meeting in person, maybe I can fly up there over the weekend."

"Is this a new case?" Jalinda asked, brushing a piece of lint from her dark blue business suit. Theo had noticed she always dressed well for events in which she might appear in the background on TV news.

"Maybe," Theo replied. "A woman from a prominent family in Newport just found out her husband's part of a heroin ring. She wants to turn him in, but she's afraid the feds will confiscate her house."

It was an intriguing case. The wife's "innocent owner" defense was on shaky ground, since their new home had clearly been built with funds from a criminal enterprise.

"Are we ready to roll?"

Jalinda nodded. "The press got the video about half an hour ago. They were told to show up at Harwood's main entrance at two for an explanation."

Theo checked her watch. "That's only fifteen minutes from now. You blurred the image, right? We can't let that out there with Hayley's face." Though the public wouldn't be able to see that her eyes were closed, her motionless body and limp arm made it obvious she was passed out.

"Done. Hank left an hour and a half ago to pick up Donald Lipscomb. They'll meet us there. And I've got four of Hayley's sorority sisters, including Sarah Holcomb, lined up to stand behind us so they can hold the pictures."

They'd blown up one of Hayley's publicity head shots and mounted it on foam core board. Young and lovely, she was a compelling victim—a fact Theo was forced to play up in order to win the press's attention. The second photo showed the Harwood Hornets, all with celebratory smiles as they hoisted their championship trophy. The faces of the three known rapists were circled in red.

But today's press conference wouldn't be about rape, but its aftermath. Naming Haley as a suicide victim while releasing the video of her rape was walking a thin line. Should Theo be accused of violating the privacy of a rape victim, she planned to argue the technicality—that no one was being charged with rape.

As they arrived at the entrance to Harwood's campus, she wrapped up her review of the facts of her case. Their twenty-page written complaint was meticulous, listing forty-three respondents, including three players, two police officers and two supervisors, the chancellor and finally, the entire board of trustees. For good measure, she'd added unknown defendants she might identify through discovery. After each group of defendants, she laid out a detailed accounting of the actions that established their liability for Hayley's mental distress and subsequent suicide—sexual assault, negligence, and intentional or reckless conduct.

She'd rehearsed a forceful speech similar to the one she planned to give during opening arguments if they made it to trial. Except today, the defendants wouldn't be there to rebut. It would take the players and university at least a day to digest the complaint, hire attorneys and issue a preliminary response. By that time, the video of the rape would have gone viral with her version of events taking root.

A small crowd had gathered on the corner of Northside and Harwood Boulevard, where four satellite TV trucks were already set up. Hank was standing off to the side with Lipscomb. Jalinda summoned the detective to carry the collapsible podium from her trunk while she handed out the giant photos to the women who waited.

Theo was rushed by a handful of reporters the moment she stepped out of the car. "Will you be announcing a civil suit against the three Harwood basketball players shown in the video assaulting a woman?"

As she strode toward her client, she smoothed a crease in her black silk suit, purchased the day before especially for this appearance. "I'll be making a statement in about ten minutes, and I promise to take your questions later."

On Theo's advice, Lipscomb was wearing a mismatched gray tweed sport jacket with a pale yellow shirt and striped tie. They were going for a humble look. According to Hank, it's exactly what he'd have worn if left to his own devices.

"Thank you for coming, Mr. Lipscomb. Did you have a chance to review my notes?"

He nodded, swallowing nervously. It was easy to think he'd never been part of something so public.

Once she made her announcement, he was to read a short statement concerning his grief over Hayley's death, and how it was worsened by news of her sexual assault and the university's deliberate refusal to investigate the matter on her behalf. Theo had coached him over the phone to limit his comments to scripted remarks, and to speak only when she gave him permission to answer reporters' questions. They couldn't afford to have him go off the reservation and accidentally say something that undermined their case.

She took the podium precisely at two o'clock, positioning herself so camera operators could frame her with the elaborate gate into Harwood University over her shoulder. The crowd had grown to over a hundred onlookers, about half of whom appeared to be students. "Thank you for coming. I am here today on behalf of Hayley Burkhart, a young woman who took her life on the night of April fifth in her sorority house on the campus of Harwood University. That same night, the Harwood Hornets won the NCAA basketball championship. It is our contention those two events are related."

She referenced the video that reporters were already buzzing about, briefly describing its contents and confirming it was her firm that had released it to the media in advance of their announcement.

"Today, Constantine and Associates will file a civil complaint in Georgia Superior Court against Matthew Frazier, D'Anthony Caldwell…" She read the names of all individual defendants except the board of trustees. "…on behalf of Donald Lipscomb, who is named by the State of Georgia as the personal representative for the interests of Hayley Burkhart's mother, her next of kin. We allege the acts committed by the defendants resulted in Hayley Burkhart's wrongful death. These are the facts as we know them."

Methodically, she ticked off the chronology of events, beginning with the party at Henderson Hall following the Vanderbilt win on February third. She indicated they were pursuing information on the person who supplied Hayley with a drugged drink, and believed him also to be the one who took the video. Though he wasn't listed as a defendant in the complaint, she fully expected to add him to the suit once his identity was confirmed.

"We have documented that Hayley Burkhart suffered great mental distress during the period from her assault to her death. For that, we ask the court to award damages for her pain and suffering in the amount of ten million dollars. We ask the court to award an additional five million for her family's pain and suffering. We believe Harwood University—in particular, its police force, administration and board of trustees—acted with reckless disregard in its failure to deliver due process to Hayley Burkhart in order to preserve not only the assailants' reputations, but also their eligibility to play collegiate basketball, in order that they might win a national championship for the university. Because of this belief, we ask the court for punitive damages through disgorgement. Harwood University should relinquish all profits from that win, which we estimate to be in excess of thirty million dollars. We contend those are unjust profits derived through unethical conduct."

There as an audible gasp from the crowd, and a smattering of expletives from within the crowd of students. The usual misogynistic crap—*cunt, bitch, slut*. Theo paused a beat while the reporters tried to identify the source of the slurs.

"Furthermore, because these actions were undeniably in reckless disregard of Hayley Burkhart's right to due process, we ask the court to award treble damages on all counts." That brought their total to one hundred thirty-five million.

Theo introduced Donald Lipscomb and stepped aside as he read his statement.

A small cluster of young men, one of whom was wearing a championship T-shirt, stood to the side of the crowd. Their allegiance to the players was evident from their scowls and head shaking.

"Bitch!" The voice came from someone in the back, and it wasn't clear if the heckler was referring to Hayley or Theo until he added, "She deserved it."

Seething with fury, Theo took the podium again when Lipscomb finished, grasping the edges firmly and steeling her voice. "The young men who assaulted Hayley Burkhart felt *entitled* in their roles as basketball players. They were *enabled* by Harwood's police and administration, and *exempt* from accountability. Whereas Hayley Burkhart was *raped* during what should have been a joyful celebration, *rejected* by those whose job it was to bring those rapists to justice, and *repudiated* for daring to speak out." She glared deliberately at the young men who'd created the disturbance. "There are those in the crowd who have gathered here today—I'm sure you heard the obscenities they just shouted about Ms. Burkhart…that she somehow *deserved* what happened to her in this heinous video. They represent a mutant strain of humanity that believes a sports trophy is worth more than a woman's dignity, more than a woman's life. That attitude is exactly why we've filed this suit—to hold Harwood University accountable for the fact that such repugnant views are at home on this campus."

* * *

Seeing Theo on live TV was getting more and more surreal. She had a special quality the camera picked up and cast out to everyone watching. In Hollywood, they called it star power, an electrifying charisma that would have producers fighting one another to turn her into their branded property. No wonder the press showed up en masse for her staged events.

Only one of the news networks had covered the press conference live. However, it was the lead story on all the local channels at six o'clock, and earned a prominent mention on all the major networks during their evening newscast. Most interesting were the words they used to describe the charges— explosive, shocking, staggering.

More than five hours had passed since the announcement, enough to be certain everyone in Harwood's administration had read the claim. Celia expected her phone to ring any minute with news of her suspension or a demand for her to appear before the board. So far only Bill Auger had called, assuring he was on call should she need him.

Unable to open page.

The message on her computer screen confirmed her fears— the blowback had begun. She took a screen shot and forwarded it to Bill. It couldn't possibly be a coincidence she'd lost access to the university's server the very day Theo's lawsuit cited an intimidating meeting with a faculty member who attempted to engage the university's help. It didn't matter that her name wasn't listed in the suit—they knew exactly who'd reported their threats.

If they'd cut off her computer access, there was little doubt they'd locked her out of her campus office too.

Fortunately, she was prepared, if not emotionally then professionally. After tearing herself away from Theo after breakfast the day before, she'd gone to Forbes Hall to gather her personal effects and relevant work materials. Back at home, she'd spent several hours downloading work files and copying twelve years of correspondence to an offline email client.

Her sharp ringtone startled her and she looked at it anxiously, relieved to see Theo's office number. "Oh, it's just you. I've been sitting here all afternoon waiting to be fired."

"*Just* me, huh?" Theo chuckled. "So the bloom's already off the rose."

"Hardly. You were awesome today. Not that I was surprised, but you kicked even more ass than I expected."

"It went well. Good turnout. Plus we had some assholes in attendance who made the press even more sympathetic. They took off before anyone could interview them on camera, but look for their sexist taunts to show up in the papers."

Celia listened with disgust as Theo described the behavior of the young men who'd gathered to heckle her. "I'm not surprised. That creepy mindset's all over campus."

"We have to expect reprisals."

"Oh, they've already started. Looks like I've been frozen out of my Harwood account. Good thing I downloaded everything last night. Except anyone who writes to me now won't get a response. It all goes to the ether."

"Good to know." Theo already had her gmail address and promised to send a schedule of TV interviews she should watch for. "I'm doing a few of them tonight here from our office, but they won't air until tomorrow morning. Oh, and I wanted to give you a heads up that I might have to go out of town next weekend for another case."

"And you said the bloom was off *my* rose. You're already making plans to sneak off with someone else."

"You could always come with me. Newport, Rhode Island. We'll find a nice B&B."

Before Celia could accept, she was interrupted by her doorbell, injecting a jolt of anxiety and paranoia. "Uh-oh, somebody's at my door." A peek through the window revealed Kay Crylak's Subaru. "It's a friend of mine. Looks like she's heard the news."

"I'll let you go. Call me at bedtime. We'll talk dirty."

Celia chuckled to herself as she bounded down the stairs for the door.

It wasn't uncommon for Kay to stop in unannounced. She lived nearby, close enough that they sometimes carpooled to the MARTA stop. Obviously she was coming from her office on campus, since she was dressed in a pantsuit with polished shoes instead of her usual warmup suit and sneakers. But the glower on her face made it clear this wasn't a social call.

"Did that lawyer send you to pump me for information? Is that what our little lunch was about? I thought we were friends."

"Whoa! What's going on?"

Kay stormed past her and whirled around. "I just came from an emergency meeting of the entire athletic department. Coaches, assistant coaches, trainers—every last one of us. They threatened to fire anybody who suggested there was a special arrangement between the campus police and the AD. There was a list going around of people we weren't supposed to talk to. Lo and behold, *your* name was on it. I'm going to lose my job the minute somebody figures out I know you."

"That's bullshit. There *is* a special arrangement between athletes and the cops, but I knew about it before you ever said a word to me. I saw it myself with Hayley. She even handed the cops a video of those guys raping her while she was passed out, and they still didn't bother to investigate."

"You expect me to believe it was just a coincidence you sat there all through lunch talking about jocks and their privileges?"

"Think whatever you want, but I wasn't pumping you for anything." Suddenly reminded of her thin walls, she lowered her voice. "Besides, if I remember correctly, you're the one who brought it up. Your girls who were trying to pass algebra? The bicycle thief?"

Kay's frown gradually eased as she recalled the conversation. "You could have told me you were a witness, Celia. I didn't have to read it in a memo."

"I'm not just a witness." It was too late to take back her words. She had to trust that Kay would see where she was coming from, or their friendship could be ruined forever. "I'm the one who took the case to Theo Constantine in the first place. The girl who was raped…she was a theater student. You saw her on stage last year when you brought that woman from Marietta to see our show. Hayley came to me for help, but Earl Gupton and Norman Tuttle wouldn't listen. Instead, they threatened me to keep my mouth shut. The reason I didn't tell you was because Theo was still investigating. She hadn't decided yet whether or not to take the case. If word had gotten out too soon, they could have destroyed evidence or pressured witnesses. There wouldn't have been a case at all."

"All the more reason…"

It was one thing for Kay to feel betrayed that she hadn't confided in her about the case. But Celia wouldn't stand for one of her friends being so callous.

"You can't possibly mean that, Kay. A girl is dead because of what those players did. And what the university did to cover it up." She heard her voice rising again but this time didn't even try to control her anger. "Hayley Burkhart was *my* girl, the same way your players are your girls. You go to bat for them when they screw up, but somehow you expect me just to let it slide when one of mine gets raped by a bunch of ballplayers. And then gets fucked over by the people who are supposed to protect her?"

"Well maybe there was a good reason. Did you think of that? What if those guys are telling the truth? What if she came on to them?" Kay threw up her hands defensively. "I'm not saying she did. Just…maybe there are two sides to this story and you only heard the one you wanted to hear."

"For God's sake, Kay! Did you even watch the video?"

"I—" She shook her head and spun away to pace the small living room. "I haven't been at my computer today. I just heard what Coach T said about the players…that she was throwing herself at them."

"Have a seat. You're going to watch this video and see for yourself who's lying." Celia scraped a dining chair out from under the table before starting upstairs for her laptop. It was all she could do not to stomp her feet.

Kay was sitting when she returned, her arms folded defiantly.

"The one that's going around has Hayley's face blurred so people don't recognize her. This one's the real deal. I dare you to look at her face and tell me she wanted this."

She clicked on the link and stood back with her hands on her hips, silently counting the seconds until Kay's moment of realization.

"Get out the way, man."

Kay's eyes widened with obvious horror as the video came to an end with Matt Frazier laughing into the camera. "You are fucking kidding me. I had no idea. How could anybody see that and not call it rape?"

"Now you know why I took this case to Theo. Those bastards ought to rot in jail. If I had my way, Gupton and Tuttle would be in the cell right beside them."

"If you'd heard what I'd heard today, you'd want the whole athletic department in there with them. I swear to you, Celia… this is not how they described what happened."

"So now you know they're liars. You should tell Theo what you told me, that the athletic department has a fixer whenever one of the players gets in trouble. That's all part of this culture of entitlement, and it has to go."

Kay went quiet for several seconds, her lips tightened as she contemplated the request. "I can't, Celia. My contract is at-will. They'd fire me in two seconds."

"Theo says they can't do that. Harwood takes federal funds. That means you'd have whistleblower status if you reported wrongdoing."

"Right…we both know it wouldn't be for that. They'd fire me because twenty and ten wasn't good enough, or they were getting complaints from players. They'd find a reason even if they had to make it up."

The audiotape Celia had made of her meeting with Gupton and Tuttle was proof the administration was part of the coverup.

If they had Kay's testimony about the athletic department having a special attorney to get charges dropped against players, it would make their case even stronger.

"I have my own lawyer, Kay. He could protect you too. Theo says I'll have the most secure job on the whole campus. They won't dare touch me."

Kay shook her head. "It's not the same, Celia. Don't get me wrong—I get it now. I want you to win this case. It's time some of those cocky bastards went to jail. But I can't afford to go against the athletic department this way. It would poison me. Not just here, but anywhere else. I'd never work again."

Dejected, Celia slumped in the adjacent chair. Tempted as she was to force Kay to watch the video again, she conceded to herself there was good reason to fear the backlash. "At least promise me you won't do anything to hurt us."

"I'm sorry I came over here with guns a-blazing. I understand why you're doing this." Kay held out her hand until Celia took it. "You don't have to worry about me. I'm going to keep my head so low, they won't see anything but the back of my neck. I meant what I said, Celia—I hope you win."

CHAPTER TWELVE

Unable to open page.

Bill Auger had assured her the shutout would only be temporary, that this was an ill-advised knee-jerk response by the university to make her life miserable. He was prepared to write a cease-and-desist letter if she gave the word, but so far she'd resisted escalating the confrontation.

Not all problems would be fixed so easily, he said. Promotion or not, fall semester would likely find her back in front of the lecture hall introducing theater to a crowd of listless freshmen. And with the worst possible schedule—eight a.m. or six p.m., whichever was deemed most punitive. But that was a battle for another day.

Celia wasn't interested in battles at all. No matter how tenuous her job, her main thoughts were centered around Theo. For the first time ever, she had someone who made her feel there might be something more important in her life than her job. She would never have believed she could fall in love so fast, that her academic career would tumble so quickly to a distant second place.

Theo was the kind of woman she'd always wanted. Powerful, independent. Someone selfless enough to answer a higher calling. The fact that Theo thought her a hero too made her all the more determined to be one.

She closed her computer and went downstairs for coffee, settling in front of her TV with the remote. The morning news shows were about to begin. Theo's list contained six interviews in all, including two cable sports programs.

Sipping her coffee, she scrolled through the channels listening for news of the lawsuit. Ironically, the story was presented first by TNS's Teresa Gonzalez, the reporter at the heart of the sexual harassment suit Theo recently had won. Despite the acrimonious court battle, the network obviously knew a hot news commodity when they saw it.

"From a studio in Atlanta, we have with us renowned women's rights attorney Theodora Constantine. Yesterday, Ms. Constantine dropped a major bombshell on the sports world, filing a multimillion-dollar sexual assault claim against three players on Harwood University's national championship basketball team. Two of those players, Matt Frazier and D'Anthony Caldwell, were until now expected to go very high in next week's NBA draft. Welcome, Ms. Constantine."

This was one of the interviews Theo had taped the night before from the teleconferencing studio in her office. Wearing a brown suit jacket over an amber top, she easily held her own against Gonzalez, a doll-like talking head. "Thank you for having me, Teresa. Before we get to your questions, I need to point out this suit is not about sexual assault. It's a wrongful death claim. Nor is it only against the three players directly implicated by the astonishing video that was released yesterday. Our suit equally charges the administration and board of trustees of Harwood University, who viewed this video and, by abdicating their responsibilities to provide this young woman with the due process to which she was entitled, directly caused the mental anguish that led her to take her life. Had the university responded in a reasonable manner, I have no doubt Hayley Burkhart would be here with us today." She held up a piece of paper Celia assumed to be the affidavit from Hayley's roommate. "Instead, they threatened to expel her from the university and support her rapists in a defamation suit should she go public with the allegations."

Gonzalez stuttered, trying to interject a question.

Theo continued over her, as was her apparent style. "In all my years as an attorney trying cases for women's civil rights, I've never seen such an abominable example of institutional misogyny. Who could possibly be surprised if we learned there were other women—other students at Harwood—who reported this sort of attack only to see it swept under the rug as well? Are there other athletes or prominent campus figures who've escaped justice? We know what Harwood University will do for a basketball championship. What else do they value more than their female students?"

The newscaster tried again to jump in, but she wasn't quick enough.

"That championship, by the way, is expected to result in a windfall of thirty million dollars for the university's coffers in increased donations from alumni, sale of championship merchandise and television rights. We're suing to recover that amount—to wipe it away as fair punishment for the depraved decision to trade the life of a young woman for a basketball trophy. And because that decision was both willful and reckless, we expect to be awarded treble damages of over one hundred million dollars."

Gonzalez finally cut in. "University officials issued a statement late Monday afternoon appealing to the public to withhold judgment until all the facts come to light. They insist student privacy laws prohibit them from releasing specific information, but there have been suggestions the woman at the center of this case may have been predisposed to mental health issues."

Celia had read that statement in the *Journal-Constitution*'s story. Their concerns about her privacy were bogus, as they'd selectively leaked details about her family situation and the fact that she'd been seen multiple times at the student counseling center, including during her freshman year for what a therapist intern had called mild depression.

"We agree completely with those suggestions, Teresa. Harwood was well aware of Ms. Burkhart's emotional history, and that's precisely why this tragic outcome was foreseeable. That makes their failure to protect her right to due process utterly indefensible."

In one segment after another, Theo delivered her blistering indictment. Over and over, she repeated her charges against the university, holding up various props to support her statements. The affidavit, a sweet photo of Hayley from the press kit for *The Pirates of Penzance*. Perhaps most impactful was the front page of the *Journal-Constitution* showing the on-court trophy presentation following the championship win—with the exuberant faces of the rapists.

By the time they got to the sixth program, a roundup of the top stories in sports, Celia had practically memorized Theo's talking points.

The host of the show was Cliff Reynolds, a thick-necked former football star with a reputation for stoking controversy. "It's been suggested by some, Ms. Constantine, that your entire case is being underwritten by one of Harwood's rival universities, someone trying to tarnish the team's victory. Others say it's a general protest by some of Harwood's ivory-tower academics who are upset over the university's emphasis on athletics. How do you respond to those critics?"

"Oh, my god," Celia said aloud. "The guy's an idiot."

Theo also took exception to the question, shaking her head with obvious disgust. "Those suggestions are beyond ridiculous, Cliff. And they obviously come from someone who has absolutely no understanding of the law. If I came face-to-face with those critics, I'd ask them if they believe the ability to play basketball entitles someone to commit sexual assault. Or if they believe a trophy—which, let's face it, is just a wooden slab with a gold-plated circle on it—is worth more than a woman's dignity. Worth more than her life. Sadly, I'm sure there are people watching this show right now who'd say yes to both of those. We need to send a message through our courts that it's unacceptable to act on such morally bankrupt beliefs."

"Whoa! Watch it there. My wife already thinks I'm a caveman," he said with a boyish chuckle. It was a transparent effort to identify with his "bro" audience. "But here's a different question. I confess to not being a legal expert, but isn't it true that your entire case is predicated on the fact that this was actually a rape? All three of the players implicated have since claimed the sex was consensual. Furthermore, the university did in fact investigate the allegations and found there to be insufficient—"

"Have you watched the video, Cliff? If you haven't, you're missing a key piece of information. And if you have, I'm going to agree with your wife. Hayley Burkhart is undeniably unconscious during the assault. Facedown, eyes closed, arms limp. When the jury in this case sees this video and then hears that Harwood police also viewed it and declined to press charges—that someone claiming to represent the university threatened Ms. Burkhart with a defamation suit and expulsion from the school if she made her allegations public—they'll understand exactly why this case is being brought against the university as well as the players."

The TV jock spun toward the camera as her split-screen image disappeared. "We'll be following this breaking story throughout the day. In the meantime, what do our viewers think? Guilty or innocent? Visit our website and cast your vote."

Celia grumbled, "Great, let's wrap up with a little whimsy."

That was the last program on her list. With unflappable passion, Theo had effectively bolstered her case, eviscerating the players, the university and anyone who dared to hint their actions were even mildly excusable. It was the show of force Theo had promised from the start, one that would incite enough outrage to bring about the results they wanted even if they lost their case.

* * *

Gloria wrinkled her nose as she wiped the excess makeup from Theo's face. "Stand still or you'll have this crap all over you. Whose idea was it to use bronzer?"

"You know I hate looking washed out on TV." Theo eyed herself in the ladies' room mirror, noting the brown streaks across her cheek.

"What do they make this stuff with? Baby shit?"

She could always count on Gloria for a frank opinion of anything. "Forget it. I'll do it."

"Hold on, I'm almost done." She'd already gone through half a box of tissues. "I know you don't want to hear this, but you need to ease up a little. Philip thinks you hit it out of the park, but I couldn't stop thinking about your jury pool. That take-no-prisoners approach isn't going to work with men, especially sports fans."

And especially not in Atlanta, where many of the potential jurors were Harwood fans.

"Yeah, I know." Theo usually showed more restraint on TV. The "angry woman" played well in the feminist blogosphere and social media, but not on the network news. "I'm trying to thread a needle here. There's a better than average chance this case will never get to court. I need to provoke enough outrage to get something that looks like justice for a rape victim."

"You mean the DOJ?"

"Or the DA. You know Justice won't investigate unless the public demands it. And by the way, Ms. Women's Studies Scholar, this is where you come in. We need to stir up a few of your militant women's groups. Get them started on petitions, protests and vigils for Hayley. Preferably without having our fingerprints all over it."

Gloria mumbled a curse at finding a smudge of makeup on the cuff of her white blouse. "I'd be surprised if they didn't stir themselves. Your problem is timing though. All the campuses—Harwood, Emory, Georgia Tech—they're out for the summer. It might be hard to get critical mass."

"A community group then. Get Jalinda to help."

Theo checked her face one last time and deemed herself fit to be seen in public. As she left the ladies' room, she ran into Penny.

"There you are, Theo. A woman called in a couple of minutes ago, says she's a sophomore at Harwood. She saw you on the news and wants to tell you something. She left a number."

Gloria nudged her from behind. "If she's a Hornets fan, that something will probably be 'Go to hell.' Our phone's going to ring all day."

"True," Theo said. It wouldn't be the first time they'd been inundated with calls, faxes and emails complaining about one of their cases. Some of the more vicious trolls threatened to rape and kill her, and they'd posted her home address on the Internet inviting the unhinged to follow through. "But I did just tell a few million viewers there were probably more women out there with stories like Hayley's. Try to screen them if you can, Penny. Get this one back on the phone and put her through."

As she waited, she checked for messages on her cell phone, finding one from Celia. *CB* was all it said. Call back, their usual exchange. She'd do that after talking to the caller.

Who would have guessed she'd have fallen so hard for someone after just one date? A date that had lasted nearly two days. By the time Celia had left for her office on Sunday to pack up, Theo was already hopelessly in love. It was crazy. And yet she'd never been so certain of her feelings.

The phone jarred her from her thoughts. "This is Theo Constantine. To whom am I speaking?"

"My name's Kelsey Cameron. I'm a sophomore at Harwood. At least I used to be. I'm transferring to Georgia Southern in the fall. I saw you this morning on TNS."

"Hello, Kelsey." Theo paused to see if the woman would continue on her own. The fact that she didn't suggested she was unsure of herself. "Is there something you'd like to talk about?"

"I wasn't sure if I should call or not. What you said…you know, about there being other girls this happened to…it did. It happened to me too. Last year right before Christmas break at a keg party. Except it was a football player."

Theo's pulse began to race but she tempered her excitement. "I appreciate you calling, Kelsey. Would you mind if I asked you some questions?"

"Sure, but I don't want to press charges or anything. That's why I'm transferring...so I can put this behind me." In pain-filled detail, Kelsey told her story.

Though it was vindicating for Theo to hear she was correct in her guess that other women had suffered the same fate, there was nothing to celebrate in Kelsey's quivering words. "Did you report it like Hayley did?"

Penny tiptoed in and placed a steaming mug of coffee on her desk.

"Not to the cops. I went to student health to get the emergency pregnancy pills. When I told the nurse I didn't remember what happened, she went and got this other nurse who came in and talked me into doing a rape kit. Just in case, she said. A bunch of swabs and a blood test. But I'd already had a shower so she said it probably wouldn't show much."

Kelsey spoke with a down-home cadence that Theo noted was different from the other students she'd interviewed. Harwood was an expensive, exclusive school, popular among what she considered the Southern aristocracy. Most of the women she'd interviewed came off as sophisticated and even a bit entitled, but not Kelsey. No wonder she was seeking refuge in a public university.

"Anyway, she asked me if I wanted them to call the police, but I felt like an idiot. Like it was partly my fault, you know? Drinking beer around a bunch of people I didn't know. That was stupid. Plus I couldn't say anything about the party because I was only nineteen at the time. A lot of us were underage. It probably would have gotten everybody in trouble."

"Kelsey," Theo said slowly, distinctly, "it wasn't your fault. Let's just get clear on that. You aren't responsible for someone else's bad behavior." It was an endless source of frustration to hear women express the internalized criticisms leveled against them for going out and having a good time. "How much do you remember about the assault?"

"Not a thing. I guess that's good. But he was there when I woke up. In the bed, I mean. We were in his dorm room. And I knew I'd been...that he'd had sex with me. I could feel it. But I got up and went back to my apartment like nothing happened, and that's when my roommate said I should go to student health."

Theo made note of the similarities to Hayley's case. A party, probably a drug of some sort, an athlete. "Where did this take place?"

"Henderson Hall. It's where all the jocks live."

And where Hayley had been raped.

"But the main reason I called is what you said about the school covering it all up...that hit a nerve. See, after a couple of days, I confronted him about it. He said no, it wasn't like that. He said he thought I was into it because I went with him to his room. I don't remember any of that. But anyway, he said not to tell anybody because he was worried about getting suspended from the team before the Gator Bowl. I already told him I wasn't going to say anything. But then the next day this man shows up at my apartment anyway. Says he's a lawyer for the team, and he warns me that I need to be careful about making allegations, that I could find myself dealing with an expensive lawsuit. That I could get expelled for slandering another student. He was so cocky I wanted to smack him."

"Do you remember this man's name?"

"Austin something. He was about thirty. Drove a black Porsche."

Kelsey probably didn't realize the importance of her story. Essentially she was describing an institutional culture of impunity when it came to athletes, in which victims were intimidated to remain silent. If she were willing to go on the record, her testimony would bolster their case.

"This is all extremely interesting, Kelsey. And important. I expect to hear from more young women like you now that the news of Hayley Burkhart's circumstances have been made public. Would you consent to do a detailed interview here in our office? I'm not asking that you commit to being a witness, just that you help us clarify the details for our records."

She made arrangements to have Jalinda follow up with a detailed interview, where they'd assess Kelsey's composure and credibility. If she held up to closer scrutiny, she could be a powerful piece of their case.

CHAPTER THIRTEEN

The MARTA stop that served the Harwood campus was nearly half a mile from her office, a pleasant walk in decent weather. Even in the rain or cold, it beat driving, as Celia's assigned parking space wasn't much closer.

It was her first visit to campus in five days, since packing up her office on Sunday. Wild horses wouldn't have dragged her in had it not been for the call from her textbook editor asking if she'd received the galleys for proofing. After getting blocked from campus email, she fully expected to find her mailbox empty and her office fitted with a new lock.

Only a dozen or so students milled around Forbes Hall, typical for summer. In the administrative office on the first floor, the secretary gave a cordial nod as Celia entered. It wasn't an exuberant welcome by any means, but it was hardly the way one greeted a pariah.

Her mailbox was surprisingly jammed, thanks to the bulk of the galley proof and a handful of letters and memos. Celia was tempted to collect it and head right back to the MARTA station before having to face her department head, but curiosity got the best of her. If they hadn't stopped her mail, perhaps they hadn't locked her out of her office either.

Not only did her key work, her office appeared exactly as she'd left it. Nothing out of place, and no sign anyone had rummaged through her drawers or files. As she stood before the bookshelf trying to decide if anything had been moved, she was startled by a man's voice.

"Celia, did you see where PSI picked Atlanta for its conference next year? Finally, an international conference we can afford to attend." It was Paul Blumenfeld, a colleague who'd joined the faculty the same year she had, yet received his promotion to full professor two years sooner. He honed his hipster image by sporting a soul patch on his chin and wearing his long dark hair in a man-bun.

"I haven't seen it yet. I just picked up my mail."

"Good ol' snail mail. Sure comes in handy, doesn't it? I couldn't believe they didn't tell us ahead of time they were taking the server down for maintenance. You'd think those IT guys could plan better than that. At least it's back up again. I had emails out the wazoo."

She smiled weakly as it slowly dawned on her what he was saying. If the server had been down across campus…perhaps she hadn't been deliberately shut out of her account after all.

He continued his blather but she'd stopped listening. When he left with a cheerful wave, she hurried to her desk to check her access. Sure enough, she was back online. A preliminary glance told her nothing had been deleted, not even the correspondence related to her meeting with Gupton and Tuttle to discuss Hayley's allegations.

Once again she'd fallen victim to her own paranoia. While it was highly unlikely she'd be welcome at one of the chancellor's dinner parties, it was clear they weren't going out of their way to make her life miserable. At least not yet.

Leafing through her mail, she found the memo explaining the maintenance work on the university's server and apologizing for the temporary disruption. Had she come to her office on

Monday instead of lying low at home, she would have spared herself the indignity of feeling scorned by school administrators.

She then came across a thin sealed envelope bearing the return address of Andrew Barker, the performance studies department head and her immediate boss. Inside were her course assignments for the fall semester—Intro to Theater at nine a.m. on Tuesday and Thursday; and at one p.m. on Wednesday, Performance Overview, a second-year course for prospective majors.

If anyone was out to get her, they were practically killing her with kindness. Only two courses—the same teaching load as other full professors—and the first time in six years she had two days free from classroom duties.

Then again, the date on the letter was last Friday, before Theo's charges went public. It wouldn't surprise her at all if she got an addendum telling her they were adding an introductory class or additional duties beyond getting ready for the spring stage production.

No, she was being paranoid again. Maybe Theo was right—they didn't dare punish her because it would make them look guilty or vindictive. The university didn't need any more bad press, not with the news stations still talking about the rape and coverup.

One of their tactics for shutting down the chatter was playing out this very afternoon in a courthouse downtown. Theo had been called in to respond to a defense motion for a gag order that would prohibit the attorneys or parties to the case from speaking about it in public or with those not directly involved. That would end Theo's appearances on news shows, where she'd stoked public outrage to the point that women's groups were demanding a criminal investigation and NBA fans were pleading with their teams not to draft Frazier or Caldwell. Considering that might be all they won, it would be a shame to see her silenced.

On the other hand, it would give Celia the best possible excuse for not responding to questions or comments from colleagues and students.

* * *

Technically, today's meeting was only for the attorneys—the motion for a suppression order, where the defense would argue in the judge's chambers that Theo's myriad appearances on news programs were prejudicing their defense. Theo didn't expect any of the named defendants to attend, and had made it clear to Donald Lipscomb his presence wasn't required.

As she stepped off the elevator on the seventh floor with Jalinda, Sonya Walsh emerged from the ladies' room. Sonya was general counsel for Harwood University and the personification of aging female conservatism, with shoulder-length brown hair that flipped up at the ends and a polka-dotted silk blouse knotted in a bow at her collar. Theo suspected she was in court today in a supporting role. This case was too big for Harwood University to leave in the hands of someone like Sonya, who lacked experience as a litigator.

"Theo, so nice to see you again. I wish it could be under better circumstances."

She knew Sonya only casually from the local bar association, barely enough to exchange pleasantries. "You know how it is, Sonya. You practice long enough, you're bound to meet everyone you know in the courtroom."

Jalinda waited quietly by the judge's door, ready to roll in the giant briefcase that held the case law and notes they might need for arguments. Theo knew implicitly she neither wanted nor expected an introduction to Harwood's attorney.

They entered the stately office to find two rows of folding chairs wedged into an arrangement facing the judge's desk, with a narrow aisle separating the plaintiffs from the defendants. To her surprise, the second row on the defense's side was occupied by the three players named in the suit.

All three were clean-shaven, dressed in ties and sport coats. Matt Frazier's signature red locks had been shortened to his collar, and D'Anthony Caldwell had covered the spiderweb tattoo on his neck with a wide bandage. Tanner Watson, all seven feet of him, looked nervous as hell.

She should have anticipated the defense would bring them in for star power in case the judge was a Harwood basketball fan. Not that it changed her arguments against the gag order or her plan to excuse Donald from the proceedings, but she might have sharpened her statements to provoke an immature outburst from one of them.

Their case had been assigned to The Honorable Jeanette Henry. Petite and in her early seventies, Judge Henry spoke with the voice of a kindergarten teacher. An unfamiliar attorney could be excused for thinking she was gentle.

Theo knew better. The woman had written scalding opinions against powerful institutions, including corporate giants Nations Oil and Surety Healthcare, and even her own employer, the State of Georgia. She wouldn't be intimidated by Harwood University.

Theo shuddered with a sudden chill as a familiar voice caught her attention. She turned toward the front row of the defense, where Sonya was speaking with a man who had his back to everyone else in the room. Tall and broad-shouldered, he'd shaved his head in surrender to male pattern baldness. He was James Somers, from Walcott Dupree, a powerhouse firm based in New York—and the last attorney to beat her in court.

The case was litigated three years ago, a class action suit against Dowd Textiles claiming the company funneled all of its female job applicants onto the floor of the sewing room, from which there was virtually no avenue for promotion. Despite the overwhelming evidence and sympathy from the judge, Somers had won on a statute of limitations technicality.

He turned and smiled, barely masking a sneer, as though he relished their rematch.

"Is that who I think it is?" Jalinda whispered.

"Lucifer himself, in the flesh."

Judge Henry arrived directly from the courtroom and paused to hang up her robe. Without greeting anyone, she scurried behind her desk to sit in a high-back leather office chair. "Are all parties present?"

Proceedings in chambers were less formal than in a courtroom, allowing the attorneys to keep their seats when they spoke.

"Theodora Constantine for the plaintiff, Your Honor."

"Sonya Walsh for the defense."

"And James Somers for the defense."

"Then let us proceed." Peering through the lower half of her blue-rimmed glasses, she eyed the motion on her desk. "Looks like defense wants a suppression order. Convince me, counselors."

Somers, with his legs crossed and hands in his lap, spoke in what could only be described as a scolding tone. "Plaintiff's counsel has been conducting a shameless media campaign clearly orchestrated to poison public opinion against the defendants, and it greatly impinges on our clients' constitutional right to a fair trial...should this ridiculous claim ever actually proceed to court."

He shook his head in a way Theo found infuriatingly condescending.

"She's conducted fourteen television interviews in the past four days, and has been quoted in no fewer than one hundred twenty-two print outlets, many of which are Internet news sources accessible to hundreds of millions of potential readers. Her wrongful death claim presumes the guilt of these three young men, who haven't been charged with any crime whatsoever, let alone convicted. A great deal of damage has been done to these young men's lives and to the reputation of one of our nation's premier universities, and it must stop."

Theo waited patiently until Judge Henry nodded in her direction. "Your Honor, the preponderance of media coverage merely indicates a high level of public interest in this case. More importantly, the publicity related to this case has produced additional witnesses who will testify to having encountered similar circumstances as those our victim, Hayley Burkhart, experienced following her assault."

"She just did it again!" Somers said indignantly. "She's claiming effects from an assault that hasn't been proven in a court of law."

"I'm not prosecuting a criminal rape case, Your Honor," Theo said. "This is civil litigation. I'm fully prepared to go to court and present a preponderance of evidence to the effect that Hayley Burkhart was sexually assaulted and the university actively suppressed her claim. That includes a graphic video that shows these three young men having sex with a woman who was undeniably incapacitated and therefore unable to consent. Following that, I'll demonstrate—"

"I get the point, Ms. Constantine. We aren't trying the case today. We're here to decide the issue of a gag order. I'm not convinced at this point your fishing expedition for corroborating evidence outweighs the importance of these defendants receiving a fair trial."

Theo glanced at her talking points. "With all due respect, Hayley Burkhart deserves fairness too. As we made clear in our filing, the main reason this wrongful death case exists is because Harwood University cynically valued its reputation more than her right to due process, and Mr. Somers is asking the court today to allow the continued suppression of discussion of wrongdoing—not in pursuit of justice—but because it serves the university's interest."

"She has a point, Mr. Somers."

"Ms. Constantine speaks of justice as if Hayley Burkhart is the only one deserving such a result. My clients are entitled to the presumption of innocence—"

"In a criminal court," Judge Henry interjected. "I'm sure you're well aware there is no implied presumption of innocence in a civil case."

"Of course, but my clients enter the courtroom disadvantaged by a media that has already convicted them of uncharged acts in the court of public opinion. It's fundamentally unfair."

Theo couldn't let that one go unchallenged. "But media coverage of Harwood's recent basketball championship elevated the defendants to a vaunted status the plaintiff in this case has not enjoyed. By publicly expressing viewpoints that counter that positive spin, we only level the playing field in a venue where potential jurors are quite likely to be fans of Harwood basketball, and therefore deferential to the players and the university."

"You don't get to tip the scales, counselor." The judge contorted her face as she readied her pronouncement. "You're entitled to continue seeking additional witnesses through referrals, but not through the news media. I'm granting defense's request for a suppression order with regard to public statements, effective immediately."

"Your Honor, if I may," Somers said. "I fear this horse is already out of the barn. Ms. Constantine just admitted her intention all along was to bias public opinion through media appearances designed to undermine my clients. Even if she ceases these self-aggrandizing interviews, the subject is likely to remain salient in the news. Commentators will continue their unfounded speculation, and consumers of this pseudo-news will be swayed by uninformed discussion. In light of the damage already done, I urge you to dismiss this case in its entirety."

"Am I to consider this your motion for dismissal as well, Mr. Somers?"

The question seemed to catch him off guard for an instant, but then he flashed a boyish smile. "Only if you're willing to grant it, Your Honor."

"Then let's pretend you didn't ask." She pushed herself out of her chair to stand barely taller than she'd been while seated. "Now if you'll excuse me, I need to get back to court."

The last thing Theo wanted was a personal confrontation with Somers, something he appeared to relish. "Good to see you again, Theo."

"Sorry, James…not really feeling it." She grudgingly respected the job he'd done on the Dowd Mills case. It had truly pained the judge to decide in the company's favor, but the law was on Dowd's side. "You can't find enough work in New York?"

He laid a hand on his chest. "What can I say? Harwood's my alma mater. It'll always hold a special place in my heart. This is my chance to give something back."

"Couldn't you just write them a check? Dowd Mills must have paid you handsomely."

"Feisty...I like that about you, Theo." Obviously he was feeling cocky at coming out with a win.

Whereas she'd expected all along to lose today. Jeanette Henry had a reputation for being restless during jury selection. While she was required to suffer the process, too many dismissals for cause strained her patience, and no attorney wanted to enter a trial before a ticked-off judge. Shutting down pre-trial media coverage was her way of heading off potential problems with tainted jurors.

All in all, this was a minor defeat. Somers was right about the damage being done now that the lid had been blown off Harwood's efforts to keep the story under wraps. While it was a shame she couldn't continue to beat the drum until the NBA draft, she was pretty sure the sports commentators would do it for her. If that somehow kept Frazier and Caldwell from a big payday, it would be a victory.

CHAPTER FOURTEEN

With the thrum of her climax fading, Celia lifted the sheet to see Theo resting a cheek against her thigh. Until now, she'd never considered herself a morning person.

"You taste even better than coffee," Theo said, crawling up to share her essence with a kiss.

"Mmm…you're forgiven for not whisking me away to Newport."

"What can I say? That's the downside of teleconferencing—fewer chances to mix business travel with pleasure." She rolled out of bed, dragging the sheet with her. "I have an appointment this morning with my treadmill. Something tells me it's feeling neglected."

Theo had warned the night before that sleeping in wasn't an option on Monday morning, since she started each week with an early staff meeting. Nor was it feasible for Celia, who had to finish her textbook proofs and update the syllabus for her fall performance class.

Celia showered and dressed in cotton pants with a sleeveless knit top, suitable for working alone in her office since she had no appointments on her schedule. By the time Theo finished her shower, she'd set out breakfast on the bar—soft-boiled eggs, toast and coffee.

"And you said you couldn't cook."

"This hardly qualifies as cooking," she answered, straightening the collar on Theo's terry robe. "But never let it be said that I can't boil water."

Theo nodded toward her suitcase by the door. "I take it you're leaving me. Was it something I said?"

"I figured we both ought to focus on work during the week. I need to rest up for Friday." She pulled Theo into a hug. "I have a feeling we're going to do this every weekend."

"Damn straight. I've already gotten used to you being around. Next time you come over, how about bringing a few extras in case you feel like giving in to your lust on a weeknight? Be spontaneous. Campus isn't that far from here. Just call me and I'll come pick you up."

"I'll take that under advisement, counselor. Have you told anyone in your office about us yet?"

"Nnnn-not exactly. But I'm sure Hank—he's my investigator—he's probably figured it out. Which is good, since he *is* a detective, after all. And since he walked in on me talking to you on the phone a couple of times. Those kissing sounds are a dead giveaway."

It was curious Theo would keep their relationship a secret from her co-workers. She'd told the magazines she thought it best to keep her personal life private, but surely that didn't extend to people she claimed were as close as family. "So what's up with that? Are you still worried they'll think it's a conflict of interest?"

"Yes and no. I suppose I need to let them know the details eventually, that I put you in touch with another attorney before we started dating. The problem"—her voice faded briefly as she went to the door to retrieve the newspaper from the hall—"is that I'm the boss, so I have to set an example for everyone who works there. I don't want anyone thinking they can socialize with one of our witnesses without running it by me. At the same time, I hate being one of those 'do as I say, not as I do' bosses."

"Just wait till I bring you along to something on campus. Won't that ruffle a few feathers!"

"By all means, save me the seat next to your chancellor. I promise to be just as nice as I was to their asshole attorney."

"How about a front-row seat for our production next spring? I haven't gotten my theater budget yet, but it looks like we'll be doing *Music Box Review*. Irving Berlin. It's out of copyright and they never give us enough money for anything else."

"It'll be even worse once we shake them down for treble damages. You'll be lucky to stage a sock-puppet show in a cardboard box."

"That's nothing. I directed a play once where the only prop was a wooden door. Nine characters played by three actors, where they put on different coats or hats depending on who they were supposed to be. We picked up everything at a thrift store, so the entire production budget was less than—"

"Son of a bitch!" Theo had found something in the paper.

"What?"

"This story on the sports page by Ivan Wallace. He covers the local colleges. Obviously a fanboy. Says he interviewed some of the basketball players—not one of which he's calling out by name—and they said Hayley was a groupie. That she hung around the team all the time, showed up at their parties and came on to all the players."

"That's a lie. Every word of it."

Theo's jaw twitched with anger as she ground her teeth. "Of course it is. It's a classic smear campaign, and whoever's behind it knows we can't push back because of the gag order."

"Then somebody should write a letter to the editor. I bet I can get Michael to do it."

"Michael's one of my witnesses. I'd be in jail for contempt two seconds after it showed up." She abruptly scraped the rest of her breakfast down the garbage disposal, apparently having lost her appetite. "I can't believe an editor let that story through without any sourcing. That tells me whoever planted this has some powerful friends."

"Is there anything we can do?"

Theo shook her head. "No, the damage is done. I won't get anything out of Wallace about who said this, but you can bet I'm going to put the whole team on my deposition list. No one's going to own this, so Ivan's going to come off looking like a hack."

Celia followed her into the bedroom and watched as she continued getting ready for work, the sensual start of their day forgotten. With the gag order and now this, it was undeniable the momentum had swung to the side of the defense.

When Theo emerged from the bathroom, her hair dry and makeup in place, she tugged Celia back onto the unmade bed. "You know what? Screw it. I'm not going to let a pack of lies ruin a day that started with me making love with the sexiest woman on the planet."

A series of increasingly heated kisses threatened to derail their plans for getting to work, especially when Theo's hand wandered up her shirt to squeeze a breast.

Though Celia had no schedule to keep, she couldn't let Theo miss her meeting. "You're going to be late...and it will be my fault."

Theo murmured, "Everything is your fault. Like the fact that I can't go three minutes without thinking about you. Like I won't be able to sleep tonight because you aren't here...unless I touch myself."

"Just promise me you'll pick up the phone when you do."

* * *

Alone in her office, Theo polished the legal argument she expected to make in response to the motion for dismissal. Though she hadn't yet received the defense's reply to her suit, she had a reasonable idea what it would contain.

The point of the defense's motion wasn't to argue the facts of the case, but its legal merits even if all the facts were assumed to be true. Without admitting anything, they would claim as a matter of law that they weren't legally culpable for Hayley's suicide even if the players had committed the sexual assault, even if the campus police had ignored the evidence and denied her due process, and even if the chancellor and board of trustees had taken no action to help her.

Four out of five judges would probably agree. That's how difficult it was in Georgia to hold anyone responsible for someone else's suicide. Would Judge Henry be the one who opened the door to the suit? Only if Theo could convince her Hayley's suicide was both foreseeable and a direct result of the defendant's actions.

After a soft knock, her door opened to Penny. "Theo, your ten o'clock is here early. Can you see him?"

She'd been so busy, she hadn't even glanced at her schedule. "Shane Satterfield? Are you kidding me?" He was a Senior District Attorney from the Felony Division. "Any idea what he wants?"

"A criminal matter. That's all he said."

Theo knew Shane from a pro bono case she'd argued several years ago, a domestic abuse victim who'd poured scalding water down her husband's back while he was trying to choke her. The DA's office had conceded the abuse, but pressed forward with charges due to the extreme nature of the man's injuries. After a jury acquitted the woman, Shane urged the husband into a domestic offenders program and advised him against further contact with his wife. Theo counted Shane as one of the good guys.

"Shane, how in the world are you?"

In his late forties, he was six-four at least, thin and wearing a suit that looked two sizes too large on his round shoulders. His offered hand was free of calluses but strong just the same. "Doing just fine, Theo. Great to see you again."

"I read about your promotion—Senior District Attorney. Congratulations."

"You stick around long enough, the other guys die off. They have to kick you upstairs eventually." He followed her gesture to one of the wingback chairs and, gentleman that he was, waited for her to sit. "Our office has been following your case with considerable interest. I suspect you know that…and that you've been expecting me."

"Let's just say I was hoping someone would come around wanting to know more. That video was pretty compelling, wasn't it?"

"I'll say. And I'm betting you have a copy that isn't blurred." He crossed an ankle over his knee and continued in a Southern drawl that was obviously born and bred. "Don't suppose you'd be interested in telling us how you acquired it."

"Does it matter?"

"Mmm…not really, I guess. We'd still have to corroborate its origin and authenticity to know whether it's been edited to show something that never actually occurred…as some have suggested."

Theo had heard that theory bandied about on sports talk radio but gave it no credence. The man who posted the video never meant for it to be seen by millions of people. "I'm willing to share the evidence that led us to believe Ruben Vargas was the person behind the camera. With your ability to subpoena the contents of a private social media group accessible only by members of Harwood's basketball team, I'm betting you'd be able to confirm that. It's also likely Vargas was the one who supplied Hayley Burkhart with a drugged drink."

He nodded along as she spoke. Theo knew what he already was thinking—if Vargas hadn't physically participated in the rape, he might be a candidate for a plea bargain in which he testified against the others. Letting him off easy would be an outrage, especially if he'd been responsible for rendering her unconscious.

"And I can show you a copy of the receipt for Hayley Burkhart's rape kit. I'll also provide a physical description of the campus officer who collected it from the student health center. You'll need that, since his signature isn't legible and you won't have any other way of knowing who it was. For what it's worth, that kit may or may not be held in evidence at the Harwood police station. Our private sources tell us it's presently unaccounted for."

"That would be very bad news for a potential criminal investigation."

"Unless you're trying to prove obstruction of justice. Then it's a pretty clear case. I'm telling you, there's a lot of blame to go around."

He leaned forward and pressed his fingertips together. "Hypothetically speaking, I might be persuaded to look into whether or not certain individuals acted as accessories after the fact. But I'll be honest with you, Theo. What I'm really after is those boys who assaulted that young woman. If that video holds up as evidence, it's easily enough for a sexual battery conviction."

"Sexual battery!" She felt the blood of rage rush to her face, and almost leaped from her chair. "Christ, Shane. That's a misdemeanor. Twelve months max. What they did to Hayley was straight-up rape."

He shook his head. "I agree with you but I'm not sure it'll fly. Physical contact without her consent, yes. But the rape statute says 'forcible and against her will.' We can't prove either one."

"That's such bullshit." Thanks to Jalinda's research, the relevant case law was top of mind. "*Dorsey* says neither substantial violence nor vigorous resistance is required if force is otherwise found. Did it look to you like Hayley Burkhart invited those men to join a rape line? Or did they force themselves on her?"

"You know it's not that simple. If we overreach, all it takes is one juror to sink us. And those guys'll walk."

"Not if you turn around and try them again. You can do that over and over if there's a hung jury. I guarantee you're never going to get an acquittal."

The oldest emotional trick in the book would be to ask if he'd settle for misdemeanor charges if it had been his daughter instead of Hayley. But then Shane knew all the old tricks too and would manage his detachment with cool logic.

"Whereas if I had a rape kit that showed this young woman was drugged," he went on, "well, that might be a game changer. We're talking an extra five to fifteen years for illegal possession and administering of Schedule II narcotics. I'd probably only get one of them for that though."

She appealed next to his territorial nature, a common theme across jurisdictions. "I might as well take this to the US

Attorney...try to get them to file felony charges against all of them for drug-facilitated rape. The video and that sadistic photo they left on Hayley's phone might net the full sentence of twenty years."

He held up a hand. "Not so fast. I want to try this case, Theo. I'm just looking for the best outcome. All I'm saying is we'll know more when we get the rape kit."

Unless the rape kit was missing. "You may not need it if all you're looking for is drugs. Check with the coroner's office. They should have hair samples from the autopsy. Test them for GHB."

Gamma-Hydroxybutyric acid was the most common date rape drug on campuses, and it was detectable in hair strands even months after use. The fact that it also was used to enhance athletic performance made it the likely culprit in this case.

"Good, that's a plan...I can do that this afternoon. And you can bet I'll be talking to these young men. Their friends too. Somebody's bound to know something. It's my experience that when push comes to shove, everybody's first instinct is to save their own hide. But it would help me a lot if I knew where to start. Somebody on the inside...like the one who gave you this video."

Theo wasn't convinced anyone besides Michael's boyfriend, Gavin Sandifor, would turn on the others, and she couldn't give him up. That didn't mean Shane wouldn't get to him eventually if he interviewed all the players. Harwood only carried sixteen on its roster. "I already told you—start with Ruben Vargas. I'll have my paralegal send over a copy of our evidence this afternoon." Minus Gavin's confirmation, of course.

Shane stood and pushed his hands in his pockets. "We're on the same side, Theo. It's good for both of us if we're sharing information, 'cause if I convene a grand jury and don't get an indictment, it's gonna sink your case. No rape means no responsibility for wrongful death."

Walking him to the door, she replied, "Come on, we both know you'll get an indictment if you want it."

"But will I get a conviction?"

"I have faith in you. But I can't help you any more than I already have. Not right now, anyway." Though the possibility of seeing Frazier, Caldwell, Watson and Vargas arrested and charged was worth going back to Michael and Gavin to ask if they were willing to cooperate with Shane if she vouched for him. Especially since he had subpoena power and could compel their testimony anyway.

She'd lost her window for calling out the US Attorney's office through the media, shaming them for not taking up the case. But now that the DA's office had responded, at least she could hope for a criminal conviction on rape charges if her wrongful death case went down the tubes.

* * *

With her phone tucked under her chin, Celia turned out the light in her office and closed the door behind her, twisting the knob to be sure it had locked. "I can talk to Michael again if you need me to, but you'd probably have better luck if you went straight to Gavin—cut out the middlemen. Once he realizes the DA's going to track him down eventually, he might decide to come forward on his own."

"I could probably get Shane to meet with him off the record," Theo said. "But no matter what, it's good news, right? The DA's going to do the dirty work. In my book, that's a reason to celebrate. How about dinner on my terrace again? I'll make it worth your while."

Celia groaned. She could honestly say she wasn't looking forward to going home to an empty house, but a voice in her head warned her not to let her feelings for Theo—no matter how strong—tempt her away from her school duties, especially since the higher-ups probably were waiting patiently for a screwup. "I can't, Theo. I want to, but I've got lots of work to do. If I bear down during the week, I won't have to feel guilty about playing on the weekend."

"Spoilsport. My calendar says that's only a couple of days from now." Which meant Wednesday.

"How about Thursday? That'll give us an early start."

"You can't see me but I'm pouting." With a garbled voice, Theo added, "My lower lip is sticking out so far I can't talk plain."

"You're officially nuts. Call me later. We'll talk about that crazy calendar of yours."

On the way out, she stopped by the administrative office to check her mail. Conference announcements, calls for papers. And another sealed envelope from her boss.

She hadn't seen Andrew since the case was filed and had no idea how he felt about her involvement. She wanted to think he'd be supportive—Hayley was one of their brightest and most talented students, after all—but he was forced by his position to straddle the line between administration and faculty. With a quick glance she noted the lights were out in his office. He'd already gone for the day or was in a meeting in another part of campus.

Her hands trembling slightly, she slid her finger through the seal. A one-page letter congratulating her on her promotion.

In reviewing our spring production budgets for the past several years, I find a disturbing pattern of diminishing support. As the celebration of stage performance is an integral component of our departmental mission...

She was stunned by the amount he'd awarded for next spring's performance, the most she'd ever received. Plenty for scenery and props, costumes, marketing and advertising. Best of all, he'd authorized enough to secure the rights for a modern musical.

The letter was dated several days ago, but well after the news broke that she was cooperating with a lawsuit against the university. This couldn't possibly have happened if the administration was out to get her.

Or maybe they were, and Andrew was using his discretionary budget to push back against them on her behalf. Nearly all of the academic departments resented the special treatment afforded athletics. The men's basketball coach was the highest-paid employee at the university, making four times as much as a Nobel Prize-winning professor of chemistry.

She liked thinking Andrew was on her side, that he was protecting her from the fallout. Whether that was true or not, good things were happening career-wise, and she was determined to enjoy it while it lasted.

CHAPTER FIFTEEN

Celia staked out permanent space on the right side of Theo's double vanity. Makeup, cleansers, toothbrush. Everything she'd need for those days when Theo talked her into a spur-of-the-moment overnight stay. Or a longer one, she conceded, eyeing the open suitcase in the closet behind her. She had no intention of returning home until Monday.

Theo had taken her suggestion to kick off their weekend on Thursday as fact, setting up an impromptu NBA draft party. The sportscasters were in a frenzy over rumors Atlanta's District Attorney's office was considering sexual assault charges against four players, one of them Ruben Vargas. How far would Frazier and Caldwell fall in the draft?

It was also a coming out party, since Theo had invited several of her co-workers, including both of her law partners and everyone working on the Hayley Burkhart case. Tonight they would announce their relationship.

She aimed to impress in black leggings and a sleeveless white tunic, with gold sandals showing off her deep red pedicure.

Classy but casual. Though she was pleased with her overall look, it did little to calm her nerves. Her concern wasn't what they'd think of her, but how they'd feel about Theo seeing someone who'd brought them a case.

The phone rang as Theo was stepping out of the shower. "That's the caterer. Can you let them in? I'll be out in five minutes."

Celia supervised the arrangement of a Southern feast—pulled pork and all the trimmings. By the time they finished, Theo arrived to sign the receipt and fork over a generous tip.

"This is enough to feed an army, Theo. How many did you say were coming?"

"Probably only five or six. Kendra and Rob couldn't get a sitter. And Jalinda—that's my paralegal—she doesn't usually go in for social things with people from the office. The only reason she comes to the Christmas party is because that's when I hand out bonuses."

They set out dinnerware, then carried the love seats from the bedroom and terrace into the living area, arranging all the seating so everyone could see the large-screen TV. It was already set to the sports station but muted.

After three days of incessant sports chatter, there was nothing new to be said. Tonight would tell if the allegations were enough to torpedo the players' draft stock. In response to news about the DA's office opening an investigation, the Department of Justice had released a statement saying it too was monitoring events.

"Did you read Ivan Wallace's column in the paper today?" Celia asked. "It's just bizarre to think the public is divided over this. But I'm not surprised. Jocks get away with anything."

"I doubt what they're printing is representative," Theo scoffed. "The sportswriters go looking for quotes from Average Joes to fill up space in their story. If they talk to a supporter, they feel like they have to include a critic too. They don't tell you how many people they have to talk to so they can scrounge up someone willing to turn a blind eye to a gang rape. What they print or put on the air always makes it look fifty-fifty. It's misleading as hell, but that perception becomes reality. On the other hand, as long as there's conflict, our story stays on the front page."

The phone rang again and Celia anxiously checked herself in the foyer's full-length mirror. It was silly to be so nervous about meeting new people, but there was a lot at stake tonight. If Theo's friends were put off about them seeing each other, it could drive a serious wedge into their relationship.

Theo pressed the entry code for the security door downstairs. "They're all here. Gloria says they've been fighting over the guest parking spaces in the garage."

"You told them we were seeing each other, right? What did they say?"

"I think they were glad to hear it if you want to know the truth. It's good for office morale if the boss is happy." She pulled Celia into a kiss. "Besides, no matter what they think, they'll pretend to love you because they know I can fire them if they don't."

First through the door was a paunchy man who carried a six-pack of bottled beer. "I figured you'd put out wine and cheese, Theo," he said mockingly. "I wanted to be sure you had the good stuff." Offering his other hand to Celia, he introduced himself as Hank Maloney.

Celia recalled his name as the investigator Theo had mentioned. The young man with him was his son Mark, mid-thirties and clean shaven with glasses. He wore khakis and a T-shirt that read *BYTE ME*.

Theo nudged forward an elegant woman in her sixties, dressed in a flowing orange pantsuit that nearly matched the color of her hair. Celia recognized her immediately. "Oh, my gosh. You're Gloria Hendershot. You used to chair the Women's Studies department at Harwood. I audited one of your classes about ten years ago." Looking to Theo, she added, "You never told me she worked with you."

The woman covered a brief look of bewilderment with a smile. "I'm Theo's best kept secret. Did I put you to sleep in my class?"

There was no reason Dr. Hendershot would have remembered her, not among the thousands of women she'd taught in her long career. "Not at all. I've read both of your books. They're wonderful."

With the determination of a border collie, Theo herded the group into the living area. "All right, introductions. You've met Hank and Mark, and you know Gloria. This is her husband Lewis."

Lewis was slim and as well-dressed as his wife, in slacks and a polo shirt with a sport coat. He greeted her with the charm of a Southern gentleman.

"And this is one of my law partners, Philip." A handsome, tanned man in his forties with a younger, very pregnant woman on his arm. Theo placed a hand on the woman's stomach. "This is his wife Sofia and their soon-to-be daughter, Theo."

Philip interjected, "Theo's convinced we're going to name the baby after her."

"Well, why not?" Celia mustered. "The Theo I know turned out pretty solid."

Theo seemed genuinely pleased to greet the last guest, a young woman who apparently had come by herself. "And this is Jalinda Smiley, hands down the best paralegal in Atlanta."

Jalinda *Doesn't* Smiley was more like it. A round-figured African-American with faint freckles, she looked positively miserable to be there.

"And this lovely lady, in case you haven't figured it out," Theo said as she draped an arm around Celia's shoulder, "is Celia Perone. *Doctor* Celia Perone. Professor of performance studies at Harwood, and the person who brought us Hayley Burkhart's case. She's also near and dear to my heart, so please try to make a good impression. I don't want her sneaking out with her suitcase after she's met my friends."

Hank answered cheerfully, "Here, Celia. Have a beer."

Cheap domestic beer wouldn't have been her first choice, but she wasn't about to refuse and risk anyone thinking her a snob.

"Grab a plate," Theo commanded. "The NBA draft starts any minute."

The mound of food fell steadily as they filled their plates and carried them into the TV area. The selection show had begun with a slate of prospective draftees and their families abuzz in Madison Square Garden. Sacramento was already on the clock with five minutes to make the night's first pick.

As hosts, Celia and Theo waited until everyone was seated. That left them with chairs on opposite wings of the room. Hank had squeezed onto the couch with Gloria and Lewis, leaving his son to sit with Jalinda on the terrace love seat. Celia caught Theo looking at the pair with a faint smile.

"Look at that," Philip said. "Frazier's strutting around like it's business as usual. He must be pretty confident he's going to get picked."

Confident didn't begin to describe his swagger. He wore a designer suit that probably had been purchased by a booster, and sported a diamond stud in his ear. Laughing, back-slapping.

"He makes me sick," Celia said. "I'm telling you right now, if he has a good night, I'll have a miserable one."

Lewis Hendershot, who worked as a corporate attorney, said, "I heard on sports talk radio that Caldwell wasn't even planning to be there. Guess his agent's been working the phones all week and not getting any takers."

The NBA commissioner took the podium, silencing the chatter in both the Garden and the sportscaster booth. "With the first pick, the Sacramento Kings select JaMarcus Hightower, from Indiana University."

The camera switched briefly to Matt Frazier, who'd plastered on a smile the whole world had to know was fake.

"At least he didn't go number one," Theo said.

The next pick and each one thereafter took another excruciating five minutes. In between announcements and brief interviews with the players, the studio commentators speculated on the fate of the Harwood duo, who'd so far been passed over by the first eleven teams.

"Frazier looks pissed," Hank observed. "He ain't even trying to smile for the cameras anymore."

After more than a hour into the coverage, Cliff Reynolds, the sportscaster who'd challenged Theo regarding the athletes' version of events, opined from the sportscasters' booth, "I can promise you, Ed, these teams will rue the day they snubbed Frazier and Caldwell. Both of these players have the talent to turn a franchise around."

"What a dick!" Gloria spat. "Talk about tone deaf."

Ed Wainwright, the second commentator, wasn't quite so bombastic in his support. "They're talents, all right. But clearly, teams have done a lot of research on these guys. Let's go to Derek Osgood for a perspective on what some of these GMs are thinking."

The screen split to a remote reporter, a crisp-looking preppie type standing on the sidewalk in front of the Garden. "Thanks, Ed. I've talked to about ten sources in the league today and they're all saying the same thing. Frazier and Caldwell are toxic."

"Woo!" Theo yelled, adding a fist pump.

"I just don't get that," Reynolds whined. "What's their deal exactly? I know there's talk out there about the DA filing charges, but I have to think if these players were going to be arrested, it would have happened already. The evidence just isn't there. It's all going to come down to who you believe—there's not a single witness who can claim they saw what went down."

Philip huffed. "That's right. It's just a video, dickhead."

"And even if charges are filed," Reynolds went on, working himself into a lather, "there's no certainty they'll be convicted. Are you telling me there aren't two GMs out there willing to take a chance on guys this skilled with a basketball? This whole fiasco could go away tomorrow and nobody's going to have the right to sign them."

"Douche bucket!" Gloria screamed.

"What part of toxic don't you understand, Cliff?" Osgood retorted with a chuckle. "Convicted or not, no one I've talked to wants to take a chance on angering their fan base, particularly their female fan base. GMs are telling me their wives have watched that video too, and they aren't happy with what they saw. It doesn't matter how skilled Frazier and Caldwell are, convincing families to come out and get behind a player who participated in an incident like that…let's just say that's a hard sell for the ticket office."

Ed interrupted. "Let me jump in here. I've just been alerted that Matt Frazier has left the Garden with his family. We don't know if he got a call from his agent…or maybe someone in the league. Whatever the reason, we're down to the eighteenth pick of the night, and he's apparently decided to sit the rest of this one out."

Jalinda suddenly blurted, "That's right, jerk wad. Go home and watch with Caldwell. You're both nobodies again."

* * *

It couldn't have been a better night as far as Theo was concerned. Good food, good friends, good times. And a pair of assholes getting their due.

Best of all, Celia seemed to have hit it off with everyone. She'd laughed heartily at Hank's absurd story of busting into what he suspected was a drug deal, only to find a white collar junior executive learning dance moves from a couple of gang bangers. And she'd listened intently as Philip and Sofia described their birthing plans in intimate detail. But her best connection was clearly with Gloria. They shared a scholarly curiosity about the world and the joy of their role in shaping it.

True, Celia was an experienced actress who could put on whichever face she wanted. If this was an act, it was Oscar-worthy.

Theo waited for a lull in the conversation. "Celia, I think you should tell everyone about your first job."

"I can't believe you brought that up!" she squealed.

She watched their faces as Celia revealed her Hollywood career. The only hint of recognition came from Philip, who vaguely remembered his younger sisters watching the show. All the others were too old or too young to know of *Little CeCe*.

"I think we're all actors to some degree," Gloria said. "We want to make people believe everything we say is absolutely real. Teachers perform every time they step in front of a lecture hall. And Theo…you should see her in front of a jury. I wouldn't be surprised if some of those people come out of the courtroom feeling as bad as the victims."

Celia nodded along with every word. "It's amazing, isn't it? I've seen her on TV. You'd think after thousands of years of developing ways to communicate, our bullshit detectors would be more attuned. We'd recognize the cues and know when someone was trying to manipulate us."

Theo planted her hands on her hips. "Excuse me, did you just accuse me of being a bullshitter?"

"Not you," Gloria explained. "Or not *just* you. Everybody. Only the extremely naive trust everything they hear. The rest of us wonder if what we're hearing is a brazen lie, or if it's only selectively true because we don't have the whole picture."

Hank laughed. "That's practically my job description. Except I don't wonder about shit. I know most people I talk to are lying about something."

"But it's all in the performance," Celia added. "Some people are really, really good actors. Everything that comes out of their mouth feels real."

Mark, who'd been relatively quiet all evening—though he and Jalinda had kept up a private conversation on their shared love seat—spoke up. "It's what makes people interesting. Having to figure them out, I mean."

"He's right," Jalinda chimed in, a pleasant surprise for Theo. It was nice to see her enjoying the young man's company, and Hank probably felt the same way about his son, whom he'd secretly labeled a world-class nerd. "If everyone always spoke the truth, conversation would be boring. Or worse, there'd be fights breaking out all the time."

"Right. What do you mean you don't like my new haircut?" Theo said.

Gloria gave her a stern look. "I've been meaning to talk to you about that. And that brown suit you wore on TV the other day…tsk."

As everyone laughed at Theo's expense, the phone rang.

* * *

After noting the caller, Theo had gone into her office and closed the door, leaving Celia in a roomful of people she hardly knew. For a fleeting moment, she was uncomfortable.

"Whoever that is, it looks important," Gloria said. "Let's hope she hasn't violated the gag order. I hate it when Theo gets tossed in the slammer for contempt."

Celia laughed. "Seriously, has that ever happened?"

"Let's see," Philip started. "There was the Anderson case, where she refused to produce her client because the woman was in hiding with her daughter."

Jalinda spoke up, "And that hostile work environment case against the paint store. The judge told her she couldn't refer to the defendant as a sexist, so she called him a misogynist, then a chauvinist. He locked her up when she got to woman-hating pig."

"Come on, the guy actually had a tattoo of a woman wearing a dog collar."

"But the judge wouldn't make him show it because it amounted to testifying against himself."

Gloria shook her head, chuckling. "The best one, though…I wish you all could have been there." Her voice turned serious. "It was right after Theo won the SCOTUS case, so she was feeling invincible, really full of herself. The case was one of the most outrageous injustices I'd ever seen—and I've seen a lot. A woman who became pregnant by a rapist couldn't give up her child for adoption without the father's permission, and he wouldn't give it unless she promised not to testify against him."

Celia was horrified. "Please tell me she won that case."

"Only on appeal. The district court ruled against her. That's when she went off, telling the judge he had two conflicting statutes—parental rights of a monster versus a woman's right to due process against her rapist. He's banging his gavel and she's yelling at him that the root word of judge is just, not unjust."

"It's what I like about her," Hank said. "She don't take no shit."

Theo returned and placed her hands on her hips, as if bracing for her big announcement. "Time to get back to work. That was Penny. She just got an email alert from the courthouse that Harwood filed its answer—a motion to dismiss. We get our copy first thing in the morning."

"Any idea what it says?" Celia asked.

"I could guess. First, they're going to say Donald Lipscomb doesn't have standing to sue because he's not Hayley's next of kin. Then they'll say, even if he is next of kin, he's suffered no monetary damages that warrant remedy. If we get past that, they'll argue Hayley's suicide wasn't foreseeable. And if it was, because they knew her personal circumstances made her susceptible to mental health issues, a legal remedy would have a chilling effect on Harwood's future acceptance of applicants who come from less than ideal backgrounds."

Philip cut in, "Then they'll pick apart the defendant list, arguing why this person or that person shouldn't be held responsible. My guess is the deepest pockets want out—that means the board of trustees and the university administrators. If the case goes to trial, they'll want to whittle it down to just the players."

Theo turned to Jalinda. "I want you to pull Sabrina off the wage theft case to help us, but make sure you run that by Kendra. Have her check every citation, read them all for context. Somers likes to cite the dissent if it helps make his case, so make sure he's not trying to pull one over on the judge. And Gloria, I want you and Jalinda to look for any material disputes." To Philip, she added, "You know your job—sharpen the argument on damages. Everything you can find on profit from tort and disgorgement."

As she rattled off orders, Celia remembered her impressions from the first few times they met. Knowing her intimate side had done nothing to diminish the feeling she was watching the real Theo—professional, calculating, competent. Determined to win justice for her client, to make yet one more dent in the hegemony that said women were worth less than men.

She found it sexy as hell. Standing with her arm around Theo's waist as the last of their guests walked out the door, she said, "Do you have any idea how awesome I think you are?"

"Don't say that yet. The biggest hurdle's the first one," Theo said, sliding toward the mess left behind in the kitchen.

"You don't really think the judge will dismiss the case?"

"I'd be lying if I said I wasn't nervous. Suicide's complicated. It could go either way." Hovering above the dishwasher, she stopped midmotion. "It would kill me if we lost. I know this is going to sound selfish…I've staked a lot of my professional reputation on this case. All those interviews. If it gets tossed, there'll be blowback. They'll savage me in the press, which is bad enough. The real problem's going to be the women who decide it's not worth it to fight back."

"Theo…" Celia pulled her into a fierce hug. "You can't fight all the world's battles in one case. Look at everything you've done for your clients…and for women who didn't have to hire attorneys because you already took care of it."

Like a pouting child, Theo went limp and whined, "But I want to win for you too."

"You already have. Frazier and Caldwell lost forty million dollars tonight, and that's the least of their worries. We don't know how bad it's going to get. You said it yourself—there's still the DOJ and Title IX. All because you made noise."

"*You* made the noise, Celia. I just cranked up the volume."

They finished in the kitchen and moved on to prepare for bed. It was clear from her silence Theo was beating herself up with doubt.

When they climbed between the sheets, Celia nestled under the crook of her arm and hugged her tightly. "Look, you've done everything in your power to make this right. Stop worrying about letting me down or letting Hayley down. These bastards knew from day one they might get away with this because that's the way it is when men make the rules and enforce them. It's not your fault."

A low groan told her Theo was wrestling with deeper emotions than guilt. After a long pause, she finally said, "Sorry, this is what I look like when I start worrying I might lose. Half of it's rage. I try to keep it buried so I won't take it out on people I care about."

"You haven't lost anything."

Celia realized she'd begun a slow comforting massage of Theo's torso as they talked. From the subconscious to the deliberate, she continued her caress. Ease the worry, release the tension.

After a subtle shift, she was poised on top, looking down into Theo's anguished face. "No matter what happens with this case, I won't ever feel anything but grateful that it brought us together. I love you, Theo. I can't believe I'm saying this already, but I could see myself making a life with you."

As she lowered her lips for a kiss, her hand slid up the nightshirt and found the part of Theo she claimed as her own. She tickled it gently, feeling a surge of passion when Theo opened her legs. Every stroke was wetter until she slid inside with ease.

Theo answered with a steady rocking of her hips. One hand caressing Celia's face while the other clutched her back, pulling her tighter with each rise.

With their tongues tangled in an endless kiss, Celia flicked her thumb across the knotted nerves.

"I love you so much," Theo whispered before throwing her head back. Her body went rigid and began to tremble.

Celia felt the walls clench around her fingers, as though she were being pulled inside. In that moment, they were one.

CHAPTER SIXTEEN

Theo spun away from her colleagues and stepped out of the conference room into the quiet hall. More times than not, she needed privacy whenever she spoke with Celia on the phone. "What do you mean, 'What am I wearing?' You practically dressed me this morning."

"And I plan to *un*dress you tonight. What did it say?"

"Pretty much everything we guessed last night. The one I'm worried about most is their challenge to our premise. It was well-stated, good citations. Basically they're saying, even if everything happened exactly the way we said it did—the guys raped her, the university covered it up—they still aren't legally liable for her death because Georgia law doesn't allow the finding of culpability for suicide. Whereas we say, maybe not in certain circumstances, but this case is different and here's why. We aren't asking the judge to rule on the evidence right now, just to let us have our chance to prove it to a jury."

Left unsaid was the possibility an appeals court would throw out the verdict even if a jury found in their favor, all because

Somers had done a superb job outlining how the case law favored the defendants. Though confident she could make her case for trial, there was no question she was fighting an uphill battle.

"I need to get back to work, sweetheart. We've got about eight people looking over the motion and picking it apart. See you at home for dinner?"

"And more."

The day had begun with a front-page story hailing Harwood's motion to dismiss, as if it were proof the lawsuit was frivolous and without merit. The very fact that the paper had gotten its hands on the motion before it was delivered to Constantine and Associates meant someone from the university had leaked it. University officials had been careful to avoid being quoted on the record lest they be held in contempt for violating the gag order, but their proxies were out in force—loyal alums and their handpicked legal experts.

It made Theo only more determined to file her response quickly, if for no other reason than to get the public momentum back on her side. It worried her that almost a week had gone by and Shane hadn't yet moved to indict the players, as if he were waiting to see how her case played out. That put added pressure on her team to get the motion denied.

Back in the conference room, Kendra was lending her professional eye to Theo's draft response. "I like what you did here. Your initial filing might have focused too much on the recklessness angle. You needed this emphasis on implied malice. Harwood had seen the evidence and knew its players deserved to be investigated. Instead they acted with an abandoned and malignant heart, and that's what sets this case apart from *Appling*."

"Thanks, that's helpful. Sabrina, make sure we haven't overlooked anything on malice. Civil or criminal."

Jalinda had made copies of the motion with color-coded tabs for each of the defense's counterpoints. As expected, the university's attorneys had argued to excuse administrators and police from the case. Theo had already drafted a rebuttal, calling them conspirators in denying Hayley due process.

She picked up the section no one else wanted, another argument she'd been expecting—a motion from the players to excuse them as defendants. Their well-funded attorney, from a firm of sports agents in Los Angeles, was still clinging to the initial claim the sex was consensual. The videotape, he claimed, depicted only a portion of the sexual activity and excluded moments when Hayley Burkhart was lucid and solicitous of their attentions. As they'd not committed the precipitating offense, it was logically impossible they could be held responsible for Hayley's subsequent suicide.

"We might need somebody to help with this argument from the players' attorney. Who do we know with a strong background in criminal litigation?"

Jalinda had the information at her fingertips. After sorting a spreadsheet, she provided the names of three attorneys they'd worked with in the past. "I'll set up a consult."

All in all, Theo was pleased with where they stood. There was nothing in the answer she couldn't counter by fine-tuning her original complaint. Her anxieties from the night before now under control, she was ready to dig in and get this case back to the court for a ruling.

"Here's something, Theo," Philip said. "A malpractice case filed by the family of a woman who hanged herself after taking a prescribed drug for depression. A judge found the prescribing doctor wasn't required to know she was suicidal, only that there was reason to know."

"So a reasonable person must conclude…that a woman who is already susceptible to a degraded mental state…" She spoke haltingly as she typed the words—an actual statement made by the university to the press—into her original claim. "Such a person might attempt suicide after being raped by multiple individuals who sadistically photographed her following the attack, who recorded and shared a video of the event in which they were laughing, whose report of the incident was dismissed out of hand by the police even after it was supported with video evidence, and who was threatened with expulsion from the university if she made these charges public." She paused to silently read what she had written so far. "Therefore the actions of the players, the campus police department and the university's administration, as they concerned Hayley Burkhart, constitute intentional infliction of emotional distress and depraved indifference to her wellbeing."

Kendra peered over her shoulder. "That's it. Now bring in the malice argument. Reckless and intentional…directly causing the victim distress."

Theo read the rest. "…that led the victim to a loss of impulse control when confronted with images of the defendants celebrating their basketball victory, the rewards of which the university valued to the exclusion of her right to due process."

It was a good case. Maybe even a winner.

* * *

"You're in a much better humor than the last time I saw you," Celia said, reaching across the console to take Theo's hand. "You'd have to be to willingly drive in downtown traffic on a Friday night."

"It's a big load off. Not that we're finished with our response. It'll probably take us till Tuesday or Wednesday to wrap it up and get it back to the judge, but it was a lot like being in law school and stressing out over an exam. Once I saw the questions and realized I knew all the answers, I started to relax. It's a big relief just to know we have a plan."

"What happens next?"

"We file a response and wait."

"Then you go back to court to argue again?" Celia's knowledge of legal procedures was limited to what she'd seen on TV dramas, which she knew took ridiculous liberties.

"No, this is pretty much final. The judge's ruling gets handed down by the clerk. A phone call. If the motion's denied, we get a court date."

And if not—the case was over.

She'd been pleasantly surprised at Theo's call to pick her up at Forbes Hall so they could go out for dinner instead of eating in. It was only when they turned toward the community theater she realized where they were headed.

"Are we going back to Sammy's Pint?"

"I thought it would be fun. We can sit on the barstool and flirt with each other. Like old times."

"If I recall, that's where you told me you'd love to go out with me, but sorry. Some bullshit about never mixing business with pleasure. What do you have to say for yourself now?"

"I made your pleasure my business. How's that?" Theo pulled into a packed twenty-dollar parking lot, handily sliding her own luxury sedan between two others.

"Lexus, Mercedes, Acura. Must be Lawyers Night."

Sammy's was packed around the bar with the happy hour crowd, but their old pub table in the back was free. They ordered two white wines, same as before.

"I remember being so excited waiting for you last time. I was still paranoid about anyone seeing me talk to you, but when you walked in, you were so cool. You had on that gray suit and a white shirt."

"I can't believe you remember all that." Today, Theo was more casual, dressed in a tan shirtwaist dress with a wide leather belt.

"I noticed everything about you. Still do, in fact." She reached over and flicked the deep V of her collar. "Like when you lean forward, I can see down your dress."

Theo laughed and leaned as far forward as the table would allow. "How long has it been since we were here? Six weeks?"

"Eight. And a half. But who's counting?"

Their cocktail waitress, a young woman wearing a black miniskirt and low-necked green T-shirt with Sammy's logo on front, dropped off their drinks. "Are you...by chance, that woman lawyer, the one doing that rape case with the basketball players?"

"I am." Theo smiled thinly with a hint of apprehension.

She nodded. "Oh...I was just wondering is all. You looked familiar."

Celia shook her head as she walked away. "That was weird. I thought for a minute she was going to ask for your autograph."

Theo shrugged. "So anyway, I was thinking...you have some free time over the summer, right? How would you feel about a week in St. John's? A bungalow on the beach…sailing, snorkeling, sunbathing. The three S's." Her eyes went wide and she grinned. "Oh wait, there are four. How could I forget the most important S of all?"

"The most important S…what could that possibly be?" She loved Theo's playful side. "Sleeping, snuggling…there must be something else."

Theo wasn't listening. Instead, her eyes had followed their waitress to another table, where several men were looking in their direction. As two of them started over, she whispered, "Better brace yourself for a couple of jackasses."

"Ladies." It was said with a vague sneer by a lanky man in his twenties. He wore khakis and a blue polo shirt with a print shop logo, the name Emilio stitched above it in script. A ball cap was turned backward on his head. Looking directly at Theo, he added, "So you're that lawyer that was on TV talking shit about Matt the Stat and D'Ant."

"Talking shit? You mean about them raping an unconscious woman? That kind of shit?"

Celia suddenly realized she was trembling, that her fight-or-flight instinct was kicking in for the latter. "Theo, we should go."

"No, we'll stay. These gentlemen will go." She waved her hand as if to shoo them away.

The other man, slightly older and wearing the same company uniform—Tim was his name—ignored her and leaned his forearms on their small table. "It ain't fair what y'all did to those guys. All this talk, this…this bullshit ruined their chances at making the NBA. Matt Frazier's probably the best point guard to come out in ten years. Now his career's practically over and he hasn't even been convicted of anything."

Emilio wedged himself between Celia and Tim, his thigh brushing hers under the table in a way that felt deliberate. "That's what sucks about this country's rape laws. Girls get to make up shit and everybody just takes their word for it."

Theo rolled her eyes dramatically. "You can't be serious, Emilio. I may be just a shit-talking lawyer myself, but I know my rape statistics. Only three percent of all rapes end up with somebody going to jail. That's ninety-seven out of every hundred where no one does time. Where are all these police and prosecutors and juries who take a woman's word for it? Please share that little nugget with me. I want to file all my future rape cases there."

Tim wasn't having it. "You don't have any idea what it's like for these guys, these sports stars. Girls throw themselves at them all the time."

"Yeah, I heard somebody say that on one of those talk shows," Theo said, nodding as though she were having a serious conversation with a reasonable person. But then she poked a finger at him, not quite touching his chest. "Did you ever stop to wonder why they didn't choose to have sex with one of those girls instead? You know, somebody who was actually awake?"

"How do you know she didn't come on to them? Were you there?"

"Were you?" Celia finally spoke up, "It so happens I knew the girl they raped. She wasn't like that."

Theo shook her head, a barely seen warning not to say anything else. "Come on, guys. Do you have any sisters who like getting gang-banged while they're unconscious?"

"This ain't about my sister," Emilio snarled. "That slut flat out begged 'em for it so she'd be popular. Then she went crying to everybody so they'd know she got it. You can't just take her word against three guys."

"I don't have to. I have a video…because one of those idiots was stupid enough to record it and post it for his friends. You saw that, right?"

To Celia's eye, Theo was enjoying herself. Her voice was lively and engaged, and her eyes bore accusingly into theirs as if demanding they account for themselves.

"Tell me something, Emilio. What is it about men who like having sex in front of each other? Does it turn them on? I mean, do you get excited thinking about watching your friend Tim here pounding away on somebody?"

"Now you're just being rude," Tim said, jutting out his lower lip and acting wounded.

"I'm sorry…seriously, I am. I'm sure your friend here knows you wouldn't do something like that. You took it personally, what I said. I can see how that would bother you. It's like when I come across a woman I know for a *fact* was raped, and I hear other people who don't know shit call her a liar."

His face reddened as he shifted his weight from side to side. "I didn't call her a liar. I'm just saying there's two sides to every story."

"Tim, what if I told you her toxicology results showed she had a date rape drug in her system? Would you still think there were two sides? I mean, who takes a date rape drug on purpose? 'Hey, I want to have sex with a bunch of guys but I don't want to be awake for it.'"

Celia was shocked Theo would give away inside information, but then realized she was drawing him into a competing narrative, the way she would a jury.

"Or if I told you there was a witness? An actual confession from someone who was there, who participated?"

Tim's jaw twitched and he finally said, "If you showed me all that, I'd be forced to believe she was telling the truth."

Theo nodded slowly. "So you'd have to see all that ironclad evidence before you'd believe her. But you don't need any evidence to take those guys' word for it even when you have a video staring you in the face." She looked past them and waved a menu at the waitress to signal they were ready to order dinner. "We're done here, guys."

Emilio stepped away and mumbled under his breath, "Cunt."

Celia's fury surged. Drawing courage from Theo's defiance, she called his name. As he turned to face her, she snapped his photo on her phone and went to work on her keypad. "I'm sharing this on Facebook. Next time you make an ass of yourself in public, you might want to wear a different shirt."

He took a step toward her but was caught by Tim. "Cool it, dude."

"It'll probably go viral…hundreds of thousands of people will see it and know exactly what you think of women. Good luck getting a date after tonight."

"Bitch isn't posting my picture anywhere."

No longer intimidated, Celia added, "And then there's all the one-star Yelp reviews for your print shop. Good thinking."

Tim shook him. "Stop being such a dick, Emilio. Apologize, or we're both going to get fired."

Emilio sputtered in protest before realizing Tim had him in an iron grip. "Okay, fine. I'm sorry."

"Maybe with a little less hostility?" Celia said, noticing his glare had turned to panic. He truly was an idiot for not realizing the trouble he was in.

He gathered himself and sighed. "I apologize...to both of you."

"That was pretty lame." She grudgingly trashed the photo.

"Apology accepted," Theo said firmly. She waited until Emilio had retreated and addressed Tim. "Thanks for sorting out your friend."

Tim shrugged. "He's not a bad guy. Just a little immature."

"He just called me a cunt for representing a rape victim who killed herself. You really ought to look for a better class of friends."

Celia waited until he was gone to speak. "I can't believe you didn't tell me about the toxicology results and the witness. Theo, that changes everything."

"It would if it were true." Theo raised her eyebrows a couple of times and smiled. "All I said was, quote, 'What if I told you?' I never said any of that actually happened. But I've sewn a couple of doubts. Who knows? It could even be true. A friend will tell a friend will tell a friend. Next thing you know, it gets worked into a newspaper column. Somebody on the players' side planted that story about Hayley being a basketball groupie. For all we know, it could have come from somebody in the administration. That's how the game's played."

It was hard to imagine a guy like Emilio changing his mind. Clearly he had no respect for women. "Do you ever wonder what these guys' mothers would say if they heard their sons talk like that?"

"Scary, isn't it? If you ever want to know what constitutes a hostile work environment these days, you should read through some of our depositions. That was perfect what you did, by the way...taking his picture. People who behave like that need to be called out."

"So how come you shushed me when I said I knew Hayley?"

Theo took her hand, running her thumb across the knuckles. "Because you were letting him know it was personal. Guys like Emilio...they love getting under people's skin. Women in particular. You can't show them any vulnerability or they'll exploit it for all it's worth."

Celia recalled the day she'd been waiting for Theo, when the man came over from the bar and told her to smile. "I always wanted to see you in action. I bet you're a holy terror in the courtroom."

"Only if I think holy terror will play well for the jury."

CHAPTER SEVENTEEN

Penny leaned across the desk with an appointment calendar as they mulled Theo's possibilities for vacation time. "This week you have the BPW luncheon, and you promised to present one of their awards so you can't cancel. This one's a bar meeting but you can skip those."

Other than the Harwood case, Theo was working a smattering of client files with estate updates, court appearances and business filings. Nothing that couldn't be rescheduled. The potential problem was the woman in Rhode Island, whose hearing could get postponed at the pleasure of the prosecutor.

"Three weeks to pick from between now and the end of August," Penny said. "You want me to see what kind of package I can get?"

"Perfect, thanks." Theo didn't like the idea of using her administrative assistant for personal tasks, but Penny knew her schedule better than she did and would make sure she didn't miss a critical appointment. She handed her one of Celia's business cards with ticketing info scribbled on the back. "Celia's okay with any of those weeks. Call her cell if you have any questions."

Sex. The other S was for Sex. In the bed, in the hammock, on the sand—wherever they found themselves alone. It would be oh-so-nice to leave the stress of their work behind for a few days and focus only on each other.

Celia had managed to enter her life at the very moment her heart was open for love. Could she possibly know after barely two months that she'd want Celia in her life forever? In the moments after making love they'd revel in their closeness. Their afterglow was getting longer. It was time to talk about the next step...about—

"Theo!" Penny appeared again, smiling and breathless as though she'd run down the hall. "I just got an alert from the courthouse. Motion for dismissal denied! Trial is set for January thirteenth."

A sense of triumph surged through her as though she'd actually won the case. Despite her hard work and optimism, she'd never truly expected to get this far, not with the legal precedent stacked against her. "Get my team in here. We need to get started on discovery. Oh...and book the terrace at the Weller Regent for this afternoon. This calls for a celebration."

* * *

Though an afternoon rainstorm had come and gone, the result was a virtual steam bath that had all but shut down the rooftop terrace lounge at the Weller Regent. Only the covered bar was open, the same hideaway where Theo had met Celia to hand her off to Bill Auger so they could date.

"Cheers!" Kendra clinked her glass to Theo's as she passed on her way to a table.

Nearly thirty of her staff and a handful of significant others had stopped by for happy hour after learning she was picking up the bar tab to celebrate their case going forward. Even Hank's son Mark had joined them, apparently at Jalinda's invitation. They were tucked away in the same intimate corner where Theo had sat with Celia.

Standing so she could watch the hostess station for Celia's arrival, Theo chatted with Sabrina, who wore a black silk shirt that showed a line of cleavage. A few months ago, that would have been a temptation...or at least a regret. With Celia now holding her heart, no one else could turn her head.

"The Marietta case you gave me last week," Sabrina said, "the woman who said her boss fired her after she asked him to stop giving her shoulder rubs...the day after I filed, he threatened to fire anyone at the agency who talked to me. I was thinking it was time to pull a page from the Theo Constantine Playbook—a press conference in front of their insurance office."

It was exactly what Theo would do but she had doubts about whether Sabrina would have the clout to command the media's attention. "What's your hook?"

"My hook? You mean other than highlighting what a pig he is?"

"I mean why should the press care? What's in it for them?" She took mercy on the young attorney, whose legal skills outweighed her public relations talents. "You have to persuade them to come out and cover the event. Make it so compelling they can't afford not to be there—tease them that you'll have an important statement that could significantly impact local insurance rates. Then announce you're amending your suit to include the parent company, and will be seeking punitive damages in the amount of whatever Philip tells you is workable."

"Whoa! That's a big deal."

It certainly was, considering the plaintiff had asked only for reinstatement and back wages. Sometimes it took asking for much more to get what you really wanted. "Convince your client you have to go big. Make sure she's okay with the publicity because this elevates it to a major case. *Your* major case...so you should do the press conference."

Sabrina obviously was stunned by her newfound authority, since Theo and Kendra usually handled the firm's dealings with the press. In fact, Constantine and Associates needed another voice and Sabrina's was perfect. She was attractive, well-spoken.

Philip leaned over Theo's shoulder and said, "There's your girlfriend. She looks almost as happy as you."

Indeed, Celia was wearing a broad grin as she greeted the hostess and scanned the small crowd looking for familiar faces.

Though Theo had insisted the impromptu party was "come as you are," it was clear she'd rushed home to change into something she hoped would impress—black skinny jeans with a sparkly sleeveless top. No way had she worn that to Forbes Hall.

Theo waved her over and wrapped an arm around her waist. "I was about to send out a search and rescue team."

"Our train went out of service, so I had to wait for the next one," Celia explained, taking a flute of champagne from a passing cocktail waitress. "Looks like I have some catching up to do."

"And some more people to meet. This is Sabrina Dawson, one of our junior associates." She nudged Celia forward. "And this is my...uh-oh, we haven't traded friendship rings yet, so I'm not sure what I'm supposed to call her. Oh, what the hell... Sabrina, this is my *girlfriend*, Celia Perone."

"Hi Sabrina. I guess I've graduated from star witness."

"I'll say. We've all been dying to meet the reason Theo's in such a good mood these days. I even heard a rumor she's planning to take a vacation."

"Except now that's iffy because we have a case to prep for," Theo said. "I can't wait to start discovery. A few thousand emails, text messages. Something will turn up. Finding one person who'll sing a different tune is all it takes to make their whole story fall apart."

"Celia!" Gloria materialized with her husband Lewis in tow. "Welcome to our little soiree. A good excuse for Theo to bring you out and show you off. But forget the fun stuff. Those days are over for a while. Things get crazy once we finally get access to evidence."

"If she gets any crazier, we're in a world of hurt."

Theo was pleased to find Celia relaxed and brimming with self-assurance around new faces and others she'd met only once. Again she reminded herself Celia was an actor by training.

"Hello again, Philip." Celia stepped forward to receive a kiss on the cheek. "Is Sofia here too?"

"Working late. I swear she's going to have that baby in her office." He squeezed Theo's shoulder and offered a toast. "Congrats, Theo. I know you were worried about this one being a loser."

She glanced at Celia, clearly wishing he hadn't been quite so blunt. Yes, she'd worried they wouldn't make it this far. But while she'd warned Celia this was a tough case, she'd been careful to mask the depth of her pessimism.

"Let's just say I'm relieved."

Celia touched her glass to Theo's. "That makes two of us. You said you were worried about it, but you always tried to be optimistic. I had a feeling it was even tougher than you were letting on."

Philip, who clearly had no idea he was talking out of school, went on, "This case has always been tricky, at least from a legal standpoint. A long shot if you want to know the truth. We needed all the stars to align—the right judge on the right day after a great lunch. Those go against us sometimes, so it's nice when they break our way."

Desperate for a change of subject, Theo spun Celia around to the couple in the corner. "And look at that. Hank's son Mark showed up to celebrate with Jalinda. I think love is in the air."

"I could have told you that. Those sparks were flying on draft night."

Theo whispered so the others couldn't hear, "I seem to recall some other sparks flying that night too."

"You think that was something, wait till we celebrate this."

"I like the way you think."

The hostess slithered through the group at the bar and presented an envelope to Theo. "This came for you just now. A courier. I asked him to wait but he said it wasn't necessary, just to make sure you got it."

Theo frowned as she looked at the return address. "Hubbard-McCaffrey. They're local, aren't they?"

"Mostly estate law, if I'm not mistaken," Philip said. "Barry Hubbard's a runner. I met him a couple of years ago when we did the Hotlanta half-marathon."

She tore into the envelope and unfolded its contents, a brief letter. "Son of a bitch."

Gloria snatched it from her hands and began to read. "… is to inform you that Donald Lipscomb has retained our legal services to represent him in his case before the District Court of the State of Georgia, *Lipscomb v. Harwood University, et al.*, effective immediately."

Struck by a sudden wave of fatigue, Theo slowly lowered herself to a padded bench in the center of the cocktail lounge. Knees shaking, stomach roiling. "We've been fired."

* * *

Within seconds, word rippled through the bar and the chatter stopped. All eyes were on Theo, her red face, her cracking voice. And the angry *slap-slap-slap* of the folded letter against her palm.

"What does this mean?" Celia asked.

"That we no longer have a case," Philip said. "It's over before it ever started."

"For us, anyway," Theo added. "My guess is Hubbard-McCaffrey has already negotiated the settlement. Lipscomb will walk away with a few hundred thousand dollars and sign a confidentiality agreement."

Gloria leaned against a bar table with her arms folded, staring disgustedly at the floor. "Then Harwood will put out a statement announcing a settlement with Lipscomb out of sympathy for his loss. An undisclosed sum, of course. But not admitting any liability."

For Celia, it was a devastating outcome. "Why would he do that? Your case is for millions of dollars."

"Because they convinced him we would probably lose." Theo rubbed her face briskly and groaned. "It's my own fault. Lipscomb as plaintiff was never that strong to begin with. Hubbard-McCaffrey noticed and jumped on it."

"But isn't that unethical?" Celia asked.

She shrugged. "Depends on how you look at it. They offered to put money in Lipscomb's pocket right now. He has the right to take it if he's worried about rolling the dice."

Gloria sat on the cushion beside Theo and patted her knee. "And let's face it. They probably told him Harwood would never settle with you in a million years because of all the damage you've inflicted on their reputation."

Celia could well imagine such a backroom conversation among the board and administration. Even those who were offended by Harwood's handling of Hayley's rape had a fiduciary responsibility to protect the university. It was nothing short of shameful that didn't include protecting the rights of female students to be safe.

"At least we won a couple of rounds," Philip said. "Frazier and Caldwell missed out on their big payday. I'd say we struck a forty-million-dollar blow right there. Plus they might be going to jail. That's a bonus."

It was fine to find consolation in that, but Celia found it ultimately meaningless if it meant this could happen to another woman at Harwood. And there was the matter of blowback— if the case ended with the university escaping liability, what did that mean for her status as a whistleblower? Was she still protected or not?

"I'm sorry, Celia. I was always worried about getting your hopes up too high."

"No, Philip's right. We got a win. And I won't be surprised now if Harwood throws these players under the bus. I'm not saying they'll order the campus police to investigate, but maybe at least now they'll cooperate with the DA."

"Don't count on it," Theo said, utterly dejected. "They can't afford to do anything to implicate themselves if the feds decide to launch a Title IX investigation related to sexual assault. No, this is exactly what they needed—a way to put it to bed without having to admit anything."

After a long silence, Philip glumly added, "Bastards."

"And on that dreary note…" Gloria slapped her knees and stood. "It looks like the party's over."

It wasn't over for Theo, who set aside her champagne and ordered a Crown Royal on the rocks.

Philip leaned into Celia and murmured, "Look out. Theo's not much of a drinker."

"Don't worry. I'll see that she gets home."

With the party atmosphere shattered, staff began trickling away, most stopping by with condolences to Theo. She was well into her second whiskey when Gloria and Lewis, the last of the revelers, left.

"You've probably...noticed this already." Theo's words were faltering and deliberate. "I'm on my way to getting sort of... uncharacteristically...drunk."

Celia put an arm around her waist and nestled under her chin. "Under the circumstances, I'd say you're allowed."

"I don't usually drink this much. You know why?"

"I assumed it was because there were so many people out there who'd get too much pleasure out of seeing you picked up for DUI."

"S'part of it. But the main reason"—she paused to polish off her whiskey and wave for another—"is 'cause the last time I did...I was with Gloria and Lewis. Drinks, dinner...more drinks. Then we went on this gallery walk in Buckhead...and I met thissss fascinating artist."

The puddles had dried on the terrace bar, enough to entice the hotel's business guests out for a drink. Their waitress however remained loyal to Theo, who'd just run up a thousand-dollar bar bill, ignoring them in favor of fetching her refill.

"Charla Peok...she did that purple and gray portrait that's over the bed in the guest room. I found her riveting. Until we got to her place...and I met her husband. He was so excited... like she'd brought home a puppy for both of them to play with." She said it almost forlornly, staring off into space while shaking her head.

It was all Celia could do not to laugh.

"I really liked her...but no. Just no. How did I not see that coming?"

"How could you have known, Theo?"

"But I...she thought I was into it. I wasn't mad or anything. I just felt stupid." Theo, her face flushed from the alcohol, was clearly making a concerted effort at proper enunciation. "But I was too drunk to even ask if there was somebody else. So I don't get drunk much anymore. Except now."

"It's okay. I'm here to make sure you don't go home to someone else's husband." Celia nursed her club soda, which she'd ordered after Lipscomb's news. "Consider this a public service. You're keeping me sober tonight, because I'd be the one getting drunk if you weren't."

"I know. I'm sorry. I let you down."

"No, that's not what I meant. This wasn't your fault." She brushed Theo's hair from her eyes and placed a light kiss on her temple. "It occurred to me though...with this case over, Harwood doesn't have to be nice to me anymore. I could walk in on Monday morning and find my theater budget slashed to nothing. Or all my travel funds canceled for next year. And my teaching schedule changed. They probably can't fire me but they can make my life a living hell."

"I dare them. If they so much as look at you sideways, I'll have them back in court so fast they'll pee their pants. They better leave you alone...if they know what's good for them."

Celia would never admit it, but she found Theo's inebriated fury frankly adorable. "The thing is though, if Harwood gets out of this without having to admit they did anything wrong, there goes my whistleblower status."

"If they do anything—*anything*," she practically yelled, "I wanna know about it. They'll be sorry they poked this bear."

The drunken threats were reassuring if only as proof Theo loved her. Celia was sick to realize Frazier and Caldwell, with their lost multimillion-dollar contracts, were the only ones facing the music over what happened to Hayley. Some of the sportscasters had speculated that if the pair managed to escape conviction, they could play the upcoming season in Europe or China—then declare for next year's draft as though nothing had happened. A mere footnote for everyone involved.

CHAPTER EIGHTEEN

With her wireless headset and microphone in place, Theo paced her office to stretch her legs. The conference call was well into its second hour. Nine participants representing the nurses' association at Mercy Hospital Group, a national corporation that controlled over two hundred community hospitals. They'd been impressed by her commentary on TNS, which had been widely cited in newspapers and on websites, and wanted to sue their employer for equal wages.

"Our next step is to assemble whatever data is in the public domain and determine which findings might be legally actionable. I can start my team on that as early as this afternoon," Theo said, knowing Gloria was already salivating to get the case underway. "Ultimately—once we file the suit and reach the discovery phase—we'll ask the court to grant us access to MHG's employee data, but there are a number of legal hurdles between now and then."

Like Gloria, Theo was thrilled at the prospect of landing a case of such magnitude, especially now that Hayley Burkhart's wrongful death suit was over and Kendra's wage theft case seemed to be moving toward settlement.

"What will you need from us?" The question came from the executive director of the MHG association.

"For now, detailed information from the complainants. My paralegal will conduct in-depth interviews with each of them. Work history, salary, duties…whatever our research advisor tells us she needs in order to start building a framework." Jalinda and Gloria were listening in on the call, trading private notes with Theo through intra-office chat.

Like many employers, Mercy Hospital Group tried to manage controversy over differential pay by prohibiting workers from discussing their salaries with co-workers. The policy, though illegal and unenforceable, had an intimidating effect on most employees. But not on four of the nurses on today's call—each was married to a male nurse with less experience who made more money.

"We can do a lot of the preliminary work by phone, but at some point, we'll schedule a strategy meeting here in Atlanta for the principal parties." She gave them a canned speech on the importance of confidentiality and signed off.

The instant she pulled off her headset, Penny knocked and entered. "I've been watching the light on your phone, waiting for you to get finished. There's someone here to see you about the Hayley Burkhart case."

The Burkhart case had been over for two weeks, at least for Theo. "Who is it?"

"An attorney with Hubbard-McCaffrey. Says his name's Austin Thompson."

There was something curious about that but she couldn't place it. "Have him wait a couple more minutes. I'll buzz you when I'm ready." She dialed Jalinda and asked her to do an electronic search through her files for the name.

"Nothing for Austin Thompson, but here's something from your interview with Kelsey Cameron, the young woman who said she was assaulted by the football player. She claims she was approached by an attorney. 'Austin something. About thirty, drove a Porsche.' He'd warned her about making allegations, told her she could find herself facing an expensive lawsuit."

In a search for attorneys associated with Harwood's athletic department, Theo had turned up an article about such a guy at one of the big football universities in Texas. A "jock sniffer," which apparently was a thing. He hung out on the field or in stadium suites with big-moneyed boosters, and swooped in whenever one of the athletes got in trouble with law enforcement.

That didn't mean Austin Thompson was the same attorney Kelsey had encountered. But it occurred to Theo for the first time that Hayley's warning to back off from her allegations might not have come from someone in Harwood's administration, as she'd originally thought. It could have come from the same guy who'd intimidated Kelsey.

"Send him in, Penny."

He certainly fit the description age-wise. Undeniably a good-looking young man, he was clean-shaven with a boyish dimple, his short hair styled with gel. Unlike most trial lawyers, who wore low-key suits in case they were called to court, he was dressed in dark chinos with a pink shirt, striped tie and gray tweed sport coat.

"Thanks for seeing me," he said, smiling as he offered his hand.

"Sorry you had to wait. Conference call. What can I do for you?"

"It's what I can do for you." He drew a piece of paper from inside a black portfolio embossed with his firm's name. "I have a check made out to your firm for two hundred fifty thousand from my employer, the law firm of Hubbard-McCaffrey. That represents the amount of your contracted fee with Donald Lipscomb. As you probably know, he settled with the defendants in the wrongful death suit involving Hayley Burkhart."

So this was the weasel who'd cut in and wooed Lipscomb away with the promise of a quick payday. The fact that he'd chosen to deliver the check in person rather than by courier meant he'd come to gloat.

Controlling her indignation, she snatched the check from his hand and placed it on her desk. "Congratulations on your quick resolution, Mr. Thompson. I'm betting that was the easiest money Hubbard-McCaffrey ever made."

"Mr. Lipscomb was satisfied with our counsel. In the end, that's what matters, isn't it?" If his phony smile meant anything, it was that he clearly relished the meeting, so much that she almost pressed him on how he'd become involved in the case. If he was, in fact, the same person Kelsey Cameron had encountered, his ethical lapses weren't limited to poaching—his association with university athletes posed a serious conflict of interest as a representative of Donald Lipscomb.

"Thank you for taking the time to deliver this payment in person. Please give Mr. Hubbard and Mr. McCaffrey my sincere appreciation for their professional consideration. Be sure to have Penny validate your parking." She needed to stall him long enough to find someone in the office who could follow him to the parking garage to see if he drove a Porsche.

"It's okay. I valeted."

She pointed him back toward reception and walked briskly down the hall to Jalinda's office. "Austin Thompson's picking up his car at valet. Pink shirt, gray jacket. Get down there and find out what he drives."

Back in her office, she buzzed for Hank.

"What's up, chief?"

"I want to know everything there is to know about Austin Thompson." She gave him a quick rundown of her suspicions. "If he's the same guy that's been running interference for these players, then he was working for the other side when he poached Donald Lipscomb. I'm filing a complaint to have him disbarred."

* * *

For the first time since reluctantly taking over the spring production eight years ago, Celia was genuinely thrilled about their selection. *Spamalot* was the musical version of the Camelot parody, *Monty Python and the Holy Grail*. Its irreverent tone and cultural cachet would appeal more to Harwood's students than Sondheim or Berlin.

She examined each item on the clothing rack for its potential as a medieval costume. "Nope…nope. Maybe. There ought to be more than this considering how many times we've done Shakespeare."

Michael, who was digging through boxes of fake weaponry, replied, "Maybe that's the problem. We've done so much Shakespeare, the costumes are worn out."

Given their department head's obsessive interest in the Bard, that wasn't likely to change. He staged a Shakespeare festival every summer.

"Whoa! I think I just found Excalibur." He drew a bulky sword, its wooden blade spray-painted silver. "Whoever plays King Arthur better be tall."

Celia had assumed Michael would audition for that lead, since it had so many musical numbers. Truth be told however, he'd make a better Lancelot, a character who turned out to be gay.

Today was the first she'd seen Michael since the DA's office got involved in the rape investigation. She'd heard from Theo they were starting off with interviews of the basketball players. "So how's Gavin these days? I haven't heard you talk about him."

A wistful smile crossed Michael's face. "He's doing okay, considering. Coach T told him he might even be the first guard off the bench next year…but then all this business came up with the DA. Who knows what's going to happen when they find out he's the one who shared the video?"

It was a relief to hear he wasn't planning on stonewalling the prosecutor. That was good for the case, but they were probably right to worry. It was hard to think Gavin would last once the others learned he'd ratted out their teammates.

"He's doing the right thing, Michael. I know it's hard to accept the fallout now…I have no doubt you'll both feel better for it in the long run."

He shrugged. "At least one thing's easier now. He finally came out to his parents."

"How'd they take it?"

"Not too bad. His mom cried and his dad went out for a few beers. Pretty much the same way mine did. But he thinks they'll get over it." He leaned against a sawhorse, his attention directed toward finding the exact point of equilibrium that would allow the sword to balance on one fingertip. "Straight people don't get why that's such a big deal. They have no idea what it's like to have a secret that could destroy their whole life. Gavin used to worry his folks would cut him off. If he got kicked off the team, there'd be no scholarship to fall back on. It would have been the end of Harwood for him."

While she was touched by his candor, it occurred to her he might not know she too was gay. Gina had been gone nearly a year before Michael and Hayley entered the performance studies program. "I remember when I came out to my mom. She said, 'Well for God's sake, don't tell anybody.' She was sure I'd never work in the business again. Looking back, I guess she was right…but that had nothing to do with me being a lesbian."

Michael lit up with a broad grin. "I had no idea. No wonder I always thought you were so cool."

His remark reminded her of what Theo had said about Little CeCe. That particular secret would stay in the closet where it belonged.

"It's kind of how I ended up at Harwood. I was in a relationship with Gina Worley when she was hired to be the women's basketball coach. We came here as a package deal."

"That's so amazing." His brow wrinkled. "But didn't she, like…get fired?"

"She did, and now she's coaching at Garfield College in Ohio. Doing pretty well, in fact. Twenty-four and six last year, so I'm guessing she'll get another crack at a major program one of these days."

"So you're…"

"No, we split up right before she left. I'm actually seeing someone else now. Someone you know, in fact." She couldn't suppress her smile. "Theo Constantine, the attorney who took Hayley's case to court."

"Oh, my God!" The sword crashed to the floor as he slapped both of his cheeks, clearly hamming it up for dramatic effect. "That woman is so hot. I told Gavin he better not let me talk to her by myself or who knows what might happen. I can't believe this."

"No offense, but something tells me you aren't her type," she answered, laughing as her face grew warm from what had to be a colorful blush. It felt good to talk with someone about Theo, even in a joking manner. "It just goes to show, we never know when the people we meet will turn out to be important."

"So true." He went on to talk about Gavin, the first guy he'd ever dated who was a popular athlete. "The best part was finding out he was a decent human being too. It could have gone either way."

She nodded, feeling the same about Theo. "Those are the kind of people we need in our lives...people who aren't afraid to do the right—"

His phone played a brief drum roll with a cymbal, apparently a text notification. "Wow. Gavin says two Atlanta cops just showed up in the weight room and arrested Tanner Watson and Ruben Vargas. I hope that means they got Frazier and Caldwell too."

* * *

"Thanks, Shane. I appreciate you taking my call." Theo disconnected and dialed Celia back. "Okay, here's what I know. All four are being charged with both rape and sexual battery... which I happen to think is a shitty idea, since it gives the jury an avenue to compromise. Sexual battery is just a misdemeanor, twelve months max. I'd much rather see them go all in on the rape charge, but they're worried they might not get a conviction at all with so many Harwood fans in the jury pool."

"What's that other one...the shield law?"

"The Rape Shield Law. It's against Ruben Vargas for publishing the identity of a rape victim in the video. Kind of a stretch but I like it. I think they're using it for leverage." She suspected the preliminary investigation had shown Vargas was also the one who supplied Hayley with the drugged drink. "He's the youngest and he's facing the stiffest charges. Shane might offer to drop the shield charges if he agrees to testify against the others. That happens—they all confess. Everybody gets five or six years in the state prison instead of twenty, but at least they do serious time."

All that said, the announcement of an indictment was hardly a reason for a victory lap. Harwood University had shirked its duty to Hayley Burkhart and faced zero consequences. The next woman assaulted on campus had no reason to think they'd support her.

"Oh, by the way, I had a visit today from the asshole who poached my case. You won't believe this—I think it's possible he's the same guy who threatened one of the women who called me after I went on TV. She was raped by a football player last year before Christmas…said this attorney showed up out of nowhere and told her she'd get sued for defamation if she went public. Just like Hayley said happened to her. I wouldn't be surprised if it was the same guy."

"Any way you can find out?" Celia asked.

Jalinda had arrived downstairs too late to see what he was driving, but Hank was checking with his DMV sources to see if Thompson owned a Porsche. "We're working on it. What are you doing?"

"I'm here in wardrobe with Michael trying to pull together stuff we'll need for our show. April will be here before we know it."

"Maybe I should rephrase. What are you doing tonight? I can't think of a single reason not to kick off our weekend on a Wednesday. You want me to swing by and pick you up?"

"Sure. Just call me when you're in front of Forbes Hall."

Over the past couple of weeks, Celia had accumulated several changes of clothes at her apartment, enough that she could last for several days without going home. Living together couldn't be far behind, but Theo didn't want to push the issue, since Celia had always been firm about going back to her place on Monday. Some people just needed time alone.

"Hey, chief." It was Hank, who'd begun shaving on a regular basis after a couple of dates with Raynelle Willis, Harwood's sexual assault specialist. "Just got a call from Bobby Hill, my contact over at the campus PD. He said the DA came by last Friday and picked up Hayley Burkhart's rape kit."

"You've got to be kidding."

"Bobby thinks they might have been holding it somewhere else 'cause it damn sure wasn't in their evidence cooler. Interesting they held onto it though, like just in case it got subpoenaed."

"Right...they had to hold onto it somewhere because they couldn't risk an obstruction of justice charge on a criminal case. But no way would they have produced it for us in a civil trial if we'd been allowed to go through discovery. 'Unable to locate at this time, Your Honor. Our filing system, blah blah.' I wonder how many more rape kits go missing."

"Probably all the ones involving athletes," he scoffed. "Looks to me like Harwood's cutting their losses with these guys."

It made sense. Once they settled the wrongful death suit, there was nothing to be gained by sticking with four men who'd obviously carried out a brutal assault on an unconscious woman. They could go back to polishing their trophy.

CHAPTER NINETEEN

"Welcome back, Theo. Nice tan." Kendra held out her ebony forearm to compare.

"Someone better tie me to my desk today. I'm ready to go back to St. John's."

Theo generally chaired the Monday morning meetings with her senior staff. But after a week in the Caribbean with Celia, she had almost no idea where things stood in the office. With hopes of handing the task off to Kendra, she'd arrived a couple of minutes late for the meeting and found Kendra in her usual second chair, forcing her to the head of the table.

With help from Gloria and Jalinda, she'd spent the second half of the summer laying the groundwork for the case against Mercy Hospital Group, which had yet to be filed. Class actions were time-consuming and required an enormous amount of work, all of it unpaid unless they won a settlement.

Sprinkled among that work were several pro bono cases—restraining orders and divorce filings for women too poor to afford an attorney. Her only major media moment was a press conference in LA on behalf of an A-list actor's wife to announce he'd violated the "forsaking all others" clause of his prenup and was on the hook for an enormous divorce settlement.

With vacation behind her, she was ready to throw herself back into her work. "Good morning, all you social justice warriors—and I mean that in the best possible way. I hope your week was as good as mine."

Her jovial greeting brought an end to the side conversations, and all eyes turned toward the head of the table. Two partners, ten associates, Gloria, and at the far end, Sandy the accountant, who was there to keep them from spending money they didn't have.

"Kendra, how about starting us off with your good news?"

The attorney smiled triumphantly. "Most of you already know. Friday night we heard from BoRegards' attorneys on the wage theft case. They've run up the white flag."

Philip butted in, "They couldn't afford to wait this out any longer. Their stock's been in free-fall since the day we filed our case. Investors crunched the numbers and speculated a jury award might go as high as eighty million."

Kendra added, "So we held the line at thirty-one million and they've accepted it."

The announcement brought a hearty round of applause. The firm's share was one-third plus expenses—a hefty payday.

"We're not home free until the contracts are signed and the check clears," Theo reminded. "But because of Kendra's leadership on this case, we've been negotiating from strength. The document analysis, those weeks on the road doing depositions all over Florida, Georgia and the Carolinas... they're about to pay off for thousands of workers."

"Eighty-six percent of whom are women," Gloria added.

"Well done, everyone. What else do we have this week?"

Sabrina was working with Hank to investigate the case of a Georgia state trooper who'd asked a young woman for oral sex in exchange for letting her out of a stop sign violation. They needed supporting evidence of past behavior with other women to make a case, since the courts were usually deferential to law enforcement officers.

"Next up, we'll be finalizing preparations to file the Mercy Hospital Group case," Theo said.

Such an announcement of progress on a major filing usually stirred excitement in their meetings. Today however, it was clear her team was exhausted from the BoRegards case and looking forward to a break.

"The good news is that Gloria and the paralegal department have done an excellent job on the initial data gathering, so we won't be looping anyone else in for several weeks. Unless your name is Philip, that is. That should give you all a little beach time when you wrap up BoRegards."

As her staff filed out, she was met at the door by Penny. "I just added an appointment to your schedule for this afternoon. A young woman, Jordan Cooke. She said you asked her to call when she got back from Europe."

It took a moment to place the name. She was a Harwood student, a woman who reportedly had been assaulted by a date after he put something in her drink.

Theo debated having Penny call back and cancel. For all intents and purposes, the Burkhart case was over. At least as far as Constantine and Associates was concerned—the case against the players was set for trial in six weeks unless they agreed to a plea.

On the other hand, Ms. Cooke had expressed an eagerness to talk and had kept in regular contact during her trip through Europe. She might appreciate knowing they'd made a diligent effort to force Harwood University to take claims of sexual assault more seriously. Theo could do her the courtesy of a brief meeting.

* * *

Celia mindlessly climbed the stairs to her office as she read the letter from her department head for the third time. With only ten days before the start of fall semester, Andrew had changed her course assignments. Instead of Intro to Theater and Performance Overview, which she'd prepped over the summer, she'd been reassigned to Advanced On-Camera Acting and a senior seminar in performance theory. A pair of dream classes—exactly the sort of assignments she'd hoped for when she made full professor. Though getting them at the last minute meant starting the semester behind the eight ball.

After dropping her briefcase on her desk, she carried the letter back downstairs to her boss's office. "Not that I'm complaining, Andrew, but this is quite a surprise."

A Shakespearean actor originally from London, Andrew Barker had singlehandedly founded Harwood University's performance studies department twenty-two years ago. Celia thought him a capable administrator, though his scholarly contributions to the field left something to be desired. That was typical of faculty who came from a performance background as opposed to a PhD program.

"I thought you'd be pleased," he said, leaning back in his chair and clasping his hands behind his head. His girth called to mind the character Falstaff.

"Oh, I am. I just don't understand why this is happening so late. The On-Camera Acting class has always been Paul's, and the senior seminar was Eric's."

"What has always been need not always be." His years in the Deep South had done little to diminish his proper British accent. "I've grown increasingly concerned that senior faculty have lost touch with the fundamentals of our discipline. We all could benefit from the occasional foray into the introductory lecture hall. How else do we learn to appreciate the point at which our students begin?"

Celia had made that argument also, but only to herself as she'd longed for the opportunity to teach upperclassmen. It was unheard of within the department to protest against the fortunes of one's peers. Full professors had earned their rank, and with it, the privilege of working with the most advanced students. But now she too held that rank.

"The syllabi have already been submitted," he continued. "You're free of course to make minor adjustments to accommodate your personal interests. However, bear in mind the students who signed up for these courses over the summer have certain expectations and may already have purchased materials on the reading list."

"Thank you, Andrew. I appreciate this opportunity more than I can say."

"Yes, well…let's hope your colleagues are as appreciative of theirs." His worried look suggested that wouldn't be the case at all.

As she reached her office, Eric Butler stormed out of his. His eyes blazed with anger, and he carried a letter like hers.

It was a remarkable end to a most memorable summer, one in which she'd even thought she might be fired. Not only had her promotion gone through, she'd received a spring production budget well beyond her request. And now to get two of the most coveted course assignments on the fall schedule. Someone at Harwood wanted her to be happy, and she had a feeling it wasn't Andrew. What she didn't understand was why.

The schedule change posed a unique challenge. Rather than enter the semester fully prepared for each class meeting, she'd have to put in extra time week by week to stay ahead of her students. There were books on Paul's syllabus she hadn't read in years. Lots of work but she was more than willing to do it.

A text came in from Theo asking her to call when she got a chance. That remained their habit, left over from the days of avoiding written correspondence.

Theo answered the call right away. "Can we hit the rewind button? I want it to be last Sunday morning in St. John's again."

It was hard to beat a lazy day in bed in a beachfront bungalow. Especially since Monday marked the start of their forced sabbatical from each other before they'd come together again on the weekend. Still the same old nonsense about needing structure so they could focus on work. Instead they talked so frequently they might as well be together.

"I have an appointment this afternoon with a young woman named Jordan Cooke," Theo said. "Did I ever mention her?"

"It's not ringing a bell."

"Her name came up when I was doing interviews on campus with some of Hayley's friends. Apparently, something similar happened to her not long after Hayley's attack. A party where she passed out and woke up the next day in bed with some frat guy. I wanted to interview her, but she was in Europe all summer with her mom. Now she's back and wants to talk."

Just the mention of Hayley's case triggered an uneasy feeling. Even though the players were now facing criminal charges, it sickened her how the university had gotten off scot-free. Gupton and Tuttle still sat at the helm, neither held accountable for their threats and refusal to take action against the players.

The worst part was Theo, who'd been angry and despondent for over a month, not only kicking herself for her own perceived missteps, but obsessed with getting revenge on the twit from Hubbard-McCaffrey for his breach of ethics.

Theo wasn't the only one in a funk. It was only after the case ended that Celia realized how much stress she'd been under from the constant fear of retaliation. She was in no mood to go through that again. "I don't see what good it's going to do at this point, Theo. That ship has sailed."

"I know, me neither. But I figured I owed her the courtesy of an interview since she followed up like I asked her to. Who knows? Maybe she's had some time to think and wants to file a case of her own."

And Theo could tell her she was wasting her time.

"I got some news this morning too." Celia went on to describe her meeting with Andrew. "This can't all be coincidence. It's like somebody upstairs is going out of their way to make sure I'm the happiest professor on campus. Not that I'm looking a gift horse in the mouth. But my colleagues won't like this preferential treatment if it comes at their expense."

"I've seen this kind of thing before, Celia. Institutions are notoriously afraid of litigation. Not only like the case we filed, but the one we would have filed on top of it if they'd punished you. This is why I always said you had the safest job at Harwood. They're afraid of you. Enjoy that power. It won't last forever."

"Easier said than done. They're going to turn me into a pariah."

"And sometimes, that's part of their master plan. They can't retaliate, but it's no skin off their nose if your working environment becomes so unpleasant you decide to leave on your own."

Celia chuckled cynically. "I can tell you right now, it'll have to get a lot more unpleasant than this."

* * *

Jordan Cooke's designer dress and TAG Heuer wristwatch made it clear she came from money. She was classically pretty, with long brown hair, high cheekbones and full lips painted with a tangerine gloss. According to Jalinda's research, she was a native of suburban Boston, where her father was CEO at one of the nation's largest pharmaceutical companies.

"What are you studying, Jordan?"

"Business administration. If all goes as planned, I'll start my MBA at Harvard next year. That's where my father went so he's kind of insistent, if you know what I mean. But my mom went to Harwood, in case you were wondering how I ended up here."

Though she had the confidence of a woman with money, Jordan appeared mildly nervous, twirling a sapphire ring on her right hand and swinging her foot across her knee. That made it all the more surprising she'd followed up with the interview, especially since Theo had been clear all along she wanted to talk about Hayley Burkhart. Everyone knew that case was over, so she easily could have demurred.

"Jordan, when I first contacted you, I was working on a case involving a young woman at Harwood, Hayley Burkhart. Did you know her?"

"Sort of, but not all that well. She was a Tri-Delt. I'm Chi Omega. We had a few events together, fundraisers mostly…a couple of parties maybe." Her face fell as she dropped her gaze to her lap. "But I heard what happened to her. Everybody did. She didn't deserve that."

"No, she didn't."

"I looked for news about the case practically every day while I was gone. I was glad to see they all got arrested. But it won't surprise me if they get off, especially since Hayley isn't here to tell people what they did."

Theo nodded along, recognizing the bitter tone of resignation. Women giving up in the face of what felt like insurmountable odds.

"As I'm sure you know, Jordan, I reached out to you because one of Hayley's friends told me something similar happened to you. She said you were pretty open about it. Would it be okay for us to talk about that?"

"Sure, I assumed that's what this was about. It wasn't exactly a secret. I told lots of people because it pissed me off so much. It was different for me though. I wasn't at a party with a bunch of strangers. I was on a date with this guy I knew from my economics class. Grant Rodgers. We'd gone out for Chinese food and ended up back at his frat house to watch the Hornets play Michigan. It was the tournament, so there were a lot of people crammed into their TV room." She paused, shaking her head as if scolding herself. "And yeah, we were having a few beers. I should have known better than to take a drink somebody handed me, especially after what Hayley said happened to her. It was literally only a few weeks later, so it was still fresh on everybody's mind. But you don't think about it happening to you when you're with people you trust."

"So you're sure that's what happened? He gave you a drink."

"Positive." She looked away and narrowed her eyes, as if seeing the night again in her mind's eye. "I got the first one out of the cooler myself. But then Grant got up and brought me the second one. I'm not saying I drink a lot or anything, but I've had four or five beers in one night, and I still knew what was happening. But that night...I don't remember a thing after a couple of sips of that second beer. One of my friends was there. She said we just got up and walked down the hall. It wasn't even halftime."

"And then you woke up in his room the next day?"

Jordan nodded. "That's right. All my clothes on the floor. It was obvious we'd had sex because there was a used condom hanging over the trashcan."

"Did you talk about it with him?"

"Yelling is more like it. The son of a bitch woke up and wanted to make out, like we were in love or something. And here's the thing that really pisses me off—if we'd dated a couple more times, I probably would have done that willingly. Instead, he had to go and be a creep about it."

Theo had seen this dynamic play out in many of her cases. Trusting women turning disillusioned and angry to realize men had taken advantage of them.

"Your friend told me you didn't report it to police though. Is that right?"

"What would have been the point? By that time, we'd all heard what happened to Hayley. People were talking about her like she was trash—even some of the girls in her own sorority—and the cops didn't do anything to help her. So there I was with Grant Rodgers—as in the Rodgers Library, paid for by his great-grandfather. I figured I didn't stand a chance. I didn't want my name dragged through the mud for nothing." She dabbed at a tear in the corner of her eye, but Theo sensed it was anger, not shame or sadness. "If I'd spoken up…hell, if all of us had spoken up, maybe Hayley wouldn't have felt like nobody cared."

"All of us…who does that mean?"

"We have this group on campus. We call ourselves the Surviving Sisters. Last spring there were about ten or twelve of us who came to the meetings regularly, but we have a lot more members than that. It's a support group for rape victims on campus. Right after what happened to me, I noticed this flyer in one of the dining halls…you know, the ones where you tear off the number at the bottom. It was like a rape crisis hotline. I was just so mad…I wanted to yell at somebody. The woman who answered invited me to a meeting."

"A meeting on campus?"

"No, turns out you have to register as an official organization for that. Bylaws, officers, the whole nine yards. I heard they tried to get a charter a couple of years ago but Harwood turned them down." Cynically she added, "Can't have people knowing there are rapes on campus."

"Looks bad in the annual report, I guess."

"Exactly. So we're informal, like a private club. We have a cell phone we pass around, depending on whose turn it is to take the hotline calls. And we usually meet at different people's apartments off campus."

The recent White House directives had spurred a growth in rape crisis centers on campus. Staffed by licensed nurses and therapists, they were accountable to the university administration. Harwood didn't have one. According to the information Jalinda had gathered for the wrongful death suit, rape victims were funneled through the student health center with no formal aftercare. Hayley had sought treatment at Celia's urging, as opposed to what should have been an automatic referral from student health. It was no wonder a private group had risen up to fill the void.

"Did Hayley ever contact your group?"

Jordan shook her head. "Not that I know of. At least she never came to any of our meetings. But we all talked about her, especially after she killed herself. At least she had the guts to go to the police. Most of the Sisters didn't. Like me. And the ones who did, hardly anything happened."

It was shocking to think not one of the women in the group had seen her case pursued by law enforcement. "This support group though…it's open to any woman who's been sexually assaulted, whether their rapists are prosecuted or not?"

"That's right, anybody who tears off the number and calls."

"And no one in your group ever had charges filed against their attacker."

"Not criminal charges, at least not that I'm aware of. A couple of them got referred to the Honor Court. That's made up of other students, so they can't put a rapist in jail or anything like that."

Theo recalled the statistics Gloria had cited off the top of her head. Emory University, a Southern Ivy school across town with approximately the same enrollment as Harwood, had reported twenty-six campus rapes last year, while Harwood listed only four. If Harwood's victims were systematically ignored or otherwise discouraged from reporting their attacks, that would go a long way toward explaining the discrepancy.

"Jordan, the women in your group...what's their mindset? I've come across plenty of women who make the conscious choice to protect their privacy. They don't want people to know them as victims, or they don't want to share what they think of as an intimate violation. What I'm getting at is this..."

She lowered her head to force eye contact with Jordan, who'd been focused intently on twirling her sapphire ring.

"Do you think any of them would be open to talking to me if it meant fighting for the justice they didn't get?"

CHAPTER TWENTY

Theo extended her hand to the coed as she left. She was a light-skinned African-American with ultra-short hair and enormous hoop earrings. "Thank you for coming in, Ms. Berry. And for sharing your story. It was helpful. I appreciate how hard it can be to talk about painful experiences."

"You can thank Jordan Cooke for my being here. She's the one who convinced us we should tell somebody what happened to us. I just wish we could have helped Hayley."

"We all do."

Jasmine Berry was the twelfth Surviving Sister to share her story. A new boyfriend had ignored her pleas to stop after refusing to use a condom. Predictably, campus police declined to file a report—citing the fact she'd initially consented to sex—even though a physical examination found bruising consistent with the use of force.

When Jasmine left, Theo asked Jalinda, "Will you see if Gloria's free for a meeting?"

In each of their interviews with the members of Jordan's group, they'd searched for another case like Hayley's, one so blatant it defied reason as to why it wasn't prosecuted. Though none had actual video evidence, a handful produced copies of vague, coded taunts on social media, and in one case, an apology. All without meaningful consequences for the assailants.

The number included Kelsey Cameron, the young woman who reported being drugged and raped by a football player, and intimidated afterward by the player's attorney. She too had joined the Surviving Sisters, a detail she'd failed to mention during her summer interview.

Gloria trudged in absent her usual gusto. "I hope you've called me in here to fire me. Extrapolating salary data for a quarter-million nurses is a statistical nightmare."

"I have great faith in you, Gloria." Theo nodded toward Jalinda, who was backing out the door. "I want you to sit in on this too. You know as much about these Surviving Sisters as I do."

The three of them clustered around the head of the conference table, where Theo opened her file to a spreadsheet she'd created to tick off the specifics of each story she'd heard. Where it happened and under what circumstances, presence of alcohol or drugs, whether or not it was reported to police. Fifteen general indicators in all.

"Here's the problem, Gloria. I have twelve victims—not counting Hayley Burkhart—and still no actionable case."

"Hunh. Maybe you're the one who needs to be fired."

A barely audible snort escaped from Jalinda, and she looked away and pretended to whistle.

"There are two clear patterns though. First, each victim who talked to the police said the officers were sympathetic at first, but then started asking questions the women felt were geared toward getting them to implicate themselves in what happened. Was it someone they were friendly with? Were they drinking or doing drugs? Was it possible they were sending mixed signals? Saying yes—or even maybe—to any of those questions almost always resulted in the cops backing off."

"And if the answer was no?"

"That's just it. The questions went on till they got the answer they were looking for. Did they clearly remember every detail of the night it happened? Did they scream and try to fight back? All of them said they felt they were treated like accomplices, not victims." She leafed through the transcripts from earlier interviews and pulled out a note she'd made of the similarities. "Of the five who reported their rape to campus police, four say they got a call from someone in administration warning them that allegations of sexual assault were very serious, capable of ruining the lives of everyone involved. A couple of them remember being advised they could be vulnerable to costly defamation suits by the accused and subject to suspension or expulsion from campus should their situation become disruptive to the university's educational mission." It underscored the fact that it wasn't just athletes who were getting this kind of support.

"Isn't that basically what Celia said they told her?" Gloria asked.

The mention of Celia jolted her. Though she'd been working on this case for almost three weeks, she hadn't told her about it. And she wouldn't until they'd built a solid case. No reason to get her hopes up again…or to set her on edge about the potential blowback from Harwood.

"Yes, but their message to Celia was even more to the point. They said if she went public with allegations that were ultimately unsustained, she not only risked being fired for failing to uphold Harwood's mission, she could be sued *by the university* for damaging its reputation. The only reason none of that happened was because we dared them to try."

"Whereas with the women who got these threats, the university can say they were merely advising them of the potential consequences."

"Or worse," Jalinda interjected. "They could simply deny making the calls."

"Which is what makes Celia's audio recording of their meeting so critical to this case," Theo said. "There's no written record of any of these communications. In the case of Kelsey

Cameron, the threat was delivered in person by an attorney who said he represented the player. Why didn't he do the same to Hayley?"

"Because Hayley reported her assault to police and Kelsey didn't," Jalinda said. "So Hayley's had to go up through channels. Her call could have come from anybody. With Kelsey, the guy who threatened her was taking his cues from what appears to be an established practice of the university, something he'd come across while representing the interests of other athletes. Same legal bullying but in an unofficial capacity."

"Smart, Jalinda. I bet you're absolutely right."

It irritated Theo no end that she hadn't been able to prove beyond a doubt the attorney was Austin Thompson. His personal car turned out to be a Nissan, not a Porsche, though they were very similar in styles.

She continued with her spreadsheet. "The women who wanted to pursue charges against their attackers were referred to the Honor Court, which is run by fellow students. Three of them followed through. Two had their claims dismissed for lack of evidence, and the third saw her attacker verbally reprimanded and placed on probation for one semester. Apparently, that's all a rape's worth at Harwood."

"I pulled in Hank to do a little research of my own," Gloria said. "In between my number crunching for the nurses, that is. In the past three years, campus police at Harwood turned over eight cases to the DA's office for sexual assault prosecution. The suspects all had one thing in common—they weren't students. Most were on campus visiting friends or they were locals who crashed parties. One drove a delivery truck."

Jalinda began nodding slowly. "In other words, Harwood has an unwritten policy against charging its students with sexual assault."

"Bingo." Gloria tossed her pen on the table and folded her arms, her face filled with disgust.

Theo scribbled their observations in bullet points, and said, "That goes to the first pattern. The university as an institution is hostile to the principle of holding male students accountable.

The second pattern I picked up is a result of that. Six of the women we talked to didn't even bother reporting their assault to campus police. When I asked them why not, each one cited personal knowledge of another victim who reported a rape and nothing happened."

"Because they knew their rapist wouldn't be charged," Jalinda said.

Gloria added, "Not only are they not likely to be charged, the university rushes to their defense and portrays them as potential victims of false allegations."

"In legal terms, that's called a chilling effect," Theo said. "The relevant body of law could be whistleblower statutes, but this goes way beyond whistleblowing. This is a civil rights issue that impacts an entire class of people—female students at Harwood University."

"Are you thinking class action?"

Theo shook her head. "I don't think we have enough plaintiffs for class status. Jordan Cooke could be our best bet as a test case because her case indicts the whole system. She's a recent example, and her decision not to go to the police was a direct result of what happened to Hayley Burkhart. That lets us bring in all of those horrific details as evidence."

"You want to know what chaps my ass?" Gloria wagged her finger as she spoke. "I spent thirty-eight years on that campus and never heard one word about any of this. Do you know how many colleges are under Title IX investigation right now for how they handle sexual assault? One hundred six. And Harwood isn't one of them."

"Maybe because the other universities don't threaten their victims into silence." That was undeniably having an impact at Harwood, but Theo also had another theory. "I bet if you look closer, the trigger for most of the Title IX investigations was having someone on the inside turn on the administration. A dean who tried to help a student and couldn't. A student health nurse ordered to bury evidence."

"Am I imagining things, Theo, or are you seriously thinking about opening this can of worms again?"

"Call me crazy." After hashing it out with her staff, Theo's legal strategy was beginning to take shape—all except one key element. "I need to get Philip in here to figure out how we're going to get paid."

"Maybe one case isn't enough." Jalinda stretched across the table and took Theo's spreadsheet. "These women came in here and told their stories. We know how much courage that takes. I think everyone who's willing to join the suit and make their case in public deserves a piece of the settlement."

"She's right, Theo. Look at Bill Cosby. One or two women complaining gets explained away. You'd have a powerful case if there was a courtroom full of women saying the same thing. It's time to drag those bastards into court—every single administrator who signed off on it. The chancellor, the provost, the dean. All the trustees, the campus police. Anyone who knew about it and let it happen."

What they were proposing was nothing short of a circus. Except circuses were supposed to be fun. Sweeping charges against a bullying institution like Harwood—and a guarantee she'd have to face off against James Somers again—had this shaping up as the toughest case of her career.

Hank knocked and entered simultaneously. "Hey, chief. We need to go get lunch." It was an unusual request coming from Hank, especially since his insistent tone suggested it wasn't a request.

"I'm supposed to meet Celia. Can it wait?"

"You don't want to wait for this."

Over the years, Theo had developed an appreciation for his cocky demeanor. It usually meant he had something big.

* * *

Theo hurried to meet Hank in the parking garage with her phone pressed to her ear. "I'm sorry, sweetheart. It's a work thing. It came up all of a sudden."

"It's all right. I can grab a bite on campus," Celia said.

"It's not all right. I haven't seen you in"—she checked her watch and did the math from Monday morning when they parted—"fifty-four hours. How about I pick you up about six in front of your building?"

"That's a great idea. It's supposed to be pouring by then."

"I'm getting in the elevator so I'm going to lose you. Love you. See you at six."

As Hank drove through the side streets of the city, he shared the results of his morning's investigation. "So my pal Bobby called me last night about midnight. He'd just gotten off his shift. Said he got a call from none other than Tommie Egan, the head of campus police. Told him to swing by the station and pick up a rape kit."

"Let me guess—another athlete."

"I don't know anything about who it was, but apparently it happened over the weekend." He stared into space as they sat at a traffic light that had turned green.

"You can go now, Hank."

He lurched forward. "Bobby said Egan told him to take it to the police station at East Point and give it to the desk sergeant."

"East Point?"

"Don't you get it? That's where they're holding the rape kits in evidence. If the DA wants it, they have to cough it up or get cited for obstruction. That's how they came up with Hayley's. They weigh the consequences as to which could hurt them worse—no rape kit or a rape kit that nails somebody. You can bet your sweet ass they wouldn't have produced it for a civil case."

"But why East Point?"

"Because that's where Tommie Egan used to work. He must have some buddies still on the force there and they're doing him a favor."

She assumed they were heading to East Point and was surprised when he turned north toward the campus. "Where are you taking me?"

He ignored her question. "Bobby says they have seven old rape kits in their evidence locker going back three years. That's all. Plus the one from last night—like I said, they picked it up but it wasn't logged into evidence. There's no official record they have it, and Bobby was told not to put the ride down to East Point in his duty log. So I got to thinking about how many of those kits might be missing." He turned into a strip mall and squeezed the SUV into a diagonal space across from Soul of Atlanta, a small café that boasted homestyle Southern cooking.

It was useless to ask him any more questions. Hank liked to explain things in a logical, chronological way that led listeners to draw the same conclusions he had. No doubt the practice had served him well as a detective on the witness stand.

"First thing this morning I called Raynelle and asked her about it. She couldn't tell me everything on account of that hippo business."

"It's called HIPAA. It's supposed to guarantee patient privacy."

"Yeah, that. But we did a little digging on our own. I thought you ought to hear what she has to say about it. I figured you might get arrested for trespassing if you tried to talk to her on campus…what with you being famous and all. We meet here for lunch sometimes. The food's good."

Raynelle Willis was waiting in a booth, and smiled when she saw Hank. Her medium-length hair, dyed auburn and cut to frame her round face, gave her a somewhat youthful look, but the lines around her eyes put her in her late fifties-early sixties. She wore tan slacks and a slimming black sweater that went past her hips.

"Pleased to meet you," Theo said. Aware of her budding relationship with Hank, she added, "And thank you for being the reason Hank has started keeping his car clean."

"Truth! The first time we went out, I insisted on driving after one look inside that garbage truck. You should have seen him trying to control himself with me behind the wheel. Crouching down and stomping on those imaginary brakes."

They shared anecdotes at Hank's expense until the waitress took their lunch order. All the while he absorbed it good-naturedly, holding Raynelle's hand under the table.

"So I was telling Theo about the rape kits, how they got picked up and taken over to East Point," he said, turning the conversation in a serious direction. "Tell Theo what you told me about the numbers."

"I was saying we average six or eight sexual assaults a month during the fall and spring semesters. Most of the girls don't want to talk to the police at all. Of the ones who do, there's no guarantee they're going to want to press charges. Some of these girls...they just want it to go away. They don't even submit to the rape kit."

"I understand," Theo said, remembering stories from the Surviving Sisters.

"But after what Hank said, I got curious about the how many of those kits got picked up, so I looked at our records. Now I can't name names—"

"On account of HIPAA," Hank said, showing off his newfound knowledge.

"Right. But I can tell you they picked up fourteen rape kits last year from women who ended up not pressing charges. Five of them never even talked to police."

Theo let the implications of that sink in. "That means the cops came looking for them because they were tipped off by someone who knew a rape had occurred and assumed a kit was done."

"Bingo," Hank said. "So naturally, I thought of Slimeball, that lawyer who hangs around the jocks. I tracked down Kelsey Cameron and had her meet me at the student health center."

Raynelle continued, "She asked about the status of her rape kit—she can do that because it belongs to her—and I confirmed it was picked up two days after she came in for the exam."

"Same scrawly signature as the one they had on Hayley. And Bobby checked—no sign of it in the evidence room."

The pieces of a conspiracy were coming together. Someone was definitely looking out for athletes accused of rape, but the only way to know if cops were protecting other male students too was through the discovery process. Testimony from Raynelle and Bobby—if they agreed to go on the record—would go a long way toward demonstrating the process was rigged.

But she'd need Celia's audiotape to prove the administration's role. She'd been hoping the case would come together without having to involve Celia again, but without ironclad proof, it would be nearly impossible to persuade the court the university was quashing rape complaints as a matter of policy.

CHAPTER TWENTY-ONE

Rain pelted the glass and stripped the first red leaves off the maple tree outside Celia's office window. Theo's offer to pick her up outside Forbes Hall would save her from a soaking dash to the MARTA station and a miserable, wet ride home on the train.

Celia had given up her reservations about staying at the penthouse on a weeknight. Now that fall semester was in full swing—and Theo was absorbed in the pay equity suit for nurses—their jobs had cut into their private time. Even on weekends, they had less time just to relax and enjoy being together.

Shutting out the din of the thunderstorm, Celia returned her attention to a research proposal from one of the students in her seminar. "Movement for Movements: An Historical Overview of Dance as Protest." A worthwhile subject, but overly broad for a senior assignment. The student would do better to focus on a subset of the genre so he could fill his paper with insight and analysis rather than a simple regurgitation of historical events.

She'd never had the pleasure of teaching a senior seminar, and she wasn't going to waste it by letting her students get away with sophomore work.

A knock startled her and she looked up to see her colleague from across the hall, Eric Butler. Without waiting for an invitation, he smiled and took the chair in front of her desk. "Ever hear that saying about things having a way of working out?"

Eric was a wiry man in his mid-sixties. A car accident thirty-five years earlier had severed his left arm, effectively ending what had been a promising Broadway career. Though he'd made a name for himself in performance theory, his scholarly work had tailed off in recent years following the death of his longtime partner, leaving some in their department to wonder why he didn't just retire.

"I'm actually enjoying the Intro to Theater class," he went on. "It's been a reawakening, like a breath of fresh air. Who knew those wide-eyed freshmen could be so interesting?"

Celia honestly couldn't tell if he was serious. Most of her Intro students had been bored to tears, showing up for her lectures because attendance was compulsory for a humanities credit. Only a handful had a bonafide interest in the theater.

"Eric, forgive me but I have to ask. Are you being sarcastic? I can't tell because you're such a good actor."

He threw his head back and laughed. "Not at all, Celia. It's fascinating to go back to the beginning with these kids. I'd totally forgotten why I loved the theater in the first place. I can look out in the lecture hall and practically see the lights go on in their heads. Not everyone, of course. But enough that I find it exciting."

"Does this mean you're actually glad Andrew switched our assignments?"

"Frankly, yes. In fact, I plan to ask him for the spring section as well. I hadn't realized how far away I'd moved from the foundations of performance." He pushed himself up to leave, but stopped in the doorway. His smile faded. "I just wanted you to know I forgive you for poaching my seminar."

Celia was stunned to hear such a blatant accusation. "Eric, I never asked Andrew for your seminar. I was as shocked as you were."

He made no effort to disguise his skepticism, drawing a deep breath and shaking his head. "Perhaps not directly, but it's obvious Andrew put a higher priority on your request to work with advanced students than on mine or Paul's. There had to have been a reason for that."

Never mind that she'd patiently waited her turn while Eric and Paul saw their wishes granted year after year. "Just so you know, I protested this. I told Andrew it wasn't fair to you guys, especially on such short notice. His answer was what you just said—that it wasn't good to let the faculty get too far away from the fundamentals."

"Well, we all know that's rubbish, to borrow his term. What some people are saying is you got special treatment because of your involvement with that rape case."

"That doesn't make any sense," she snapped back, checking the anger in her voice. The fact that her colleagues were talking behind her back was enough to make her want to go to each and every one and explain what happened. "Why on earth would they give me special treatment when I was willing to testify against them in a wrongful death suit? Some days, I'm surprised I still have a job at all."

"Because punishing you would have been a political disaster."

"Whereas rewarding me accomplishes what? I would have testified against them if the case had gone to trial." In her heart, she knew Eric was somehow right, though she couldn't pin down the administration's motives. What mattered now was making sure he knew she hadn't set out to take advantage of her position. "You know, Eric...I don't know how any of this happened. I didn't deserve these assignments more than you or Paul, but I swear I did nothing to steal them out from under you. If you're really serious about enjoying the Intro class, then I'm happy for you. I'm enjoying the fact that after twelve years I'm finally getting a crack at leading a senior seminar. I'm sorry that came at your expense, but it isn't as if I'm not qualified to do it."

His frown slowly gave way to a weak smile. "I believe that. And I appreciate hearing you had nothing to do with how this came about. Let's hope for your sake you can convince Paul of that. You might want to reach out to him and explain. He's not as happy with his Performance Overview course as I am with Intro. In fact, he's considering filing a grievance against Andrew."

That was distressing. The process was playing out exactly as Theo had predicted—dividing her from her colleagues with preferential treatment, and ultimately creating a work environment so miserable she'd consider resigning.

"Thanks for the heads up, Eric. Something tells me this is going to get worse before it gets better. If Andrew's up to something, don't be surprised if he screws over someone else in the spring."

* * *

Theo studied the graph of nursing salaries, trying to make sense of the regression line. Her math comprehension had grown substantially since Gloria came aboard as a consultant, but hypothetical models that considered several variables at once left her at a loss. Pie charts and bar graphs were more her speed. She wouldn't dream of making her own statistical argument in court—that's what expert witnesses were for—but she had to understand it well enough to frame her case.

After throwing herself full steam into interviews with Harwood's rape victims, she was falling behind on the nurses' case. That meant bringing files home. Since Celia was staying over tonight, she hadn't intended to work more than an hour, but had been at her desk twice that long.

The dishwasher entered its rinse cycle, the roar reverberating through the wall and breaking her concentration. Her frustration boiling over, she yelled, "Remind me to buy a new dishwasher tomorrow. A quiet one."

Celia appeared in her doorway with her arms folded. She'd changed into knee-length leggings and the white dress shirt she'd purloined from Theo's closet after her first sleepover. "I'll do that. And you remind me why I said yes to coming over tonight to watch you work."

It was a fair question. Whether she blew off her work or left Celia to entertain herself, Theo was sure to feel guilty about it. But not as guilty as she felt for hiding the reason she was so far behind—that she'd begun working on a new case against Celia's employer.

Before she could say anything at all, Celia spun and walked out.

With a frustrated groan, Theo switched off her desk lamp and buried her head in her hands. There weren't enough hours in the day for the things she needed to do, especially not when Celia offered something so much better than work.

The living area and kitchen were dark. Following a beam of light that emanated from the master suite, she found Celia in the walk-in closet putting together an outfit for work the next day. Noiselessly, she crept up from behind and placed a series of soft kisses on the back of her neck. "I'm very"—*smack*—"very"—*smack*—"sorry I ignored you. You now have my undivided attention."

Celia sneered at her skeptically with one eye closed. "For how long?"

"For the rest of the night." She was disappointed to have Celia wriggle free. "Come on, I thought you'd be happy."

"I am…except now I'm the one feeling guilty. I know what it's like to be under the gun like you are. It's obvious you have a ton of work to do. I didn't mean to be pouty about it."

That was one of the many things she loved about Celia, her instinct to empathize with the people around her. It made Theo that much more determined to spend the rest of the evening with her—and to make the most of it. But first she needed to come clean.

"Come sit with me. I need to talk to you about something… the reason I've got so much work piled on my desk right now." She took Celia's hand and led her out to the love seat. "I was going to wait until I had everything ready to file, but I decided you should know what we're up to."

"What is it?"

"We're looking into reopening the case against Harwood. A general case about how they deal with rape. I've talked to twelve women so far. A lot of them got the same treatment as Hayley… or non-treatment, if that's even a word. Some reported it just like she did and the police refused to investigate. Others didn't even bother to report it because they knew Harwood wouldn't do anything."

Celia gaped at her. "What are you talking about? When did this happen?"

"There was a woman…I told you about her calling me. We tried to talk to her last summer but she was out of the country. She came back right before the semester started and called us. She knew Hayley."

In painstaking detail, she laid out the details of the case they'd developed so far while Celia shook her head with disbelief.

"Harwood basically got off scot-free, Celia. They shook out some pocket change for Donald Lipscomb and didn't do a thing about the problem. We have another chance to make them."

"Why are you just now telling me this?" There was no mistaking the irritation in her voice.

"Because…I'm sorry. I wanted to say something sooner but these last couple of months have been so good for us. We weren't stressed out all the time. You quit worrying about Harwood getting back at you. I just didn't want to put you through that again."

"Theo, you don't just…" Celia shook her head and tried to pull away, but gave in when Theo gripped her wrist. "I can't believe you didn't tell me this. This is not just anybody you're talking about suing. It's my boss. I had a right to know."

"Of course you did…you do. And that's why I'm telling you."

"Telling me? Shouldn't you be asking me?"

Theo was taken aback by the combative tone, to say nothing of Celia's suggestion that she needed permission to do her job. "No, because I work for my clients."

A long, awkward silence followed. Celia's jaw jutted defiantly and she refused to make eye contact.

"Celia, where is all this hostility coming from? If you're upset because I didn't tell you we were looking into this, then I'm truly sorry. Honestly, I didn't want to drag us both back into that spiral again, at least not until I knew for sure we were going to go ahead with the case. You and I didn't need that hanging over us."

"So why are you starting it up again?"

"Because it's what I do. You know that. But it doesn't have to be what *we* do." She scooted closer on the love seat, practically forcing Celia to lean into her arm. "These women I've talked to…they've been treated like trash, just like Hayley. It's time somebody stood up for them. I can't just walk away and leave them without a voice."

Celia didn't reply, so there was no way to know if she was upset about the case or about Theo's decision not to tell her.

"I need to know what you're feeling right now. Talk to me."

"I feel like…Hayley's case is over. It's in the DA's hands now. And you're right—it's nice not to be stressed out all the time. Things are going my way at work, and I don't want to risk messing it up by having you stir the pot again."

Her reluctance was understandable, but Theo couldn't help being disappointed by her selfish perspective. This wasn't the same woman who'd sneaked into her office fired up to bring the whole university down for the way it had treated Hayley.

"I can try to bring this case without dragging you into it." It would make her job extremely difficult though, since the audiotape Celia had made of her meeting with administrators was a critical piece of evidence of their pattern of behavior. And it was the only solid proof she had, since all the threats had been delivered in person or over the phone by unnamed administrators. She'd have to find another way to prove they intimidated victims and witnesses into keeping silent.

"It won't matter whether I testify or not, Theo. Eventually they're going to find out about us sleeping together, and they'll think I had something to do with it. It's not as if you like to fly under the radar."

Stung by the snideness of her remark, Theo abruptly disentangled from her and walked out onto the terrace. The city lights had an instantaneous calming effect. She would have felt justified at snapping back but knew she'd regret it. Her secrecy, after all, had set up this argument.

"Theo, I'm sorry." Celia approached her from behind.

"It's okay."

"No, it isn't. I freaked out and took it out on you."

"But it's my fault you freaked out. Either you're mad because I took the case or because I didn't tell you about it. I'm not sure it even matters which."

Celia stroked her arm lovingly before taking up a position beside her at the rail. "It's a little of both, I guess. But mad's not the right word. Surprised…confused. Maybe scared. And I was hurt that you kept it from me, so I hurt back. That was a shitty thing to do." When Theo didn't respond right away, she added, "Does your silence mean you agree with me?"

Theo chuckled softly. "No, I'm taking the blame for this one. Unfortunately, it doesn't change anything. I still need to do my job and help these women. We're going to have to work it out so it doesn't come between us."

"I know who you are, Theo. One of the reasons I love you is because I respect what you do."

They leaned into a gentle kiss.

"But I don't want to be a part of your case. I can't handle all that pressure again. You'll have to do it without me."

* * *

Celia rolled onto her side and backed into Theo's embrace. Despite the argument they'd had only minutes before coming to bed—or perhaps because of it—their lovemaking had been intense and filled with emotion. Now as her body relaxed, she craved warmth and closeness.

She clutched Theo's hand and kissed her knuckles. "I love you."

"I love you too. And I want this every night…you right here beside me. What would you say to moving in with me?"

Warm lips caressed her shoulder, quelling her desire to roll back over to face her. "You want us to live together?"

"No more running back and forth to your place, juggling what's where. No more fighting traffic out to Dunwoody. It would give us more time together."

It would, but she didn't want to take such a major step out of convenience. Nor did she want Theo's invitation springing up only to smooth over hurt feelings.

"Celia, I'm not the only one who brings home work every night. You've been playing catch-up all semester with your classes." Theo burrowed her hand into the warm hollow between Celia's breasts. "Up to now we've been trying to manage by dividing our time. I think we ought to share it instead. That's how we really get to know each other."

"This isn't because of our argument, is it? Because I said I was okay."

"No, of course not." She sighed and nuzzled the back of Celia's neck. "Not directly. I felt bad when you said I hurt you. And even worse because I need to work the case anyway, when it's obvious you'd rather I didn't. All of it made me realize how important you are to me, how much I want you in my life. Telling you that is too easy. I want to *show* you. So after four months of sleepovers, I think it's time for us to stop living like this is just a day-to-day relationship."

Celia rippled with joy at hearing Theo shared her feelings. "You want me in your life, huh?"

"In my thoughts, in my heart."

"And in your bed, I hope."

"Every night."

There was one word Theo hadn't used, conspicuous for its absence. *Forever*. Celia didn't need to hear it to know it was implied but not promised. They needed to take this step first, to mesh their lives under one roof and learn the give and take. "Yes, I'll move in."

Even in the dim light, Theo's smile was bright enough to see.

"But what would I do with my place?"

"Who cares? Sell it, rent it, let it sit empty so you'll have an imaginary safety net until you feel like you don't need it anymore."

It was funny she'd put it that way. Celia had taken for granted their relationship would evolve without effort, that they'd wake up someday and realize they'd been together for years.

CHAPTER TWENTY-TWO

Celia unceremoniously dumped the contents of her desk drawer into a box, the last of her office to be packed. "I can't believe I get to go from looking out over a parking lot to looking out over the whole city."

Theo was giving up her gigantic guest bedroom so Celia could have a home office too, complete with a sitting area that included a sofa bed in case they had overnight guests.

"I said that about my office downtown, but I barely get the chance to look out the window. I don't think I've ever been this busy in my life."

"When do you file the nurses' case?" Celia couldn't bring herself to ask how the sexual assault investigation was progressing. It was a subject they barely talked about.

"Hard to say. The data we really need to look at is proprietary. The best way to get access to it is to file a class action, but we can't get certified until we have data to demonstrate the class of women makes less than the class of men. Of course, the men who make more don't want to make less, so they aren't exactly volunteering to help. It's a catch-twenty-two."

"I was wondering about that. How did you even know there was a discrepancy at Mercy? Aren't their salaries supposed to be confidential?"

"Married couples. We've talked to about twenty of them so far. Gloria came up with a statistical formula that estimates what they should make if their salaries were based only on their training and experience. In all but four cases, the women make less and the men make more." Theo taped the box closed as she talked. "Getting data from Mercy is a piece of cake compared to getting it from Harwood. Not only are the numbers proprietary, there's an extra layer of privacy because we're talking about students."

They'd gone all weekend without talking about the Harwood case, and Celia wasn't about to start now. To avoid having to respond, she scooped up the box and carried it downstairs and out to her car.

Theo was on her heels with a stack of books. "The other problem we have at Harwood is that it's rape. These days, the Internet's a cesspool of animals hiding in their mother's basement and sending out threats to women who speak out about it. To protect our clients, we may have to call them Jane Roes."

Celia suddenly had the feeling she was being baited.

"It takes a lot of courage to subject yourself to something like that. A couple of the women were gung-ho at first but then—"

"Maybe it's not worth it, Theo." It was all she could do to control the ire in her voice. The last thing she wanted was another fight about this case. "All I'm saying is, Harwood knows it's under scrutiny now. You said yourself you might not win Hayley's case, but the outrage might be enough to make them clean up their act."

"Except it isn't going to get cleaned up as long as the same bad actors are there. The administrators, the cops...Harwood needs a turnover."

"And they'll get it. We passed a unanimous resolution at the faculty senate calling for accountability."

"What does that even mean, Celia? Can the faculty senate force the police to investigate sexual assault complaints? Are they going to allocate the budget to set up rape crisis centers and hire victims' advocates to help get these women through the trauma?"

To her credit, Theo seemed to be doing her best to control the tone of her voice so as not to sound as if she were on the attack. Her questions, however, were borderline absurd.

"We can keep the pressure on them, Theo. Believe me, they don't want us bringing it up over and over. They'll fix it for no other reason than so we'll leave them alone."

Theo followed her back up to the office, where she commandeered the desk chair. "But that doesn't fix anything for these women. They deserve some kind of personal justice, not only against their rapists but against the system that shut them down. Any one of them could have ended up like Hayley."

"Come on, Theo. That's below the belt."

"It's not a dig against you. But if you're taking it personally, maybe you should ask yourself why."

Celia could feel the pressure, whether Theo admitted to applying it or not. "Are we having another fight about this? It sure feels like it."

"It's not a fight. It's just a discussion. Can't I talk to you about my work? Or is this particular case off limits? That would be really weird, since it's the only case I currently have that actually involves both of us."

She was right about that, a point Celia found frustrating. Even if Theo managed to build a case without using her testimony and audiotape, there was no way she could disentangle herself, since she was the one who brought Theo to Harwood's doorstep.

"I told you the other night, Celia. I won't let this come between us. It's my job to handle it, but I don't have to talk about it if it bothers you this much."

And now Theo was being reasonable, which was also frustrating. It made Celia feel like a brat who had to be accommodated lest she throw a tantrum.

* * *

Celia looked stunning sitting across the table in her black dress, the same one Theo had tossed on the floor of her bedroom the night they first made love. Almost too sexy for dinner with friends.

They'd been invited to celebrate the Hendershots' fortieth anniversary at Aria, the couple's favorite restaurant in Buckhead. The artistic presentations of each course complemented the modern ambience of the black and white decor.

The early conversation centered around the chore of packing and moving, which Celia announced she was never doing again. "I'm serious. If this doesn't work out, I'm keeping the penthouse and kicking Theo out."

"Atta girl!" Gloria clinked her wineglass to Celia's in a toast. "I'll help you find a good attorney."

"I remember when I first asked Gloria to move in with me," Lewis said. "She was working on her PhD, I was in law school. Who had time to run all over hell and half of Georgia just for a date? But she said no."

"What I said was 'Hell, no.' On account of what happened to Margaret Bower." Gloria nudged her husband as if to force him to finish the story, but then forged ahead. "She was one of my sorority sisters. A braniac. She wanted to go for her PhD in chemistry, but ended up getting married and teaching high school chemistry so she could put her husband through law school. Two kids later, he gets his JD and files for divorce."

"So Gloria wouldn't move in with me—and she damn sure wouldn't marry me—not till I finished school."

"I had to make sure you had your own money." A prescient attitude, since Lewis had amassed a small fortune from his law practice.

Celia narrowed her eyes and nodded. "Smart. I think Theo was waiting for me to finish my textbook. She's been watching me work on it since last summer. Those eight rounds of revisions nearly drove me nuts. Add that to my class preps and getting ready for the spring performance."

"You can't wait for Theo to get finished with anything," Gloria said as she carved her lamb shank. "There's never a day when she doesn't have half a dozen irons in the fire. Right when she's juggled all the balls up in the air, some boneheaded celebrity calls because her tenth husband wants her money."

"Just like the ninth…and the eighth," Theo added with a chuckle.

"This Harwood mess though," Gloria went on, "it's going to be the death of us all. We've never taken on a case with so many moving parts. Until the university gets proactive and shuts down its rape culture, we'll be getting new clients every week."

Theo tensed, bracing for a possible eruption from Celia.

Instead, she calmly asked, "Did Theo tell you about our faculty senate resolution? We voted last week to hold the administration accountable for fixing all the issues having to do with sexual assault on campus. Starting with transparency. There's now an official faculty task force responsible for coming up with recommendations."

Gloria rolled her eyes. "Ha! Good luck with that. We did the same thing for admissions, scholarships and housing. It took a Title IX action to finally get the women's dorms renovated."

Celia said testily, "We're proposing a comprehensive overhaul."

"I'll be surprised if the trustees sign off on it. That would be like admitting they have a problem and they're all too stubborn to do that. I used to think Earl Gupton was a decent guy, somebody who'd put the interests of the students and faculty first. But his management style…when push comes to shove, he's just a puppet."

"How's the New York strip, Lewis?" Theo asked, eager to change the subject.

"Juicy. And it's got a good rub. Salt and pepper—that's it."

"Theo said the same thing today," Celia went on, not taking advantage of the out. "That the senate wouldn't have any teeth. I think we will. There's talk of implementing an orientation seminar on sexual consent so everyone's on the same page about what constitutes assault. And we have to improve the police response, and of course counseling services for victims."

By her frequent glances toward Theo, it was clear Celia was talking to her. And saying in a calm, rational way all the things she'd refused to talk about while they were packing up her office. The irony was that Theo didn't have to push back— Gloria was doing it for her.

"Here's what I think." Gloria waved her serrated knife as she talked. "Gupton, Tuttle, that police chief, Egan…somebody needs to make an example of them. Right now that's us. Nobody else is coming after them. If they get away with what they've done, there's no disincentive not to try it again."

"What's going on with the criminal case?" Lewis asked.

Theo had spoken with Shane Satterfield the day before. "Unless they get a continuance, they're proceeding to trial two weeks from Monday. The DA offered all of them a plea for five years and got no takers."

"You didn't tell me this," Celia said.

"I was going to." *If she'd shown any interest in talking about it.* Lowering her voice as she leaned forward, she added, "Right now the four of them are sticking to their story that Hayley consented, but Shane's considering sweetening the offer for one of them to roll on the others."

"Not Ruben Vargas, I hope. He's the one who started it by giving Hayley a drink that knocked her out."

"Apparently that was part of a hazing ritual for freshmen. Shane says Vargas didn't take part in the actual rape, but if they choose to go to trial and a jury finds them guilty, they all could get fifteen years."

Lewis leaned in as well, understanding that Theo was sharing sensitive information. "If the DA's office knows that level of detail about the assault already, they probably have enough evidence to convict all four of them without making any deals."

"That's what I told him," Theo said. "But if he makes a deal with Vargas in state court, there's no guarantee the feds won't jump all over it once the trial's over. Drug-facilitated rape gets you twenty years. Nobody's going to walk, not with that video out there."

Celia had stopped eating. By her sullen expression, she was none too pleased at Gloria's pessimism about the faculty senate's lofty goals. Clearly she'd hoped for an ally. "No matter what else happens, it'll be a happy day when the bars close behind those bastards."

* * *

Celia keyed in the elevator code to access the building's upper floors and leaned into Theo as they started up. Her shoulders and thighs were sore from carrying heavy boxes to and from the car. A hot shower before bed would feel great.

"Welcome home, Dr. Perone. Does it feel different this time?" Theo pulled her into a hug and planted a kiss on her forehead.

She wouldn't feel completely at home until Monday when her furniture was delivered, but there was closure in knowing she wouldn't be returning to her townhouse. She'd already found a tenant through an executive rental agency.

"Does what feel different? Me coming home to your penthouse or your hands on my butt?"

"Definitely the latter. In case I forgot to tell you, I absolutely love you in this dress…almost as much as I love you out of it."

"How about we trade back rubs when I pull it off? I probably won't be able to get out of bed tomorrow."

"I'll trade anything you want. I appreciate you saying yes to dinner tonight. I know you were tired. Gloria and Lewis are special friends of mine—I hope they'll be your friends too. It was nice they asked us to celebrate their anniversary."

Celia caught herself before saying they could return the favor. She had no idea what day Theo would mark as their anniversary—the day they first made love, the day they moved in…or maybe the "someday" when they got married. It wasn't something they'd talked about.

She had her key out already and opened the door to what was now her home. "I appreciate you too, sweetheart. Don't think I didn't notice when you tried to change the subject during dinner."

"Oh, that. I figured one steaming pile of discord was enough for one day. I was surprised when you didn't let it go."

Truth be told, she was hoping if she said the right thing, Gloria or Lewis would take her side, seeing the wisdom in letting the university clean up its own mess. "I was surprised by Gloria. I really thought she'd be in favor of letting the faculty take care of it internally."

"I don't think she was against it." She beat the same drum as before. "But even if you implement all of the recommendations, these women who've been victimized don't get their justice."

"You keep saying that. I don't think what you're doing gets them justice either. It's not as if their rapists are going to be arrested. The best they can hope for is a payday from Harwood. You punish the school without punishing the perpetrators. At least Hayley's rapists are going to trial." Celia heard the aggravation in her voice and checked her temper before their discussion escalated to another fight. "Neither you nor the faculty can force the university to get rid of the people responsible for this. The most we can hope for is reform. I just happen to think the best chance for that is from the senate, not from outside pressure."

"Fair enough."

"Outside agitation's just going to make it worse."

For the next twenty minutes, they readied for bed, the subject apparently closed. Though Theo made small talk, there was no mistaking an undercurrent of polite civility as she too tried to avoid confrontation.

Celia tossed her robe aside and climbed into bed nude as usual. When Theo joined her, she expected little more than a perfunctory goodnight kiss. Instead Theo drew back the blanket, straddled her back and began kneading her shoulders.

"You don't have to do that, Theo. I'm too tired to return the favor."

"It's okay. You worked harder than I did today. Besides, one of us lifts weights three times a week. That way, she doesn't get as sore when she has to do a little physical labor." She delivered her chide with a kiss on the shoulder.

"Kick me when I'm down."

"Come on, does this feel like kicking?"

Far from it. If her neck and shoulders could purr, they would. "I'm sorry I've been such a grouch today about your case. I know it's important to you. I'll try to be more supportive."

Theo expressed her gratitude by expanding the massage area to the muscles along her spine.

"Can I just say one more thing?" Celia asked at the risk of breaking their truce. "I've realized over the past few days how much of my anger had to do not only with Hayley being my student, but with me having so much in common with her. Her being an actress, trusting people around her…and then getting drugged and violated. It made the case personal to me. That's why I was willing to put myself out there. I was fighting for both of us. What happened to these other women upsets me… but I don't feel the same sense of personal resentment now that Hayley's case is pretty much over. At least not enough to put my career on the line again. Can you understand where I'm coming from?"

"I can." The massage continued in silence for several very long seconds. "And since we're being totally honest about our feelings, I should tell you I'm disappointed you feel that way. It's on me to get past that and I will. I love you…and nothing about work is going to come between us—ever."

The words, though delivered in a calm and loving manner, were devastating. There was nothing Celia could imagine that would be worse than knowing she'd disappointed the woman she loved.

Theo finally stopped her massage and rolled over to her side of the bed on her back. "It's my own fault, Celia. I project onto others what I want them to feel, and I know it isn't fair. When you first came to me, there wasn't even a tiny part of my legal brain that thought we had a case. But I was so taken by your compassion, your outrage…you made me want to put on armor and go to war. That woman you were when you first came into my office? I have to be that woman every day."

Celia slid her hand beneath the covers and clasped Theo's hand, her heart breaking with sorrow and bursting with joy. One of those feelings triggered her tears—either the shame of not being the person Theo wanted her to be…or relief at knowing Theo loved her anyway.

CHAPTER TWENTY-THREE

With her headphones in place so no one who happened by her office could hear what she was watching, Celia followed the live streaming feed from the morning news program. This was the third such interview of the morning, an anchorwoman speaking via satellite to Theo in her downtown office.

Theo had filed her case against Harwood the day before. Once again at the entrance gate, she'd held a press conference alleging the university had created a hostile learning environment for female students, that it had been negligent in its enforcement of laws against sexual assault, and that threats of SLAPP suits alleging defamation had produced a chilling effect on the free speech rights of victims and on the reporting of such crimes.

"What's different this time?" the anchorwoman asked.

"The suit we filed last summer involving a video that showed Harwood basketball players sexually assaulting an unconscious woman was a wrongful death case. Their victim suffered mental distress, not only from the rape…" Theo appeared to appreciate the chance to recount Hayley's heartbreaking story, but she moved quickly to the merits of the new lawsuit. "As we were investigating that case, we came upon a disturbing pattern of treatment of Harwood's female students who reported being sexually assaulted. As with Ms. Burkhart, their charges were pushed aside. We're not talking just one or two cases here, Sandra."

Theo went on to cite publicly available statistics, concluding with the fact that no male student at Harwood had been criminally charged with rape on campus over the past six years. The period coincided with Earl Gupton and Norman Tuttle assuming their respective leadership roles.

To Celia, it was the strongest argument yet for Gupton and Tuttle to be fired.

She barely heard the knock as the door opened simultaneously. Kay Crylak, her forehead wrinkled in a deep frown, entered and closed the door as Celia closed her laptop and removed the headphones.

"Hey, what's up? Is everything okay?"

"It's okay right now, but it probably won't be by the end of the day." Kay was dressed in a black and orange track suit with the Harwood softball emblem on the chest, as though she'd come directly from the playing field. She took a chair and tugged a business card from her wallet. "Remember when I showed you this? It's that attorney I'm supposed to call if one of my gals gets into trouble with the cops."

She recalled during their lunch over the summer Kay had told her the campus police intervened when one of her players stole a bicycle. "Is one of your girls in trouble again?"

"What? No, I'm talking about me." She got up and started pacing, her shoes squeaking on the marble floor each time she turned. "That case they filed yesterday...all those girls who said they were raped and the school didn't do anything about it. I called Theo Constantine's office and made an appointment for one thirty this afternoon. I'm gonna tell her about the AD's special arrangement with the cops...how this lawyer, this Austin Thompson, *Esquire*"—her voice dripped with sarcasm at his title—"is all buddy-buddy with the cops and makes everything magically disappear."

Celia was stunned by the about-face. It was hard to believe this was the same woman who'd castigated her over her involvement with Hayley's case. "You can't be serious. You're talking career suicide. It won't matter if you're right. Harwood will find a way to get rid of you. You know it as well as I do."

Whirling around, Kay threw her hands up in the air. "If that happens, I'll live with it. I was looking for a job when I found this one. What I can't live with anymore is being part of this conspiracy. Going along to get along. It's time I stood up to 'em like you."

"Except I'm not involved in this case, Kay. What I did for Hayley Burkhart was because she was my student."

"But I'm involved in this one. Do you know I have my own Wikipedia page? Says I'm the women's softball coach at Harwood. Born in Ocala, played college ball at Florida State. Here's my record, blah blah blah. One of these days, somebody's gonna go in there and add a paragraph about all the coaches implicated in this mess. I'm deciding right now what I want it to say—that I came forward and told the truth."

* * *

Theo pressed her phone to her ear as a car squealed around the corner in the parking deck attached to the US District Court. "Don't worry about this, Jordan. It's just a routine suppression hearing…a gag order. For some reason, it annoys them when I go on TV and tell the world what terrible people they are. I'll put out a memo tonight and let everyone know where we stand."

She'd expected Harwood's quick response this go-around, since they probably intended to recycle their legal arguments from the first case. Furthermore, she wasn't surprised to find James Somers waiting in chambers to argue the university's case.

"You're persistent, Theo. I'll give you that," he said curtly. He wasn't amused this time—he was annoyed. "Though one would think you'd get eventually tired of tilting at windmills."

"Not so much. I do a lot of cardio," she deadpanned. Despite the outcome of the Burkhart case, her courtroom confidence was soaring, since after all, she'd beaten Somers on their last outing—the motion to dismiss the wrongful death case.

The case had been assigned to The Honorable Leon Diggs, an African-American federal judge in his late fifties with a reputation for being difficult to read. Theo had once appeared in his court and found herself frustrated that she couldn't determine if her strategy was effective.

Without looking up from his desk, Judge Diggs flatly read the motion to suppress aloud and called on Somers to state his case.

"Thank you, Your Honor. Before we get to that, I'd like to begin by pointing out that those responsible for the atrocious behaviors upon which this case is based are individuals who are currently facing criminal charges in district court. The civil aspects of this case were settled confidentially after the plaintiff fired Ms. Constantine as his attorney when it became evident to him she was representing her own vindictive, publicity-seeking biases, and not his legal interests. That she would refile this case is evidence of more grandstanding on her part."

Diggs looked over his glasses at Theo. "Is he correct, counselor?"

"I'm not sure, Your Honor. To which criminal and civil cases does Mr. Somers refer?"

Her question forced Somers to recite the details of Hayley's case for the court reporter's transcript. Without intending to, he supplied a fresh summary that bolstered her current claim.

"And how is it you know, Mr. Somers, why the plaintiff fired Ms. Constantine?"

"I served as lead attorney in the settlement negotiations, Your Honor."

"But you just said those terms were confidential. You understand you can't claim that and use the plaintiff's position in this court to strengthen your case?" His question was obviously rhetorical, as he turned to Theo without waiting for a reply. "What say you, Ms. Constantine? Are you attempting to get a second bite at the apple in the federal courts?"

"No, Your Honor, not at all. Neither the victim in that case nor her surviving family members are plaintiffs in this complaint. It is quite possible however that we will introduce the horrific circumstances of that particular crime—the *atrocious* crime to which Mr. Somers just referred—and the egregious coverup as evidence of a pattern of disregard of the wellbeing of Harwood University's female rape victims leading us to allege a hostile learning environment."

"Satisfied, Mr. Somers? I believe I am."

It was tough to imagine Somers getting embarrassed, so the reddening of his ears was likely a sign he was agitated. He traced his notes with his finger as if struggling to find his place. "The defense also questions whether the federal court is the appropriate venue for this case. All of the actions cited by the plaintiffs are alleged to have taken place in the state of Georgia. As such, concerns regarding equal protection might best be addressed via interpretation of the state constitution."

Theo didn't wait to be called on. "Diversity of citizenship, Your Honor. Six of our plaintiffs hold driver's licenses from other states. The federal court is the proper venue for interstate litigation."

"You are correct, counselor." He looked to Somers and drolly asked, "Your suppression motion…I assume that's why we're here. Do you plan to address that today?"

It was hard to rein in her optimism at the way Diggs was dressing down Somers with nearly every remark. He usually wasn't so overt in his distaste for counsel. Clearly, Somers had pushed a button by coming in unprepared.

"Your Honor, plaintiff's counsel called a press conference yesterday to announce these inflammatory charges." He then rattled off a log of all the TV, radio and other news interview shows she'd given since the story broke, and cited case law about how extrajudicial statements to the media could materially prejudice a potential trial. The words were familiar, and when he listed the sports talk shows, the reason became clear—in his haste to prepare, he'd lifted the argument verbatim from the suppression motion for the Burkhart case.

Theo was operating at a clear advantage, since she'd had weeks to prepare for motions she knew would be filed. "Your Honor, once again defense counsel has confused this case with *Lipscomb v. Frazier, et al*. I've done no interviews with sports talk shows, as this case—unlike *Lipscomb*—does not name Harwood athletes as defendants. Regarding the substantive issues in his argument, Harwood University has unfettered access to contemporary media outlets, and thus numerous opportunities to portray itself as an upstanding institution. During the *Lipscomb* proceedings, a gag order resulted in Harwood University increasing the number of positive image ads in local press outlets by four hundred percent. Such an imbalance clearly favored the defendants."

It had been Jalinda's idea to scour the media for that data, which Theo then presented in chart form to both Diggs and Somers.

"More importantly, we ask the court to consider the fact that secrecy—in particular, the extraordinary efforts by the defendant to suppress allegations of sexual assault on its campus—is at the heart of plaintiffs' case. The secrecy at Harwood has created a culture that allows these assaults to proliferate. A suppression order would not only support that culture, it would restrict the constitutional rights of victims to speak critically of its effects."

She had no idea if her argument was resonating, as Diggs seemed to be absorbed in the media report she'd presented. Without making eye contact with anyone, he leaned toward the court reporter and said, "Let the record show this is a properly filed case that meets the requisites for federal court. In light of plaintiff's evidence that Harwood University engaged in an uptick in image advertising while under a suppression order, likely to enhance its standing should it find its case in court, I reject defense's motion for a suppression order. Counsel is advised to proceed with caution as such an order may be imposed at any time."

With every word, Somers sank deeper into his chair, the arrogance fading from his face.

Theo didn't really care about the gag order, as she had no more bookings for interviews. She cared only about getting to trial and winning her case.

* * *

Celia straightened her back against the plush upholstered chair. A work-study coed had delivered a glass of ice water and left her to wait outside Earl Gupton's office a half hour earlier. This was his meeting, not hers, and she had little doubt what he wanted to discuss.

The fresh spate of allegations had sent shockwaves through the university, sparking online flame wars in the comments section of the *Daily Hornet* and an impromptu protest by several dozen students—male and female—in front of the administration building. Celia was gratified to see so many rising up on behalf of the victims. At the same time, it was sickening proof of how the celebration of a basketball trophy had smothered the outrage over Hayley's rape and suicide. An "attention-seeking drama queen" so conveniently dismissed. People only told themselves what they wanted to hear.

By now, Theo had probably spoken with Kay. Confirmation of the athletic department's tactics would help prove part of the conspiracy, but even Celia knew the administration would try to distance itself from what they'd label a "rogue" practice undertaken in secret by minor operators. Ban the attorney from campus, suspend an assistant coach or two—all fixed.

It was Sonya Walsh, Harwood's general counsel, who opened Gupton's door and invited her in. Gupton was waiting in the sitting area of his office with none other than board of trustees chair Norman Tuttle. Déjà vu all over again.

"How wonderful to see you again, Celia," Gupton said, his enthusiasm embarrassingly forced. Last time she was in here, she was Dr. Perone. "You remember Chairman Tuttle."

"Of course." She shook hands cordially. Ignoring Gupton's offer of a seat on the sofa, she took the armchair at the end of the coffee table so as not to feel surrounded.

"So sorry to keep you waiting. The three of us have been brainstorming some ideas for letting the women on campus know we're behind them one hundred percent. Sonya reminded me earlier about our meeting last spring. As I recall, you were concerned about the university's response to an unfortunate incident on campus, one the courts are looking into right now. I wondered if you had any ideas for what we could do to meet this issue head on. Sexual assault on campus, I mean. We want our female students to feel safe."

It took a conscious effort to keep her jaw from dropping. Clearly Harwood's legal team had made note of the fact that Theo's new complaint included no mention of their threats to her if she went public with the allegations. They'd mistakenly concluded she was now on their side, grateful for her plum course assignments and generous theater budget.

"Sorry, I should have asked how your semester was going," Gupton said. "Andrew tells me we're in for quite a treat next spring. *Spamalot*."

That answered the question about whether her department head was part of the payola scheme to buy her silence. A dismal, disappointing revelation.

"Yes, we've just completed casting."

"My wife and I saw that a couple of years ago in West End," Tuttle said amiably. He'd sunk deep into the sofa cushions, so far that his feet were no longer on the floor.

Gupton nodded toward Sonya Walsh, who said, "Dr. Perone, we were concerned you may have misread our position during our last meeting. At the time, the administration faced an unfortunate predicament, caught between two parties in an interpersonal conflict. You can understand our hesitance about taking sides with one student against another without the benefit of all the facts."

Celia caught herself watching Walsh's hair, which held its place like a helmet no matter how much her head bobbed during her animated speech.

"As administrators," she continued, "we're responsible for both students and faculty. We were extremely worried you might find yourself on the wrong end of litigation without the financial means to defend yourself, and felt it best to discourage further escalation."

"That's not…quite how I remember it," Celia said, adding a smile that was every bit as fake as theirs. "I understood the threat of litigation was from Harwood itself. Plus you indicated I could be fired if I said or did anything to place Harwood in a negative light."

"Which you did," Tuttle said brusquely. "But you weren't fired, were you? In fact, you were treated quite handsomely by your department, even after you offered testimony to that Constantine woman in support of that specious wrongful death claim. Greedy lawyers."

Walsh jumped back in, ostensibly to keep the discussion from becoming acrimonious. "A claim the university ultimately paid—strictly out of compassion for a family that had lost its child. While we admitted no direct liability for her death, we fully acknowledge a certain responsibility for the wellbeing of all our students while they're on campus under our care."

"How can you say that, Ms. Walsh? You were given irrefutable evidence of a young woman being raped while she was unconscious." Channeling Theo in one of her TV interviews, Celia pummeled her with the ugly facts. "The whole world has seen that video, and your attempt to paint the administration as a neutral party is laughable. You refused to order the campus police to investigate the evidence. That isn't being neutral—it's taking sides with rapists."

"Whoa, whoa, whoa here!" Gupton held up his hands in the direction of his counsel, as if imploring his colleagues not to escalate the rancor. "There's a lot of blame to go around, and like it or not, we're on the hook for our fair share. But let's not lose sight of why we're here today."

Celia crossed a leg and let it swing whimsically. "Can you reiterate that for me, Chancellor Gupton?"

"What we need, Celia, is some guidance going forward. Sadly, Harwood has struggled with its tribulations, as all major universities sometimes do. But such adversity hardly constitutes a hostile learning environment. It's apparent to all of us, given your recent experience, you're in a singular position to help us convey that message." His earnest gaze made it clear he expected a response.

"I'm a professor of performance studies. If it's faculty advisors you want, I should think it would be more beneficial if you engaged those in the women's studies department. Or perhaps public relations." Even as she suggested other disciplines, it struck her with no small measure of irony he was in fact looking for an actor, someone who would pretend all was well.

"No…no, your contribution is…unique." He cleared his throat and glanced at Walsh.

"What Chancellor Gupton is asking, Celia," she said tightly, "is how the administration might work with you to ensure the messages from the university continue to be positive. What could we do to facilitate that on your part?"

There it was—a flat-out bribe to prevent her from testifying about their threats.

Celia shifted in her chair, leaning forward as if to pin them in their seats. "Why don't we cut the innuendo so there's no misunderstanding? Hayley Burkhart was my student and I cared about her. But I'm not part of this new case, and you'd like to keep it that way. Is that a reasonable reading of what you're asking?"

Gupton nodded solemnly. "It would be detrimental to the university if you testified as to your assumption that you were threatened. I can assure you, there was no threat intended. I hope we can clarify that today."

"You realize I could be subpoenaed to testify about that conversation. If that were to happen, you'd like me to forget that you threatened to fire me and focus instead on your assertion that you were attempting to balance the best interests of everyone involved. And you were especially concerned that I'd be exposing myself to malicious litigation from assailants seeking revenge. Do I have that right?"

All three stared at her blankly, their silence speaking volumes.

"Very well. What do you propose for *your* part of"—she used her fingers to make air quotes—"facilitating this?"

Gupton picked up a folder from the coffee table. "Andrew made several suggestions for your consideration. A permanent part-time research assistant. A paid sabbatical with one of our European partners. An endowed chair from the Harwood Foundation."

Such rewards would elevate her above other professors in her department—and make her the target of their resentment. After a measured silence, she replied, "Those would be amazing opportunities. But I'm worried there would be some…shall we say, jealousy among my peers."

A look of relief crossed Gupton's face as he realized they were officially negotiating. "You'd have to show some patience, of course. Give us two or three years to roll them into place. That should assuage the skeptics, plus we could boost the opportunities for others in your department so you won't feel singled out. Bear in mind your elected position on the faculty senate makes you deserving of a certain level of esteem. It's only fitting Andrew would reward that with a certain degree of academic largess."

Celia drew in a deep breath and threw her shoulders back with renewed confidence. "If I agree to facilitate such a conversation, how do I know those rewards will·be delivered?"

Tuttle heaved a wheezing sigh. "We can't exactly write this down in a contract, Miss Perone."

"Dr. Perone," she corrected flatly.

"Celia, look." Gupton leaned forward and clasped his hands, the picture of a reasonable man. "I understand your doubts. These opportunities, as you call them…they cost us mere pennies of our endowment. Withholding them for any reason would be foolish on our part. On the contrary, we'd be forever grateful for your help in getting us through this dispute. I promise you, we'll come out the other side a better institution."

"And you'll do everything you can to fix the way women are treated when they report being sexually assaulted?"

"Absolutely."

"No more telling the cops to back off? No more special treatment for jocks?"

"That stops today. I'll tell Chief Egan myself. You have my word."

Celia shook hands with all three again and closed the door behind her when she left. A research assistant, a sabbatical in Europe and an endowed chair. All she had to do was sell out a bunch of nameless, faceless rape victims…and Theo.

A bribe, a confession, a promise to reform. Smiling to herself as she walked toward the faculty parking lot, she took her phone from her pocket.

"How wonderful to see you again, Celia. You remember Chairman Tuttle."

Ironclad evidence the administration cared nothing about its rape victims. Wouldn't Theo be proud?

CHAPTER TWENTY-FOUR

Theo perched on the arm of her couch, adjusting the belt on her dress, a long-sleeved chocolate brown wraparound that hugged her from thigh to shoulder. The local news was set to start at any second. "Celia! Get in here. You have to see this."

When the program opened with photos of four of Harwood's administrators, she clicked the remote to pause the story.

Celia emerged from their bedroom wearing Theo's favorite, the bare-shouldered black dress, mixing it up this time with long pewter earrings. "This is getting ridiculous. I'm buying a new dress this weekend and throwing this one away."

"Don't even think about it. I'll fish it out of the trash. You look gorgeous in it." She pulled Celia toward her and spun her toward the TV. "Watch this. It's the lead story."

"Bowing to pressure today from students, faculty and alumni, Harwood University's board of trustees fired four top officials in what some say is only the beginning of a personnel shakeup at one of the nation's elite institutions. Trustees chairman Norman Tuttle, chancellor Earl Gupton, general counsel Sonya Walsh and campus police chief Thomas Egan were fired after being indicted two days ago on charges of perjury and obstruction of justice in relation to the Harwood basketball rape scandal. Sources tell us the four officials are accused of intimidating witnesses, interfering with a criminal investigation and lying to the district attorney about their involvement in the scheme to cover up the assault. Four players from Harwood's national championship basketball team face sentencing next week in the drugging and rape of Hayley Burkhart, a twenty-year-old junior who committed suicide after the assault."

"Un-fricking-believable."

"Satisfying, isn't it?" She doubted Celia's department head would survive the purge, since the audiotape from the second meeting clearly implicated him in the conspiracy to silence witnesses. Another head on the chopping block was Austin Thompson. Once Theo learned for certain he was involved with the athletes, she'd filed a motion with Georgia's disciplinary board to have him disbarred for brokering the settlement on behalf of Donald Lipscomb.

"I totally get what drives you now, Theo. It's the rush from seeing people like Gupton get their comeuppance."

"I admit I like that part. But it's nowhere near the rush I get from seeing my clients vindicated. Or my witnesses," she added with a kiss to Celia's temple. "You were so brave. Your friend Kay too, and all those women who came forward with their stories. The only way to change the system is to stand up and fight back."

"Mmm…it's not over yet."

"For all intents and purposes, it might as well be. Trust me, they don't want to go to trial. Whoever comes in to replace Gupton needs to get this lawsuit behind him—or her—as quickly as possible so they can start rebuilding their reputation."

"It helps a lot that they've cut off the head of the snake." Celia wrapped her shoulders in Theo's Burberry shawl. "I stole this, by the way. You said we'd be sitting outside."

November nights were iffy, but the forecast called for the low sixties all evening. Not that it mattered—Atlanta Grill lined its terrace with patio heaters to maintain a comfortable ambience for outdoor dining. It was Theo's favorite restaurant, and she'd been wanting to take Celia there for dinner ever since they missed out on their first date.

Tonight was a special celebration—seven months since the day Celia had walked into her office in disguise, her voice cracking with fury as she told the story of a young woman violated and denied justice. Her outrage had fueled Theo's admiration. *That* Celia had emerged again the day she handed over the new recording and announced herself ready to testify. Even when Celia doubted it herself, Theo knew the firebrand was in her heart.

* * *

Celia loved the way heads turned when Theo walked through the dining room to their table. Even if her face hadn't been all over the news, especially here in Atlanta, her striking looks and the confidence with which she carried herself suggested if she wasn't a VIP, she ought to be.

No, they knew Theo. In moments, they'd be texting their friends with news of a celebrity sighting.

She vaguely remembered what it was like to be recognized in public as a child star of ten years old. Even before cell phone cameras were ubiquitous, her agent had warned her to be on guard with her looks and behavior, that she was always on stage.

The hostess settled them at a table on the second-floor terrace across from the Grand Atrium in the historic 200 Peachtree building. An interesting ambience...urban romantic.

"What's so funny?" Theo asked with a bemused smile.

Celia hadn't realized she'd been laughing to herself. "Nothing really. I was watching people watch you. You're famous."

"Says the TV star."

"That's why I was laughing. It reminded me of something I hadn't thought about in years, back when I was doing my show. You have to understand, Hollywood's one of those places where you can run into an Oscar winner in McDonald's. I used to go into restaurants with my mom, and if nobody recognized me, she'd say something like, 'Is this table all right, Little CeCe?'"

"She actually called you that?"

"Only in public. And always loud enough that you could hear her three tables away."

"She must have been a character."

"Understatement."

"It still blows my mind sometimes," Theo said. "You being the same girl I grew up with on TV. My very own Little CeCe."

"Tell the truth, Theo. That's the real reason you fell in love with me. Your dream-come-true girl crush."

Theo laughed richly as she shook her head. "You really want the truth? I started falling way before that. A beautiful woman shows up in my office saying all the things I already believe. Raging at the machine. Ready to right somebody's wrong. I was hopeless from that day on."

Celia too had felt the attraction instantly. "You didn't let on. I'd have gone home with you that night."

"Yeah, we lost a few weeks because I was being careful. But I intend to make up for them. Just like I'm making up for the dinner we missed."

As they looked over the menu, Celia stole a long, loving gaze. Even after months of knowing Theo intimately, she still was awed by the celebrity aura surrounding her. By her hypnotic blue eyes. By how she managed to come off as charming even when she was the most forceful, focused person in the room.

Their waiter, a soft-spoken twenty-something wearing a tuxedo shirt and vest, folded his hands formally at his waist. "Good evening. My name is Stewart. May I start you off with something from the bar?"

"Vadin-Plateau," Theo answered without hesitation. "Chilled flutes, please."

"Must be champagne," Celia said after he'd left. "Are we celebrating?"

Theo held out a hand and interlaced their fingers. "Happy seven month anniversary, my love. I can honestly say they've been the best of my life."

"*You're* the best of my life. I mean that." Theo's capacity for love was greater than any she'd ever known. Unconditional, unwavering. "Sweetheart, I'm sorry it took me so long to come around to supporting you on the case. I was being selfish… worrying about my own hide. But I realized one of the reasons I love you so much is because you stand up for people. When I came home with that second recording, when I said I'd testify… God, I just felt so noble. Like I bet you feel all the time."

"You are noble, Celia. I always knew that about you."

It was a crystalizing moment for Celia, hearing not just *I love you*, but why. Theo brought out the best in her, the person she was meant to be.

"Ladies." Stewart stood an ice bucket next to their table and presented the bottle to Theo for approval. After a pop, he offered a taste before pouring for both of them.

"To us," Theo said, her eyes smiling as she raised her frosted flute.

"I love you, Theo." Only at the last second did she drop her gaze to the champagne. There was something in the bottom of her glass. "What—"

"Is something wrong?"

"There's…" She held it up to the dim light of a wall sconce several feet away. Bobbing gently amidst the bubbles was a ring. "Oh, my God."

"Why, I believe there's something in your drink. Let's get that out of there." Theo fished it out with a teaspoon, dipped it in her water glass and proceeded to dry it with her linen napkin. "Where on earth did this come from?"

Unable to speak even a word, Celia rested her left hand in Theo's palm and gasped as the ring slid onto her finger. A platinum band with inlaid diamonds.

"When I was a kid, I used to dream I'd grow up someday and marry Little CeCe. That she'd fall so deeply in love with me, I would make her the happiest woman in the world. Will you make that dream come true for me?"

Bursting with joy, she began to nod. "Yes…yes, I will."

Theo kissed her knuckles and let go so Celia could admire the ring.

"I thought I knew so much about you. I had no idea you were such a romantic."

"I wasn't…but I am now. I'm a lot of things I wasn't before. Happy, settled. Secure in knowing you're the woman I want to grow old with."

On the verge of tears, Celia raised her glass. It didn't feel right to toast the woman who'd brought them together, but she'd never forget Hayley, nor the battle Theo had waged to bring her justice. "I'm so glad I get to be here to watch you change the world, Theo. To winning."

Bella Books, Inc.

Women. Books. Even Better Together.

P.O. Box 10543
Tallahassee, FL 32302

Phone: 800-729-4992
www.bellabooks.com